SCEPTRE

Also by Stella Duffy

Calendar Girl
Wavewalker
Beneath the Blonde
Singling Out the Couples

Eating Cake

STELLA DUFFY

SCEPTRE

First published in 1999 by Hodder and Stoughton
A division of Hodder Headline PLC
A Sceptre book

10 9 8 7 6 5 4 3 2 1

All characters in this publication are fictitious and any resemblance to real persons, living or dead, is purely coincidental.

A CIP catalogue record for this book is available from the British Library

ISBN 0 340 71562 6

Typeset by Palimpsest Book Production Limited,
Polmont, Stirlingshire
Printed and bound in Great Britain by
Clays Ltd, St Ives plc, Bungay

Hodder and Stoughton
A division of Hodder Headline PLC
338 Euston Road
London NW1 3BH

for the cake makers – fat and thin alike

thanks to:
Shelley Silas, Yvonne Baker and Carole Welch for the usual (and in this case quite a lot more), the five-a-side advisory team of Ashdown, Paine, Simpson, Sorba and Whelans, and the Improbable Lifegamers for practice in real stories and generous time listening to the tedious rantings of one tied to a touring laptop.

1 S

It started with my Jesus year. Just like the man himself – perfectly normal until thirty and then building to crazy as hell over the next three. Slow burn to start, gathering speed, with a huge over-the-top finish in the last great annus miraculous of the notorious thirty-third. I gave the Galilean sea stroll a miss; I'm not fond of wet feet, far too beaches-in-Goa for my taste. I'm not a holiday backpack kind of girl. I prefer a properly run hotel with clean white sheets and on-tap room service. At least I thought I did. The delights of tacky B&Bs only became apparent after a while. Some things take the slow drip of time to grow on you. Orange carpets, cheap tea bags. Nylon sheets. Anyway, this body of flesh I inhabit turned thirty-three and I took the momentous occasion of my third eleven as a sign. Read it as a meant-to-be. To tell the truth, I would have taken any old half-mystic injunction seriously, I was so desperate. Not that I knew it at the time. I had barely begun to notice the suffering. I thought I was happy. Until the morning I woke up and remembered that I wasn't.

I never meant to be a bad girl. Or an evil woman. A bitch, slut, whore. Tart was the most I'd ever managed until then, and that only in the sixth form. Once. Because Sandra Harris thought I fancied her boyfriend. She was right, but I'd only ever told my diary, certainly had never had the courage to mention it to Ian Pearson himself. I was not made for wickedness. It doesn't come naturally. Didn't come naturally. Boredom, however, is an excellent teacher, and four years of marriage the ideal school. Something had to give.

It wasn't anything in particular at first. I didn't notice the pale slipping-away, hadn't really registered that Andy was fading slightly. The edges of him folding into our new house, getting all mixed up with sheaves of aspirational colour charts and hundred-year-old dust from the floor sanders and the dirty lint hiding in dark untorchable corners of the loft. By the time I did see what was going on, it was too late. Too late to ask for what I'd not even had the sense to know I wanted in the first place.

On a late autumn morning ten weeks after our fourth anniversary, a month after my thirty-third birthday, I woke with the blackbird's angry nest-protecting call. Brown mother blackbird pink-pinking to save her babies from real or imagined dangers. I think. Not that I know too much about birds. Andy does. Bird-watching, gardening, house plants – pick a growing thing and it's his forte. Any growing thing, as long as I don't touch it. Our relationship the prime example. Only Andy hadn't yet noticed I was going silently crazy inside of it. Not his fault. I wasn't too clear on what was really happening either – it's hard to see the kaleidoscope pattern from inside the mirror triangle. The blackbird was nest-protecting furious, or maybe she'd just picked up on my mood. The one that was about to take me over. I turned on to my side as I'd done every morning for the past seven years, three as shag monster lovers, four as happily marrieds. Turned to look at my husband, to gaze with bleary, sleep-crusted eyes upon the one true one. But he wasn't there. Andy lay beside me, still and peacefully heavy, breathing a soft half-breath of last sleep, a small frown creeping across his forehead, premonition of my next unsettling thought. Andy lay, deep-sleeping on my left as he always did, but the beloved wasn't there. I'd spent the long night curled up with the corpse of lust and woken with a crick in my neck. It wasn't an especially warm place to be.

I know the body entirely renews itself over a period of seven years. I don't know this to be a fact, of course – cellular biology is not my chosen subject for the big black chair. Like most graduates with a BA in pretty much nothing at all, I've carved a career out of talking to people and playing kid games with adults, calling it work – I leave concrete scientific evidence of my own reality to those far cleverer than I am, those with Channel 4 programmes all their own. This thing about the seven-year renewal is a suburban myth I've grown up believing. Culled from a half-remembered biology class, taught by a Jesus Christ Superstar fantasy to a room full of pheromone-rushed girls. So many would-be Magdalenes and not a single sexual experience between them. I believed it though, the story the bearded baby god squeezed into my head past a door fiercely guarded by Ian McCulloch and Julian Cope. Cells die and replace themselves and, seven years from any one day, the body is completely different from when it started seven years ago. I lay beside my husband, seven years, three months and twelve days after first meeting him, and knew he was a completely different person to the man I first met. Knew I was different too.

I got up quietly, not wanting to disturb him. I didn't know what was coming but I figured he'd probably need his rest. I power-showered with a brief rush of guilt for the drying, dying water reservoirs of Britain, dressed in Saturday ease clothes and went downstairs to the sitting room to watch the sun come up, stained-glass sunshine illuminating the bare boards and well-placed islands of coir matting. Our house is exactly the same as all the others – it's Heal's when we can afford it and Ikea and Habitat the rest of the time, and the only difference between our home and those of all our friends is that we stand in it, created it out of nothing from joint desire and imaginary budgets.

I woke Andy with a long slow kiss that welcomed his morning desire and then chose to ignore it. I gave him fresh milky coffee instead, which is normally a fairly good substitute when we don't have a great deal of time to spare. Andy and I are so well married our lust is relegated to spare time pastime. We are not unusual. I took our joint-prepared shopping list and went to Sainsbury's while he dragged himself the slow mile from bed to bath to breakfast. Hunted and gathered through the gleaming aisles like it was any other day, returned to kiss him quickly and brightly this time, put everything away in our red squirrel store cupboards, and then the two of us made a start on the vegetable garden. From house to garden, those easy things to do together when each one has a role and you know how to do it – who takes the cellophane-wrapped tea and coffee from the stretched plastic bags, who is brave enough to face the undefrosted freezer with yet another low-fat ready meal, which one of you will open the biscuits first and pass a half-bitten custard cream to the other. All this from seven years and so simple to be together and so easy now and you can small-talk and listen to the radio and answer the phone and open the mail and put away a week's worth of shopping without ever thinking about the delineation of a single action. Being together so usual and simple that the inorganic clairvoyance has grown to second nature. In the garden, weeding and mulching and preparing for the hibernation of winter grey, all the while slamming the uninvited disquiet from the front of my thoughts.

We worked hard and he was gorgeous, my husband. Old jeans, a t-shirt Andy insisted on ironing (just like his mother, nothing like mine), shiny clean hair and tanned lean limbs easily working beside me in seven-year softened harmony. Me and Andy outside in our own garden, enjoying the last of the morning sun. Working the joint-tenanted forty feet of land we possess between us. Me still marvelling that I could actually own a chunk of the earth, and lovely gentle Andy oblivious to my crazy thoughts, staking the young fruit trees to prepare for the winds to come, gathering the last few apples. We two weeding in wedded bliss, recreating a long-planned future that neither of us could possibly hope to achieve. Not that Andy knew this, you understand. Not yet. The morning passed and the door of my insanity storehouse began to creak.

We had friends over for lunch, a couple with twin sons who played in the paddling pool we'd thoughtfully bought specifically for the children of friends, inappropriate autumn warmth cheating out an end-of-summer charade. Little ones playing in the paddling pool that was meant to come in handy for our own kids one day. Saturday child-friendly lunch of fresh pasta and vegan pesto and tediously healthy fruit. With ordinary Australian beers for the adults and apple juice for the kids. Normal and unexceptional and safe. So very safe that unsafe couldn't be far in the distance. That evening we went to another couple of couples and a handful of singles for dinner. I looked around the table and knew their secrets, knew their infidelities confided over drunken glasses, late at night. They did not know mine, I had none to tell. We are role model couple, Andy and I. Years ago I chose to make the faithfulness commitment to my husband. It was a conscious decision. I would be the good wife – I placed him high on a pedestal of my own design and then vowed to deserve him, merit his love. I made that choice from a position of love over experience. I thought it was what I was meant to do. We swallowed a dinner of rocket and Parmesan and tuna steaks and cranberry soufflé and expensive wines and new-ground coffees and bitter dark chocolate mints, enjoying our friends' bounty, not allowing ourselves to mind their greater income and refusing silent comparison with their smooth walls and our done-it-ourselves plasterwork, an evening bound up in the constancy of been here before and will be here again for ever and ever amen. That night we made love – Saturday night fuck before the Sunday morning roll in the newspapers. Gently, tenderly and, with an accomplished practice born of seven years, much too quickly. For both of us. Andy fell into an easy sleep, tired, relaxed, mildly drunk and stroking a gentle 'I love you' on my back. Because he did love me. Just as I loved him. Past tension battering love into the submission of loved.

I lay beside him, this stranger husband, and cried. Partly with a late night alcohol melancholy, but under that and bubbling to the top, with an alien anger that wanted only for change. Silent tears, salt hot, rolling down my perfectly cleansed and toned high-boned cheeks. Which is when I made the wet-pillow metamorphosis, sent out a prayer for the different, the new, the exciting. In that moment I was fond of Andy, cared for Andy, did not want to lose Andy. I actually loved Andy. But it wasn't enough. And it wasn't Andy's fault either. A good man, a kind man, a really bloody funny man, a man my mother told me was 'shining good through and through'. She meant that he wasn't my dad. This new departure from the planned programme was all me, all my doing, and I take complete responsibility for it. At least, I take responsibility for it now. At the time all I wanted was change. Lisa did love Andy, had loved Andy, but Andy was a new body now and so was I. Therefore Lisa couldn't really truly love Andy any more, could she? It was the new Lisa who offered up an unvoiced imprecation for desire and passion. And then surprised myself by adding danger to the list. A dumb plea which fell flat and dead into the walled back gardens of inner city suburbia as I finally settled into another night's perjurious sleep. It wasn't my agonized prayer which mattered though, which allowed me to turn off and rest. It was the promise of hope, a possibility of glorious new. The Jesus morning awakening had made the potential potent.

And, as things turned out, that was more than enough for transformation to commence. In well-lagged loft tanks across the land, water was slowly turning into wine.

2

I went out running that Sunday night. This is not so unusual. A woman turns thirty and suddenly starts calling herself a girl/chick/babe – anything other than the mock-adult soubriquet of 'woman' she's insisted on since she was fifteen and couldn't possibly have known how to carry to term. More to the point, said babe develops a serious interest in keeping cellulite at bay. She knows it's an anti-feminist conspiracy dreamed up by the money-hungry pharmaceutical patriarchs. She knows cellulite didn't exist until the advertising lads invented it. And still she cares. I'd been running for three years. I didn't like it much. Didn't like it at all most of the time, nor did it help a great deal with my body obsessions. But it did make it look like I was trying. Hard.

Running girl. London autumn. The brief burst of Saturday's post-summer warmth and sunshine had given way to fat dark clouds and commented-upon temperatures. Global warming was fucking up the crisp autumn myth as well. Muggy air and warm rain on my warmer face, pounding through only half-dark roads, orange-streetlight-lit. Pavement hiking in time to a lurid combination of Lydia Lunch and Nancy Sinatra. Enough to disturb even the most Zen of babe-women. And God knows that's not me. Track pants, old t-shirt, hair in ponytail, Walkman and baseball cap. The closest I'm likely to get to being a Madonna look-alike is when I punish my body at one hundred and thirty frantic heartbeats a minute. Since the momentous occasion of choosing a form of exercise to take as my own, I always liked best to run at night, in what passes for dark on London streets. Andy hated it, worried about me the whole while, bit his tongue for when the edge of his 'be careful' would slip from loving husband into concerned father. And it always did. Which is probably part of why I liked the night thing so much anyway. Knowing it was fucking him up.

I did not mean to bait Andy. But he was too wonderful. Good husband, great shag, brilliant carer – what more could a girl ask for? Nothing in the first place, nothing in the first years. Everyone loved Andy and they were right to do so. He was the best catch of the year when his big brown eyes lighted on me. I wasn't. I was just Lisa, and so I was flattered and wooed and won and eventually, in the warmth of his delightfulness, I blossomed beyond girl cliché into person. I might well have done it alone anyway, no doubt would have made myself into my own woman with time, but in reality, I did it with my husband.

There is a chance I might have grown into someone else, without him, I'm sure I would have. Might have loved another, might have hated another, might have become a big-deal career woman who ran away from him the first time he whispered the baby idea, might have become a baby machine who was content for my man to go out and earn whatever pittance he could get to keep our holy family alive. What I did in reality was take on the both of us with the earning power of a job in management training so Andy could concentrate on getting the extra qualifications necessary for his real future as a career teacher. It was all he'd ever wanted and more. He loved to teach and after several years of me putting him first, he was finally ensconced in a school where he had all the support he needed and could put into action theories and plans he had dreamed up with me in long night conversations over the past seven years. In time he meant to run his own school, in time his great theories would be proven and published, in time his vision would become reality. Not that I didn't enjoy my work and not that it wasn't occasionally fairly stimulating and interesting and not even that I didn't sometimes meet quite nice people when I was working. It's just that it was never really that much of an ambition in the first place. I spent forty or fifty hours a week working at something that was never a first choice of career plan. Then again, I had no choice of career plan when I left university, or even when I went to university. All I knew was I had to find something that would interest me and challenge me and give me a career base right in the middle of London.

I fell into training through a company I was temping for. I had a degree but no solid qualifications for real work. I liked it well enough and, after attending all the available courses myself, I became fairly good at it too. But the job had always been a career by accident more than intent, until Andy, cleverly spotting a good earner when he saw one, encouraged me to go it alone and start up my own business. Then training became what I really did. After twelve years I'd had mildly interesting, been briefly challenged, and I was working from one and a half rooms, four floors up in Soho. So at least I achieved the office in the middle of London. My job was also bringing in a good two-thirds of our money, which meant it was possible for Andy to stay in the slow career progression, not earning a huge amount, but with his integrity well satisfied. The intention had always been that one day he would be doing so well in his chosen path that there would be time and money and space for me to look at what I really fancied doing for a living. Or even try out the mother thing, the baby potential. Yet another conversation Andy and I were planning to have any day soon. The two of us had grown up together over the past seven years and for a long time I used to see it as Andy grew me up. Andy grew me past him. I trained myself out of my gratitude. By the time I was starting to feel restless and uncertain about the two of us, I knew I didn't really need him to look after me any more, but I think maybe he wasn't sure what else there was to do, what other future we might have. Neither was I.

Then I went out running that Sunday night and the world slapped me in the face with the possible.

3

My night runs went past all the other Victorian terraces, each one exactly like ours and just that little bit different – stencilled wall here, authentic B&Q picture rail there, plaster-enhancing gloss of minimalist white slapped on the hall. Just that little bit different and still not a chance of different enough. In London it's the late Victorian terrace, in Edinburgh the renovated city tenement, in Manchester the thirties suburban semi. The young moderns and their wedding-list tastes have remade every suburb in their own wish-we-could-afford-real designer image right across the land. We've bought our new old houses and patterned the whole of Britain to the blueprint combination of a *Changing Rooms/Homefront* fact sheet. All so very exciting and new and all so depressingly interchangeable. Leftover alcohol swimming through my tainted organs, the crap weather of season switch, the inevitable irritation of Sunday night when Monday no longer brings fresh excitement – I was not in a brilliant mood.

At seven o'clock on that particular evening not all the bay window curtains had been drawn yet. There were families and young couples and older couples whose children had left home and students and teenagers doing that last-minute-homework-while-sneaking-a-joint they do so well. They were all really doing exactly the same. Getting ready for work and school the next day. Watching television. Finishing dinner. Cooking a later supper. Putting the kids to bed. Doing what I'd prepared to make of my life ever since I had the sense to start thinking about it. Or, as I was starting to feel, non-sense. Just doing what you do when you're coupled. When you've bought the house after all that saving and searching, those years in the too-small flat supposedly suddenly worthwhile for the little piece of London you now own together. When, despite your fears and unvoiced insecurities, you've started the family. When you've finally achieved what you broke away from your poverty-furnished childhood and exhausted parents to do. The doing-better-than-we-could that they planned for you since your mother threw up for the third time and confirmed to Dad that there was another on the way. You've got the house, the car, the career and the actual future, and even if the bank does own about nine-tenths of it and it's going to be another fifteen years before the groundwork on the career actually pays off, from the outside it seems as if you really are having that life. And then when you study it closely, none of it looks like it was supposed to. All bent out of shape through the distorted lens of no-good-reason, just-not-satisfied.

That everyday night I ran further than most, running from doubled-over desperation, running from my good man and walls closing in of the safe home into a murky darkness temporarily lit by other people's windows. I ran past God knows how many houses, turning back on myself, up one street, down another, past the first street and twisting back to make the quiet streets less same. The closing of parks at nightfall is one of the crueller attributes of caring local councils. Yes, it saves us delicate girl chicks from muggings and rapings and beatings and unexpected stabbings. Great. Those of us who prefer to sweat in public after dark are also doomed to pumping through reproduction suburban streets with no hope of a raised rose garden, pine copse or ornamental pond to alleviate the tedium of our quest for thinner thighs. And the rapist fear is no less potent for being removed to silent streets.

So there I was, running still, legs aching, arms pumping, breathing hard and leaping puddles to the accompaniment of a down-home dirty laugh. Warm rain washing warmer sweat from my face. I was actually liking it, despite the description of a woman in Hollywood starlet torture mode. For a start, I was glad to be out of the house. Turning the flush of exercise into a blush of hope. I ran out into the evening pissed off and too warm and irritated by the people we'd had over for lunch. Left Andy doing the dishes, putting away the dregs of the afternoon, settling in for a night of the unwatched videos from last week's TV. Preceded of course, by a good half-hour's concern for my welfare. And a couple of hours moaning about all the work he had to catch up on that he hadn't even touched this weekend. Like he'd really wanted to replan the next term's entire history curriculum. Actually, he probably did. I tied my shoelaces furious with him for simply being in another room that intersected with a part of my life. Not his fault and blaming him anyway. I didn't say my dissatisfaction was rational. Counting blessings has always seemed a bit too Sunday school for me. Seven years with the backing of the man I love has made me strong – I'm more your counting-the-hours kind of girl now.

Forty minutes in the muggy, wet world, though, and I was feeling better. Heart pumping, pores opened to the dim light. Hoping that the night-running good I felt would be translated into a feel good for Andy when I got home. Convincing myself with each carefully placed step that we were OK really. Everyone gets bored after a while – it's normal, it's usual, it will pass. Assuming my Saturday morning panic was just another fourth-decade trauma.

Running to thirty-year-old music and a mantra of I can do this. I could be the wife. Crossed the road without checking for cars. I could love him because he really was a good man and I would go on with it all. Ran back up the alleyway in the street behind ours, late wistaria and clematis still trying hard to perfume the damp night. I would translate honest care and settled love back into refound passion and desire. Rounded the corner, up the hilly part, where it got really dark and I proved just how much I didn't care. Breathing harder, then along the edge of the park, street side of the rails. I owed him, and if we were a little stale with each other, a bit tired of each other, then that wasn't Andy's fault, it was up to me to make it better. I could see what was wrong, so it was my problem and I would solve it. Andy had loved me to my state of present bravery, loved me into such a place that I could even see my own dissatisfaction. I owed him, I would remember that. I would be good. I would repay. Houses on my left side. Dark green trees relinquishing leaves to my right. I had no right to reject his care and goodness. I would go home and apologize for being sharp that afternoon. I would make it all OK. There was no reason for the way I felt. No solid, tangible reason. Andy had done nothing wrong. Neither had I. Yet.

And I was looking in at all the houses and they were all doing it. That thing I was convincing myself of. Going along with it, living through 'is this all there is' and believing it would do. There were the weekend decorators, taking up dustsheets and paint-cover plastic, delighted with their achievements. Habitat's new paint range reaching into their homes with perfect predictability. Finishing another fresh ordered room so that they could cross that one off the list. And start all over in a year when everything was done and they had time to sit still and panic again. There were the parents, bundling kids up to bed and focusing on the toddler's cuteness rather than daring to glimpse the terror of another twenty years of permanent parenthood and no more time to themselves ever again. There were the student flats, young bodies laid out across the floor under an unshaded bulb, in front of a wide-screen TV. I knew all this. This was my life. It was fine. Everyone else did it too. This was all I ever thought I wanted when I hopeful-teenage-planned my life in my parents' flat. When I booked myself into the getting out, getting on, getting up, and left my old life behind. I had worked bloody hard to remake me from scared girl to grown woman. I had the good job and the good home and the good man. I had another ten minutes to run and I would do this. Anything was possible, even submission to the inevitable.

And then I'm stopped short. Brought up to a screeching halt outside a house just like ours. It has the bay window with the stained-glass insets and the half-porch and the sitting room with original folding doors through to the dining room at the back. And it has them. The man and woman pair. Framed inside the window. There's a light on in the back of the house and their calico blinds have not yet been lowered. And they are half clothed. They are fucking. She has pushed him up against the reproduction fireplace and wrapped her legs around his waist. I should run on, get home, Andy will start to worry. But she is me. He is Andy. She kisses him like she's fourteen and this is her number one, the very first. I watch the quiver run from her belly button to her cunt and see her unconscious flesh demand she kisses him more. He is first morning of holiday in response, teenage boy offered woman on a plate in response. I need to get back and do my cool-down stretches, but these people are my husband and I. Their house is our house and they look like us and they are us. Except they're fucking like there's no work tomorrow and no mortgage with interest rates hitting us again every three months and no pressure for kids in a couple of years and no reason to be anywhere else. Ever. Which is not me and Andy. Andy has school and I have meetings and a potential client in the afternoon and then there's his staff meeting and my drinks party for my old boss and then we have to greet each other after twelve hours separate in the world and eat a tired sandwich together and half watch the news and decide about my parents at Christmas and put off making the baby decision yet again, too tired, not enough time to talk, never enough time and then it will be Tuesday morning and we'll do it all again. They are not us. And they don't care that the windows are bare and open to the street. That her breasts are open and bared for the street. Andy will not fuck in the open. He is private. He is careful. I should stretch – I'll get cramp, fuck up the whole point of the exercise. He is holding her up with one arm. She's clinging to him, blue-painted fingernails clawing into his worked-out shoulders like this is new and just beginning. Andy has beautiful shoulders – his body is fine and lean and strong-muscled. But I do not claw him in desperate desire any more. She is moving the man, placing him, readying herself. I've stopped running and even though the night is still muggy I'm getting cold. Sweat drying on my forehead. I can't move on, though. She has twisted around on to his back, her lighter weight doubling him over, they roll in a slow arc down to the sofa. I turn Nancy down – 'I know you're leaving babe, goodbye, so long' fades out. I can hear him – he's screaming irrepressible joy into her face. She is biting his neck, talons in his collarbones, dragging him down to her. He is big, this man, and she wants him to crush her. My legs are shaking, triceps quivering. Muscles finished too soon, not given cool-down time, cramp rippling into my left calf, my back aching. They are moving now, agitating the still air around their ravenous flesh. The fuck isn't over but it has mutated into a dance. A two-step for bodies joined Siamese at the hip and rotating on the axis of each other.

And they are laughing. Laughing like it doesn't matter. Like none of it matters. So they are not me and Andy after all. *Frasier* makes us laugh. *Friends* makes us laugh. We save our biggest belly-laughs for imported American comedy. We don't laugh like that. Not any more. Not simply for the fuck of it.

I move off. I am not running. I look like a girl who has run too far. Overtaken by exhaustion, a stitch at the very least. I am stumbling home bent over with grief. And the water washing my face isn't rain. I don't know what's coming, don't know what I can do to make this better. But somehow I know being a good girl isn't going to do it.

This is what Andy thinks:

I wish she wouldn't run in the dark. I'm worried for her. I'm worried for us. I know she's not happy. I've known for a while. I don't know how to fix it. Or even if I'm supposed to want to. I want us to be all right and I know she isn't satisfied. Neither am I. But I'm OK, good enough is OK. Good enough is better than most. I've tried the other and it didn't work for me. This will do. I don't want to think about it. Thinking about it will make it real, talking about it will let in the demons. It is just time. This happens to everyone. We'll move to the next level, do the next thing. It will be fine.

I wish she wouldn't run in the dark.

4 S

It wasn't always like that.

First sex with Andy. Wanting him like needing to swim in midsummer suburbia. Late July, London enveloped in thick heat haze. He called it smog. We'd known each other for maybe a year, friends of friends, met at a couple of parties, pubs. Nothing special, didn't yet know he was distinctive, didn't yet know he had noticed me. Didn't yet know that in noticing me, in shining his heat on me, I would love him back, love him for wanting me, love him for the warmth of his want, love him simply because he was lovely and I could.

Then a different night, two weeks before the sex. He called me from his mate Simon's house. Simon was Jaine's ex from three years earlier. He and I had nearly had something ourselves, not long after they broke up, but then I'd had a fling with Si's brother and he'd met Kelly. Kelly and Simon lasted a good three months, Paul and I managed a slightly less impressive six weeks, four days, twenty-two hours. Paul didn't know it, but he'd mattered. Three years later, though, we were all doing good friends incredibly well and with no recriminations. Or at least not unless an awful lot of drugs were involved, and then the tears could usually be confined to a controlled outbreak in the girls' loos. We had a convoluted friendship circle, no more interesting or incestuous than any other group, no less impressed by itself for that. I lived in South London, Simon lived North, Andy lived in Shepherd's Bush, but did I want to traipse over to Finsbury Park anyway as Simon had decided to have a barbecue.

I knew Simon's place well. It had been a huge squat in the seventies and most of the eighties, a fantastic old Edwardian semi with about sixteen people living in the dark, high-ceilinged rooms. Simon was maybe ten years older than us, had been in the house for ever, stayed when governments and times changed and eventually bought it from the council on a special deal. The deal being that they would get a wreck off their rate-capped hands and he would give them fresh cash. At the time of the party Simon had only just replaced the broken old tiles, made a roof garden with sapling plants and was living in the basement kitchen, three intervening floors of debris still to tackle. He showered at his neighbour's flat next door. There was an outside toilet that functioned perfectly well for one man but needed great care when guests insisted on using it too, stretching the limits of sanitation and Simon's sanity. Plumbing irregularities aside, Simon knew he was going to do well one day. Today the house that Simon built is worth more than twenty times what he bought it for. Every room is light and bright and airy, restored to either original charm or modernist cool in the places where original charm really means small windows and crap wiring. The roof garden is all climbing roses and clematis and heavy-scented wistaria, with winter heathers should reality strike that far into bliss city. His whole street is lined with elegant flats, latest-registration cars. But Simon has an entire house to himself and the best pension plan of us all, the perfect future created from the proceeds of his brother's Norfolk garden. The green, green grass of East Anglia sold especially well in concrete London in the early nineties, and it paid for an awful lot of timber and plaster. After seven and a half years of work, Simon now has a house of grass and no big bad wolf to huff and puff and blow it all away.

That night seven years ago Andy was calling to invite me to the roof garden christening. The sun had been up long and hard all day. It was four in the afternoon – I was sweltering in a shared flat five floors up in the Elephant, my third residence that year, each new home delineating a milestone on my odyssey to the epicentre. Every second move grave-marking yet another failed relationship. I left the third aborted attempt at a business plan on my bedroom floor – still trying to make my own business so I didn't have to keep temping, still failing – laid myself out for fifty grateful minutes in a scented bath and left the flat for the cooler North. Twenty minutes on the Bakerloo Line and my beautifully made-up face was sweating, my soft floating summer dress was beginning to look grimy with the touch of other people's hot breath, and I was wishing, not for the first time in my life, that I could just go out in old jeans, t-shirt and a hint of mascara like any other girl. Not like any other girl I knew – other than Jaine – but like any other girl in every magazine and telly programme, all those natural beauties who are glorious first thing in the morning and carry silent lighting men around with them in their back pocket just in case the glow of youth should slip away in a rain-darkened street. I wasn't, I didn't and I arrived at Si's house looking real. Andy later told me it was the imperfections which made him notice me. Much later. If he'd been that honest in the first year we'd certainly never have made it all the way to seven.

The roof garden filled up slowly. Thirty square feet of disparate people, joined by any tenuous connection to Simon and fine-weather worship. There weren't many of us, maybe fifteen at any one time, most people passing by on their way to or from some other event, but Simon, Andy and I were there from six in the evening until four the next morning. Ten hours of light and dark and near-light again, ten hours in which Andy came into focus. I knew him, he was nice, we'd talked before, got on OK, had a laugh. He was good-looking in a Ken sort of way – classic boy good looks, not what I'd much fancied before, but that night he changed. Slipped without warning from pleasant enough nice guy into wanting. Made the transition because he chose to, chose me and in that choosing I saw him properly coloured in. I don't know why Andy wanted me that day, why he called me, what made him think, as he says he did, that even before I answered the phone we would end up together that night. He was right, but not about that night. I wasn't going to let him be in charge of it all. Not even then.

Hot evening, where the cool air never came, even when the sun went down. Stoned and drunk people singing along to Simon's America and Fleetwood Mac albums, not even aware we'd known the words until that night. One long conversation about Thatcher as anti-feminist devil, a second on the glories of E, neither of which I cared about too much, both just passing time, sharing words. Another joint, another bottle opened, some coke, fairly new to me then and illicitly exciting. Andy outlined against set-sun sky, teal-blue memory of where the light had been, Finsbury Park trees silhouetted behind him, everything amber warm and still. Songs to make you want to fall in love. We did. Kissing like teenagers in the fading light, sharing one of Si's hash brownies, feeding each other strange-tasting dry chocolate crumble cake, then later more coke, wide gulps of whisky, last of the wine, bodies confused with the up and down of drug combination, underscored with constant ascent of desire.

We didn't sleep that night, told our rehearsed stories – my first love, his last, the worst heartbreak, the latest bastard. Parents, siblings, school, music, sex – talked the long conversations of the newly falling until the sun came up. Then everyone else had crawled or night-bussed home and Simon went down to the basement to sleep, left us his spare mattress, and we rolled into closed eyes on the roof, foetal-twinned our fully dressed selves – fully summer dressed, lots of skin – and slept through the morning.

We woke hot and bothered, ate with Si and then spent all of that Sunday together, met Monday after work and again Tuesday, Wednesday. I claimed a yoga class on Thursday only because I was so scared. Too soon, too fast, too easy, too damn good. I wasn't used to it, wanted to hold him at bay, wanted to pull him even closer. We still had not had sex. For two weeks I refused my own desire and his. I didn't have a good reason, only that I had shagged too soon too often, had read the good books, was trying to save myself from the almost inevitable future. Hoped that by waiting, even a few days, I would know more. Be sure that he could be trusted, would know he wouldn't hurt me. Even while I rationally knew I could wait two years and still not know if pain was going to follow, it felt big and strong to leave his place or send him from mine and sleep alone for those first few days. Big and strong and in control like the girls in the questionnaires, the ones who always choose the 'Mostly A's – you know what you want, all right!', the ones who know where they're going and what they're doing with their lives, the ones who choose their lovers, don't wait to be picked like claiming sides for a playground game of football. He had picked me, I was happy to be chosen, but I wanted a semblance of control. I have always been chasing after a semblance of control.

And then that seemed stupid too. Two and a half weeks after the night on Simon's roof I knew I wanted to fuck Andy, like I'd known in the first place, the minute I saw him clearly. I knew if I left it any longer the act itself would become too big, too important. We had dinner in town. He met me after work at the Dean Street office where I was bad-tempered temping. Halfway through the main course I told him I wanted to fuck that night. Neither of us ate the ice cream we'd ordered. We tumbled a slow moan of a bus ride home to his place and did it. Eighteen-day courtship ritual ended, bodies watered and fed with each other. I swam, drowning and waving in my want for him that night. And the next and the next.

I didn't really know him, not yet, but it didn't matter. The essence of falling in love is the blind leap of faith, the bliss terror of putting an ignorant offer into action and guess-hoping it might work this time, joy in the free-fall tandem paraglide, wondering which of us holds the rip-cord. I fell in love with Andy not for who he was, but for who he wasn't. I don't think I am unusual.

Andy wasn't Neil, the bi-polar ambisexual beauty of my first year out of university, half the time running faster than I could have imagined possible, dashing from one new idea to the next old party, cokehead speedhead laughing and giggling all the way, me triple-jump skipping beside him. Until he crashed down again and insisted I hide out with him in the place of cold tears, real fears, locked into the dark room so long I almost believed his pain was my own. Andy wasn't Martyn, he wasn't my third true love and best fuck ever and most beautiful boy and didn't everyone else know it, and Andy wouldn't be coming home at four in the morning, another girl's perfume on his neck, an empty hip flask in his pocket and the stench of fresh vomit on his breath, but wanting to fuck me anyway – and me wanting it too. Andy wasn't Glynn, last great desire and the fantastic town planner of our futures. My perfect would-be poet, could-be artist, wannabe film-maker. Might-be anything if only he could stop smoking before five in the morning and roll out of bed before midday and get a job where they understood him and move to Spain with me and find the two of us away from the stench of London and just explore our love in the country, in the clean air, our babies tumbling around us, tarot cards and amethyst crystals flying in the warm wind. Glynn's fists flying in a cold wind.

Andy was nothing like any of my failed loves, and different from the others as well, the one night fun-fucks, no future. Like me Andy loved *The Waltons* and hated *Little House on the Prairie*. He liked oysters and champagne and too much curry sauce with his chips. He chose to swim in rough sea and had no intention of ever learning how to ski, knew he wouldn't get on with the ski-slope people. He preferred autumn to summer and winter to spring. He had experienced death and had more reasons to cry than I did. He looked like he might know how to make it better. Andy was possibility, easy to be with, and he liked me. He was good sex and good fun and I believed I had trained myself out of a desire for stupid danger, that with him I might grow up and learn to be satisfied with happy enough. Loving him made sense and I was ready to be sensible. Sane and in love at the same time.

First sex with Andy led to only sex with Andy and always sex with Andy. And then we were a couple and then we were married and now we are seven and if we could go back to that roof garden hot night, I would, I'd jump at the chance, I'd love to want Andy like that again.

5

The scent of freesias does it to me every time. White freesias and a shadow of jasmine and immediately I'm fourteen, fifteen, sixteen, and all I am is hope and desolation and possibility and fear. Horrible, freezing fear. The unformed Lisa who doesn't yet know who she can be, but knows she has to get there soon or she'll collapse under the constant gravitational pressure of trying to work it out, dying to become. Lisa with such huge dreams and the vast possibility of going to be. The terror she inspires in her parents when she talks of all she might be. They just want a good education for her, the one they never had themselves. They don't necessarily want her to use it, to make a difference. It is surprising and touching to remember that girl Lisa. Scared Lisa, sad Lisa. Lisa who wants to belong but doesn't even know to what, let alone how.

Monday morning after Sunday night running, there was a bunch of freesias on my desk at the office. Unknowing sweet gift from Andy, who cannot have intended to make my mind spin so fast or so far from his present. Who could not know that I felt so removed from him at the time that even his name on the florist's card looked foreign. Andy will send flowers when he senses I'm not very happy. Or when he wants to please me. Or when it's my birthday. His birthday. Andy knows how to do the right things. I have tried to learn but I'm often a day or so late with the birthday card, blame it on the inefficient postal service. It was just a small grouping of the flowers but, despite the wonders of forced modern growth, four of the nine stems were a true gift of old-fashioned, authentic freesias. The thick white ones – heavy waxy petals, fatter in both trunk and trumpet width and so much more scent to them as to make a mockery of the purple and pale yellow delicacy of the others. What point could there be to a flower of pure colour and no discernible scent? The coloured freesias are probably adequate for the bees, maybe even the birds, but they remind me of nothing but paint colour charts. My wedding bouquet was a soft smudge of white and cream freesias bound together with jasmine. I was led up that aisle as much by the scent I held in front of me as I was by love and passion. These flowers didn't return me to my drunken and delicious and ludicrously enjoyable wedding, they clambered past that day of photo-enhanced memory to the years of teenage yearning.

I was not a lonely teenage girl, but I was uncertain. Part of a group and yet always feeling not really there. Part of the grooviest clique of girls at my school and yet not quite fitting. A little poorer than some, a lot poorer than others. Not quite as well dressed, well read, well informed. But they took me in and I was accepted by them, as one of them. I didn't think they ever really knew that I thought I didn't fit. I tried to talk to Sharon about it once, at a drunken grown-up girls' night. She was shocked. It had never occurred to her to think of me as a satellite to the main group of five. In her head I was always there, as much a part of it as she was, and I suppose from the outside it looked like that too. It can even sound like halcyon days when I regularly tell the tales of the group of girlfriends, best friends all. Women I now see once a year at the most, that little group, half of whom are still clumped in south-east London while the other three are scattered across the globe. Women I will never stop knowing no matter how different our lives become. We did do that best friends thing. We actually achieved the long-lasting friendship my father always said would stand me in good stead for the rest of my life. He was right. Knowing them did make part of it easier. It was far simpler to be in a gang than to be alone. It made going to school easier. It made going to the pictures and walking home across our little estate much easier. It made the first fuck an inevitability rather than the distant terror it often is at fifteen. Just as knowing I never really fitted in, knowing that I wasn't really like them, also made it all that much harder. Maybe everyone is like that really. The more drunken conversations I have, the more I am convinced that certainly every woman and maybe most of the men too think they don't really belong. Have never belonged. Scatter themselves through their days and weeks with collections of friends and lovers and husbands and wives, children too, and still know that they don't ever really belong. Or maybe I just think too much, drink too much. Certainly when I was fourteen, fifteen, sixteen I did. Perhaps the drinking too much wasn't clearly in evidence until the sixteen, seventeens. The thinking too much certainly was though. Even in the best of times with those girls, the few sparkling moments when I was sure I had my place, there was still the growing knowledge, the ghastly taunt, that perhaps none of it could ever be enough, that I could create all the new truths I wanted, but I'd never really be satisfied.

There was an old convent not far from where we lived. It backed on to my friend Heather's house. She didn't live on our estate like the rest of us. Heather's father was a doctor, her mother the practice nurse. Their medical practice was a small family business and in our area it was thriving. In the mid-teens my closest cross-group liaison was Heather. We talked university before UCAS forms and

Erich von Daniken years before *The X-Files*. We drank cup after cup of after-school instant coffee. I was in lust with her boyfriend and a little in love with Heather. According to the letter she wrote when we were in our second year at separate and distant universities, she was still in love with me. No accounting for taste. I fucked the boyfriend eventually. I know she never did. But beyond the talking and the theorizing and the maybes, and before either of us discovered the real possibilities of sex, the thing we did that made me happiest was to climb over the broken brick wall at the bottom of Heather's garden into the convent grounds. Much of my mother's own rampant Catholicism had died out with her pregnant-at-sixteen forced marriage to my father, though she insisted that my big brother and I were educated in the forms and protocol of religious attendance anyway. No doubt to breed in us the healthy disrespect we both now suffer from – and certainly had fully developed by the time we hit the hormone years. Heather's parents were staunch atheists and so, with fourteen-year-old invincibility and no scruples of sacrilege or superstition to stop us, we happily raided the treasures of the ageing nuns.

Apples and pears from an orchard of gnarled trees that had never seen pruning shears or pesticide in their lives. Trees lichen-covered in winter and heavy with fruit in the autumn. Around the edge of the small orchard, through a broken wooden door and into a walled garden. There was a grotto with a faded Mary statue on the other side of an overgrown and muddied lily pond, with a strangely sited plaster penguin in the centre of the pond. The penguin was completely out of place, maybe put there by one of the girls who had gone to the school when the nuns still taught and my mother still wanted to learn. The garden was walled on three sides, the fourth side was a ten-foot-high jasmine hedge. Now that I watch my husband be the gardener in fenced land of our own, I know this hedge couldn't possibly have grown as easily as the orchard – Andy has been trying to grow the same in our back garden since we moved in, and even the couple of small plants need constant care. Maybe there was a secret green-fingered nun who crept around her own Eden only when we weren't invading it. Maybe she was scared of fourteen-year-old girls. Fair enough. I'm terrified of them. Now. Against the south wall were the freesias. Someone must have planted them once, a tribute to the virgin, the scent wafting across her lily pond long before the penguin found its misplaced way to the position of chief acolyte. Maybe when they were planted there were even some palely scented coloured freesias in among them. But by the time Heather and I came along there were only wild white. Hundreds of them. The bed must have been a good five feet by fifteen, and all just a mass of the wax-heavy flowered scent.

We stole great clumps of the flowers, half opened, leaving those that were fully blooming so the ones we took home would open in their own time, in our lives, slowly perfuming our bedrooms. The scent was somewhat dissipated in Heather's large, detached house, but in our flat of one long dark corridor and six square rooms leading off, the freesia essence drunk-punched your nose the minute you walked in. Fat flower smell overpowering the frying bacon and my brother's aftershave and my mother's pore-clogging powder. For the three fast growing-up years the wonder of heavy freesia heightened by sweeter jasmine proclaimed spring and early summer and, until my sixteen-year-old occupation of the local supermarket in summer job tedium, heralded long days with hundreds of free hours to waste until we made it through to the magic of Adult. All this to an accompaniment of Bob Dylan. Too young to have known the music the first time round, we discovered him for ourselves when Heather's oldest brother tossed out his Dylan records to make way for his rapidly expanding punk collection. I still think we got the better deal.

The convent has been made into luxury apartments now. I expect they have wonderfully high ceilings and fine old wooden floors. I expect they cost hundreds of thousands of overpriced pounds and the new owners think they've procured themselves bargains. I don't suppose they have jasmine and wild freesias every year though. The orchard and flower-beds are a carpark.

For two weeks of my fifteenth summer I fed the cats and watered the plants at Heather's house while her family holidayed in France. We'd already been for our cheap family getaway to Majorca – easily one of the first families in our block to do anything so daring. My mother quite sensibly reasoned that if we could get nine hundred extra miles for the price of our usual week in Rye, then she could have exactly the same arguments with my father and brother, but at least she could enjoy them with a backdrop of different scenery. As it turned out, Dad and Will adored Spain while I suffered skin-stripping sunburn and the attention of too many unpleasant British lads. My mother, who quickly discovered she didn't even like paella, was forced to endure unwanted Spanish summers for the next twelve years. Now they've returned to Rye.

Afternoons alone at Heather's place that summer. Quiet, sunshine-warmed rooms. Rooms empty of people, reflecting back from the dark polished wood that must have been the unconscious impetus for the floorboards I insisted we copy the moment Andy and I moved into our own place. At fifteen, I didn't realize that the three weeks of dust and dirt and constant noise would be enough to splinter our just-mortgaged relationship almost beyond endurance. I simply thought the wood looked great. The teenage girl fantasy that this was my house – no thin-wall neighbours to disturb, no communal gardens to be intruded on. Silent afternoons when I stroked the lonely cat and wandered, watering can in hand, around that three-bedroom Edwardian house. Just an ordinary three-bedroom house. But the provision of a long hallway and central staircase made all the difference to my longing. It's why no matter how I envy the much more beautiful home of our friends Jaine and Nick, the clean lines and remodelled elegance of their excessively modern flat, I'd never choose to live there myself. Not merely because Andy and I couldn't afford it and therefore I have decided I don't like it, removing the delicious from temptation by calling it tasteless. I was born in a shared building, my bedroom wall against their bathroom, my sleeping head dreaming to the rhythm of their running bath. No matter how elegantly named the collection of apartments is, they'll always be a block of flats to me. Heather's place was a whole house, with no shared walls. It was my dream. I could make noise that no one else would hear. I played Heather's piano – I didn't know how to really, but I'd watched her often enough. Two chords up and four chords down, I was singing love ballads to possibility. Throw in a section on just the black notes and it was as if Kate Bush had moved in.

This was where I began to plan the new life, the two weeks of summer when I ran to Heather's empty house as often as I could possibly escape from my own. Where I started to design my future around what I might be instead of what I was, a life in which I had time and space, and that house was the reason all the possibilities could be made real, the place from which my future life would spill out. I never talked about it to anyone except Andy. Certain I would be laughed at for my temerity.

But it did become real, was made possible through my joining with Andy. When we chose each other, it made the rest of my dream seem attainable. The mindscape version of the fantasy house was what I later created in fact with my husband. The only problem was that, at fifteen, I had never actually pictured anyone else living in the perfect home with me.

I did try to talk to Andy about it – the uncertainty, the terror of stasis, the just not fucking knowing how to fix it. I did want to make it better. As I said, I am not the Bitch Queen. Lady-in-waiting, pretender to the throne perhaps, but basically your average wannabe goody-two-shoes. Red stilettos, of course. I tried to talk to Andy about it, but couldn't make my mouth say the words. We sat in front of a late television in the just-finished sitting room. I held his hand to distract him from the period BBC bimbo on screen. I got as far as – 'Babe, I want . . .' My husband and lover of the mystical seven years answered me, 'Yeah, I know.'

He knew? Understood the existential angst playing itself out in my fettered breast? Felt like I did, knew the unexpected, inexplicable desire to scream 'What now, what else, what is this?' to the unrelenting ether? To demand undeserved satisfaction from the universe? My darling true love understood all that I was going through?

'I'll make you another coffee when this bit finishes.'

Right. The man knows me well. I did want another coffee. As well as all the rest. Took a deep breath which lingered on into an irritated sigh and tried again. Nothing if not persistent.

'No, hon, I mean . . .'

'All right, I'm going.'

Andy got up, stalked into the kitchen, clattered plates, cups, glasses. Came back half an hour later. The programme he'd been watching was over. He sighed at the scrolling credits and smiled indulgently at me over a tray with fresh strong coffees, short, sharp shots of whisky, sliced russet apples and a great chunk of Stilton.

'Here you are, Lise. This lot should keep you going for an hour or so.'

The seven-year husband could tell I was hungry. The

seven-year husband could tell I was thirsty. The seven-year husband knew I wanted sex. The seven-year husband knew me too damn well. We threw back the whisky and sipped the coffee and turned over to another channel where a smiling girlie told us of bigotry in small-town America and Andy fed me chunks of apple laden with the biting, creamy Stilton. We kissed with lips made bitter from cheese and sweet from the juicy apples, mouths scented with smooth whisky and strong coffee. Mouths scented with seven years of knowing how to do it, knowing what to do. We fucked on the newly covered sofa, firm reupholstery beneath our backs, plump soft cushions to cushion our fall to the messy floor. An hour later we left the food and drink debris on the shiny wood and stumbled upstairs to bed. Our curtains remained firmly closed. We didn't get around to conversation.

By the time I got out of the shower the next morning, Andy had cleared up the mess, done the dishes, made the sitting room shiny and new again. Any sign of spontaneous action was tidied away, made neat and ordered by my husband, who likes things to be done properly, likes things to be put back in their place. I was famished again. Yes, I suppose I could have told him. Could have pushed back the proffered tray and his sweet-offered body and explained. Told the truth that nothing he could offer was likely to satisfy me, that I didn't even know if I could be satisfied. Could have. Didn't. Didn't want to reject him. Wanted to be with him. Just wanted so much more as well. Didn't want to upset him, had no reason to hurt him. Held back the truth because I didn't even know what it was yet. I stayed hungry. My dietary requirements were changing.

6

The week before my wedding. A week of too much alcohol and too many dress fittings and therefore not enough food – I was going to be gorgeous. Drunken conversations filling the spaces where breakfast and dinner should have been.

'One more time, Lise. You're doing this precisely why?'

'Christ, Jaine, because I love him.'

'I love Nick. That's no reason to spend three grand on a party.'

'Fifteen hundred quid.'

'And the meringue.'

'There is no meringue.'

'You're hardly the judge.'

'You'll see. The dress is no meringue.'

'I would have seen already if you'd let me.'

'I don't want to show anyone.'

'I am the best woman.'

I looked at Jaine – closest girlfriend, mouth full of chocolate, half a glass of champagne in one hand and a near-empty bottle, last dribble of tequila, in the other. 'That babe, is very debatable.'

It was my hen night, girls' night, pre-wedding girlie do. And Jaine was, as she had been for most of the past three months, baiting me about the impending nuptials. My wedding four days hence. Not a big party – the two friends from school who still lived in London, Andy's sister, Jaine and me. Five women in their late twenties, only just thirties, celebrating an upcoming ancient ritual that only one of us believed had any validity. Even Andy's sister thought that after four years of living together it was 'a little excessive to start making public pronouncements now'. Not that they had said so unkindly, or nastily. It was just that they didn't really understand why either Andy or I felt the need to do the wedding thing. My own views were well hidden under a gloss of post-modern reasoning, but at four thirty in the morning, when the others had long ago left Nick and Jaine's flat, stumbling home to nurse the beginnings of their champagne and tequila hangovers, the best woman produced half a gram of coke and started picking at the scabs.

'So you really love Andy?'

'Yes.'

'Enough for ever and ever amen?'

'Yes.'

'Enough for married person's tax allowance?'

'Hell, yeah, that's half the point.'

'Liar.'

'True, but it is a bloody good perk.'

Jaine was leaning over to hoover up her third line, snorted in derision at the inequity of the tax system that was about to benefit Andy and me – to the tune of the cost of our wedding – and managed to send five lines flying across her mirror. She picked up her John Lewis card and started reordering them.

'Bloody traditionalists. What if—' She paused as she breathed in deeply through her left nostril. 'What if you want to fuck someone else?'

'Bloody traditionalists don't fuck other people.'

'But you might.'

I took the proffered fifty-pound note. Jaine had bought

only good champagne and bloody expensive tequila and finest Swiss chocolate for the evening. She was taking her role of best woman very seriously and refused the possibility of anything merely good enough or second best for the entire night – she'd been saving the crisp new fifty just for this moment. I inhaled two lines, laid down the note. 'But I don't want to fuck anyone else. I never have done. Not since Andy. It's a choice. I want to do the monogamy thing.'

'You've never done it before.'

'Neither have any of the other blokes I've been with. If Andy can do it, so can I. I want to do the right thing. I want this to work.'

I pushed the mirror aside.

'You don't want any more?'

'Not yet. Give me a chance.'

'No. It's your hen night. It's supposed to be excessive.'

Jaine pushed the mirror back to me.

'Girls' night. Hen night sounds so bloody naff.'

Jaine pushed my head down to the mirror, held the note for me. 'Lise, it is naff, all naff, that's the point. Why bother with the wedding at all if you're not going to do all the other crap as well?'

I inhaled, felt the bitterness trickle down the back of my throat. 'So now you think I shouldn't be doing it at all?'

'No, but I just don't understand why you're doing all the traditional stuff—'

'I like the idea of the church. And Father Mike's really nice.'

'And he doesn't care that Andy's an atheist.'

'Yeah. He's cool.'

'He's a fucking hypocrite.'

'Jaine, do we have to do this now?'

Sadly, her four lines had kicked in sooner than mine and we did have to do it. Right then. Jaine wasn't letting any of it go. 'See, I just don't get it. You're doing the church and the dress and the bloody cake—'

'Chocolate cake with caramel icing.'

'Sounds disgusting.'

'But not traditional.'

'Yeah, well, you're doing all of that, but you're not doing any of the sensible bits.'

'Like what?'

Jaine swallowed down a tequila champagne slammer, then handed a last one to me. 'Wedding list.'

'Andy and I are adults.' I downed the fizzy alcohol, felt it swirl across my numb teeth and then melt into the coke at the back of my throat. 'We've been together for four years, we don't exactly need people to buy us things for our house. We haven't even got a bloody house. Having a wedding list just looks a bit greedy.'

'Don't take the tax allowance, then.'

'Don't be stupid, that's the Inland Revenue, I'm getting anything I can from them – I am self-employed remember. It's just my friends I don't want to use. No, the whole wedding list thing, it's just a bit—'

'Naff.'

'Well, I was thinking too fucking middle-class, actually, but yes, that'll do. So what else would you like to complain about?'

'You're not having a honeymoon.'

'We can't afford it and we've only got three days. It's a waste of money for just a weekend. I'd rather have a proper holiday when we've got the time. I don't want to use Andy's half-term break to fly somewhere exotic just for a day and a half. Anyway, we're saving for the house.'

'You've been saving for that bloody house for ever.'

'I've wanted that bloody house for ever.'

'What house? You haven't even started looking.'

'We can't afford to yet. We just need to save for a couple

more years and then it'll happen. When we move out of the flat I'm going to have space and time and everything I desire.'

'No you're not.'

'OK, but it's a good start. Anything else?'

'Not really.'

'Yes?'

'Well, sort of. I mean . . .'

Truth drug fighting well-brought-up reticence fighting natural desire to be nice. Truth drug won out.

'I just think that you and Andy aren't really that well suited.'

Very truth drug.

'I mean, I know you love him and I know he's made things happen for you and I know you're happy now, but . . . the rest of your life? Fuck it – how can you possibly be sure?'

Can't, wasn't, couldn't. Doing it anyway. Didn't know if it was the right thing to do. Didn't know how you were supposed to know. Loved him, wanted him, couldn't picture my future without him. Couldn't picture my future. Wanted to. Thought it might work. That was all. Hadn't felt it with any of the other loves. Just wanted to. It was impossible to explain. Even to myself. Even when sober. Andy had asked me to marry him on a sleepless night when not even a three-hour fuck was going to calm me enough to allow sleep. I was agitating about the lack of work that I could love, still not satisfied with what I was doing. I was moaning about the small, cramped flat we'd been in for eighteen months and wouldn't be leaving any time soon. I was jealous that Jaine and Nick always had extra money for playing and therefore seemed to have more fun than us. I'd spent the day with my mum and dad and had been depressed yet again by the quiet pall of their unfulfilled expectations, saddened and resentful at the same time. I was not a happy girl. Almost three years with Andy had encouraged me to believe in my dreams as he did in his own, had persuaded me that perhaps I could have it all, the perfect love, career and home. That it would be possible, even in my life, to have the triumvirate of attainment I'd always thought had to be an imaginary truth. I had learnt, through a process of crap flats and bad relationships and worse jobs, that you could have good love and nice home, or interesting work and great love, or pleasant home and fantastic work, but you could never dare to think all three of work, love and home could satisfy at the same time. But Andy disagreed, he did believe we could have it all. He maintained that with each other's support we could manage the perfect trinity. It seemed to be working for him. Just not me, because even Andy, with his strength and certainty, hadn't yet managed to love me into the degree of self-confidence that was going to let me think it was OK to have it all – to take it all if necessary.

I was tired and angry and resentful and crying. I was fed up with working too hard so I could earn the bulk of our income, freeing Andy up to continue his career-ladder climb. I hated the fact that my parents believed I wasn't living up to my early promise. All they'd ever hoped for was a lawyer for a daughter. I was clever, why hadn't I used it properly? Everything was supposed to be all sorted out, I was going to be thirty soon. I was terrified every time Andy mentioned the baby thing, because he so knew he wanted it one day and I so knew I didn't know what I wanted, but I really didn't think that being a mother was going to make it all better. I didn't know what would, but I was fairly certain that being responsible for another person, no matter what vast natural resources of love came with it, wasn't a sensible solution, not yet, maybe never. It was all wrong and all impossible and gone five thirty in the morning. And Andy asked me to marry him. And I heard a blackbird outside and said yes. Yes anyway. Yes but. Yes and. Yes. Because I could.

I was marrying Andy because I thought he could save me. And even then I knew it was a lie. Saving me wasn't his job.

I didn't tell this to Jaine. The extra slammer was one too many. Before I could get my mouth around the truth, Jaine ran off to their beautiful minimalist bathroom and threw up all over the stark white bidet. I put her to bed, tidied up a bit so it wouldn't be too horrible in the morning, and let myself out of the flat. There was sunrise and possibility. I was looking forward to the wedding, the party. I figured there was a good chance it would be all right. Which it was. For a while.

7

I met Jaine in my first week at university. We rapidly became best friends when we both realized that neither of us could bear to stay in halls of residence beyond the first term and ran away to a grotty, rain soaked, incredibly expensive flat and set about learning how to be adult. Holding dinner parties with vegetarian bakes and vast bottles of cheap red wine was our first test. We passed with flying colours, most of them thrown up on the kitchen, sitting room, bedroom floor. Same floor – small flat. Our place became a mecca for all those others left living in halls or still with Mum and Dad. At Lisa and Jaine's you could get pissed, smoke dope, eat badly cooked 'healthy' food, taste-free vegan lasagne a speciality, and still make it into an early morning lecture. We didn't guarantee that sleep was also possible. We weren't especially well suited as best mates – Jaine was far more outgoing than me, readier for a night at the pub or ten hours of dancing or a sudden-decision weekend dash to France. We were leftover best mates, a coalition formed out of necessity from a larger group which fades with time leaving just the nucleus partnership which has become solid and real, created more from what went on around it than from any initial spark of excitement. She'd been with me through two nineteen-year-old pregnancy scares – after the second one she'd forcibly marched me to her GP for the pill. I took her to the clinic when her lauded pill failed and contributed half the fee for the abortion, holding her hand all the way. We'd been drunk together, horribly sick together, holidayed in Turkey where we'd fucked the same two blokes on alternate nights, and in Greece where we couldn't find a decent man on any of the six islands we travelled to. By the time we were in our early twenties we were friends from time and experience and shared history rather than anything more specific, and once we'd both met the men who became our permanent partners, our relationship underwent the careful and occasionally creaky metamorphosis from couple to weekend foursome and 'my best friend' became 'our best friends'. There were a stumbling two years when Jaine and Nick first became a couple. Jaine and I reworked our friendship from best friend to best girlfriend as Nick took over the role of her constant companion and I continued to lurch from one unsuccessful relationship to the next. It was unsettling at first, partially losing the person who had become my other half. I didn't know if I was upset that she now had what I wanted – man, relationship, chance to plan a future – or if I was just pissed off that Nick had pinched my best mate. And while I wasn't exactly jealous that Jaine had achieved the long-desired status of couple before me, I certainly knew I wanted it too. Then Andy became part of my history and I was double too and the uneven keel was righted again. I was able to prove that while two may be company and three can quite often be an uncomfortable crowd, a collection of four individuals was fairly ideal for talking up a whole host of other adages. With partners to confide in Jaine and I no longer needed to share every secret thought. We rarely met without our men around, but we still got on easily and well, a relationship carved out of years with no need of social niceties or polite discussion. I never felt the need to cook ostrich steak for Jaine. And she'd have laughed at me if I had.

Of course, the term 'best friend' is something of a misnomer. Both Jaine and I had friends we got on better with for different things, friends we talked to about some matters and not others. But because we could go out as a foursome, because we enjoyed ourselves as a double-couple group, the 'best friend' tag stuck. We were their best friends and they were ours – we did stuff together, got on well enough, brilliantly sometimes, had holidays together. Did it all because that's what couples do – they make other couples mirror themselves so they never have to feel too damn different, too damn wrong. Surrounding yourself with other apparently happy couples saves you the bother of looking at the cracks in your own relationship. You can have a far better time scrutinizing the schisms in theirs.

After the initial period of getting to know Nick, learning to forgive him for stealing my playmate, he and I actually developed a good friendship of our own. We had to. If a girl doesn't make good buddies with her best friend's man, she's likely to lose that friend pretty damn quickly. Or she will once they've had a ten-margarita session and the girlfriend has drunkenly burbled what she really thinks about the tedious, sexist lech. A woman will forget many things after a night on the piss, what her best friend really thinks of her boyfriend is not one of them. Nick was different from Andy. Very. Where Andy was good guy and nice bloke and easy mate and all those things I longed for in my state of early twenties insecurity and terror, Nick was much more difficult. He could be funny and charming and over-the-top brilliant to be around on a good day. On others, he was liable to lapse into huge depressions at the drop of a hat, ready to launch into a mean argument at the slightest provocation, sarcastic and occasionally cruel. Once I learnt to ignore his bastard phases and enjoy the rest, I got on very well with him. And as I grew into myself and my own bravery I realized that he and I often had a similarly bitter sense of humour, regularly demonstrated the same propensity to exaggerate and were both prone to a degree of overindulgence. In anything. So I liked Nick and he liked me and Andy liked Jaine and it was all very nice and easy and cool.

The four of us did the couples together grouping really well – which is bloody useful when your social life is a dinner party rather than party party kind of place. After the first year or so of doing the normal couple thing – girls on the wine at home and boys down the pub – it slowly dawned on us that perhaps we weren't making the best use of our collective resources. We realized that ours was the turning-millennium version of new couple cosiness. Not for us the past passing of boys playing new lads at the football while the girls hung back on the warm Chardonnay alliance. We split across rather than along gender divides. Although Jaine went into advertising and I went into training, we had a shared history to base our relationship on. Nick and Andy, however, never had much in common in the first place. They were perfectly capable of conversing about politics or music or even about their women, but not very much else. Andy was much straighter than Nick – he'd had his future mapped out as long as I'd known him and more. And he was glad of it. Nick, on the other hand, was an actor. Fairly successful with several good-money ads and voiceovers and even the odd juicy role in every other televised Ruth Rendell. He was also a potential playwright, not a bad musician and quite often very wise. In a knowing-bastard kind of way. And if Jaine complained about his occasional sarcasm turning to vicious nastiness in the cold night, well, we all have our crosses to bear, right? At least Nick was awake enough to be evil. Andy was always snuggled up close and fast dreaming by three in the morning.

We split, then, as couples not along gender lines but cross-sex for shopping companionship. Nick and I would go into town on a Saturday afternoon – we'd do the Bond Street, Oxford Street, Covent Garden, Soho trawl and wind up in a smoky wine bar somewhere. Jaine and Andy would stay at home and indulge their incomprehensible love of football or do something terribly clever involving Polyfilla and power sanders and then the four of us would meet up in the evening for movies and supper and more drinks. It worked really well. It worked too bloody well.

8

Nick was tall but didn't look it and remarkably well formed for someone who'd spent years abusing his body. Fortunately, he was also just starting to develop the stomach that comes to men in their thirties when they've laughed at the rest of us and our body paranoias for so long. Something I'm only a little smug about. He hid this minor imperfection well, though, with excessive vanity clothed in big jumpers for casual and ludicrously expensive suits on every other occasion. Nick dressed far better than Jaine had ever done. Jaine was more your jeans and checked shirt kind of girl. Of course, Jaine was that kind of girl because she had no need to overdress. Because Jaine looked fucking brilliant, *marie-claire*-five-page-fashion-shoot-somewhere-in-Arizona-cowgirl-model kind of gorgeous in jeans and a checked shirt, just out of bed and hair still unbrushed. Jaine didn't run five nights a week – she was born with an ideal body and had no need to find the perfect item of clothing that could point up her good features while hiding all the rest. Jaine was all good features, long limbs, dark-brown black skin, expensive chocolate black, seventy per cent cocoa solids black, huge green eyes, startling with her colouring, pupils so naturally dilated they looked like jet, and fantastic everything else. It didn't take a whole lot of shopping to find her clothes. Whereas not only did Nick take hours to find the perfect shirt, he also loved to do so. And I did too. Mine was less to do with the joy of shopping and rather more to do with body obsession. When you're not a naturally jeans and t-shirt chick, and when you've put all the bloody effort I have into making yourself look passable, you're not going to ruin the effect with a hastily purchased and possibly inappropriate item of clothing. Besides, I long ago discovered that the best thing about designer clothes was not the label itself but the way they manage to hide all your imperfections. It took me a while to suss it, but by the time I was twenty-five I was well aware that posh girls don't just look good because of the breeding and all that fresh air down at the country pile. They really look good because anyone's arse looks better in Nicole Farhi than in Mark One.

Nick was also one of those really ordinary-looking blokes that you simply don't realize are beautiful. Unless you marry them. Or see them on screen in a particularly appealing light. Or don't marry them but happen to kiss them anyway, kiss them in a quiet corner, a secret alleyway, kiss them in a place that makes a fuck out of the question and all the more definitely desirable. And then you look up and realize that the deep-set, heavily bagged eyes you always assumed were only brown, ordinary brown, anyone's brown, are really nearly black. Ebony with halogen lights bright behind. And how could you miss that piece of birth-wrought perfection? How could I have missed it for so long?

Nick wasn't exactly my first choice for a partner in sin. When you've known someone for nine years you tend not to think of them as an object of desire. And it's even less likely that a modern, post-feminist, fully grown-up girlie is going to develop a major crush on the man who is also her best friend's boyfriend. But then passion doesn't tend to follow perfectly understandable paths, and when the love virus strikes you can't exactly claim prior vaccination and present immunity.

Fair enough. I know that's crap. I could have chosen not to get into it. Could have turned the feelings off if I'd really wanted to, if I'd tried to early enough. But that's exactly what I didn't want. I went into the affair because of the desire and excitement. I welcomed the risk. Later, though, it was much easier to tell myself I'd had no choice. Later is the time when everyone always claims they had no choice. The eternal, all-cultures myth of love-struck, love-blinded, love-lost turns you from active aggressor into passive victim. Even unwilling victim. And all those impossible love songs we were brought up with go a long way towards providing the perfect soundtrack for absolution.

I don't know why I'm making light of this, why I'm telling this story like it's easy. This was the most interesting thing I ever did. And therefore the most dangerous. This was where it started. In my state of mind at the time, though, danger just looked like a whole lot of fun. As I said, I didn't really choose Nick. It did just happen. Though I don't doubt my being up for it helped. The readiness is all – and all that.

There we were, my best friend's boyfriend and I, all shopped out, a couple of hours to go until we were due to meet the others and at least a bottle of wine to get through until then. I'd decided we should both tube that day, rather than me driving. Premonition of the need for insobriety, perhaps. I'd probably had another glass too many on no breakfast and no lunch. Far too many clothes to try on to make things worse for myself by eating as well. And there I was, a bit pissed and fairly bloody satisfied with my purchases of the day, and so was he and we were smiling and laughing and chatting and then I took his hand to make some point or other, fuck knows what it was, I don't know what it was – I can barely remember anything that happened before that moment. All I know is that from the instant we did the touching skin thing it was different. Nick. My best friend's boyfriend. A man I'd holidayed with. He'd seen me sunburnt and stupid. A man I'd been embarrassingly drunk with, and who had several times held me while I was throwing up. A man I knew all the nasty little stories about – he was my best friend's lover, after all. I knew about him and that bloke in his second year at university. I knew about him and the woman who used to work for his agent, about that girl up in Manchester. I knew too about Jaine and the man in Edinburgh. And the other one in some other city that she wouldn't give any more details on. Nick didn't. He had confided his infidelities to her early on, seeking absolution and getting hell. She had known better than to tempt him with the whole truth.

I knew all that and remembered all that and anyway it just started happening. Like in the soppy movies and the trashy girl-meets-boy books and the silly love songs, and I was just going along with it. His hand felt good. Sitting in my small hand, his long-fingered hand felt good. It was not Andy's hand but it felt like it wanted to be there anyway. I looked at Nick and I realized his hand did want to be there. Be there and elsewhere and be more of me, and I wondered how long this hand had been coming my way and if it had been coming why hadn't I seen it sooner and if it had been coming did that mean it was meant to be and if it was meant to be then fuck it, just fuck it, why the fuck shouldn't I kiss him?

So I did.

9

He kissed me back.

Oh God and then the earth moved and I knew Nick was the One True One and everything changed and it began, we began. I began again. The Saturday afternoon café around us fell back on itself, the inner city cool people crumpled into tissue paper balls and then there was only Nick and me and my mouth and his mouth, teeth-clashing tongue percussion and the hot, violent passion running through me. We entered into the torrid affair I'd been longing, begging for without even hearing my own cries. Nick became my only reason for being, my sole truth, the uncharted destination my heart had long sought.

Ah, no. We didn't. Even at that point, in the very moment of kissing him, I knew the myth that was trying to build itself around us was total crap. But fuck it, I did feel something. I felt him. I still don't know if it was because he was Nick or just because he was new. Perhaps he could have been anyman. Maybe he was anyman, but his lips on mine were brand new. The bitter taste of his smoker's tongue in my mouth was new. Andy has never smoked and his lips are full lips, juicy lips. I've loved my husband's lips more than any part of his body. Kissing someone else, wanting to kiss someone else, was never supposed to be on the agenda. Andy and I have often had those late-night stoned conversations about who would you be with if you weren't with me, and have gone through the litanies of her or him, or that one or the other, but always you in the end, babe, always you in the end. Me for his mouth, he for mine. But it had never occurred to me that I might actively choose someone else's lips over Andy's. And the specific notion of wanting to kiss Nick was even less likely. I've just never fancied Nick's mouth. Wide mouth, thin lips – odd combination. Not especially attractive. Not ugly, not unpleasant, just not really that great, nothing to write home about. Of course I'd wondered what it would be like to kiss him. He was my best friend's boyfriend – it's the kind of fleeting thought you have when you're admiring the fourth Galliano suit he's tried on in half an hour and wondering what Jaine sees in him when he's naked. But I thought about it and then dismissed his mouth as not my type. Not my type of mouth, ergo not my type of man, so I won't shag him, then. I've always liked kissing. Sometimes I've even thought that kissing was what I liked most. Sometimes. Occasionally. And my husband could kiss for England. This was fact, one constant truth of our marriage. Which at that moment, in that city café, was irrelevant. The kissing comparison from Andy to Nick was all of a sudden completely not the point. You can't carefully study physiognomy when your faces are the bare millimetres apart allowed for breath and bruise-free exchange. I say all this glibly, I know. At the time it still was – easy, flippant. It hadn't begun to matter yet. But sitting in the café, sharp-squashing my tits against the edge of the table to be closer to his skin, the taste of Nick in my mouth woke me up, shot a jagged line of potential from my navel to my cunt. I was a fourteen-year-old girl again and wanting it bad.

Was bad for wanting it. Knew I was bad. But then for the teenager that's part of the charm, isn't it? Defining the boundaries and then breaking through them. Checking out just where the end of Mum and Dad's patience lies and pushing a little bit further. After our seven long years I knew exactly where Andy set his limits. He understood mine beyond words. We'd had times of slamming against each other, often turning those breakouts into games – sex games, power games, the games you play when you're either just learning to love or desperately trying to get desire back again. Games that don't really go with mortgages and burglar alarms and planning for the baby, let alone actually having the baby, giving in to the biology and making the for ever genetic joining. Yes, and maybe we gave up on playing too soon, and God knows it certainly wasn't all Andy's fault, I was as guilty as him of giving in to the ease of easy married life, happily married wife. More guilty perhaps – with Andy I had made real the vision of what I'd always believed I wanted, what I'd been born and bred to want. Out of the estate and away from the no-challenge jobs my parents hated and vaulted into the land of urban bliss they'd promised would make me happier than them, far away from the hopeless loves I'd had to scramble through to find him. And it wasn't enough. I actually had what I'd always planned for and worked for and, just like they always say in the talk shows, it wasn't enough. Guilt. Excitement. Potential. The bad man as opposed to the good man, black hat not white hat, lure of the illicit motorbike boy, intense desire for you really know you shouldn't. The whole fourteen-year-old package. Puppy fat and zits not included. Fantastic.

So there I was kissing Nick. We half pulled away from each other and sort of laughed. Sort of. A stupid, embarrassed, wait for you to speak laugh. I waited for him to speak. I kept my hand on his. He didn't speak. So it would be up to me. I moved my fingers in his hand, entwined opposing thumbs. Lisa gets to put her big foot in it and make the first offer. Which is so crap. Fourteen again. Disparity looms and you're going to be the one to make a tit of yourself and say it out loud, you will be brave because you're the girl and you know girls are better with words, everyone's always said so. Deep breath, words finding themselves on the tip of your tongue, making a stupid break for sound and speech. So it's either got to be 'I liked that, can we do it more?' or 'Hah! That's funny!' And either one runs a massive risk. He still said nothing.

I ventured an erudite, 'Well, fuck!'

He chanced his hand with the more scholarly, 'Yeah, fuck.'

So all that education wasn't wasted, then.

I wondered if he thought 'Yes please' like I did.

And then we laughed. Together. Simultaneously. Grown-ups again. Major relief and suddenly at ease with each other – only friends, same thing, normal life, normal wife, just shopping and we can cope with this. The café can cope with this. The Saturday shoppers around us turned back to their cool wines and warm caramel lattes, instantly reassured. The fully grown people at the corner table aren't going to turn into rabid pubescents and start ripping each other's clothes off, fumbling for genitalia with the blind desire of genetics and no knowledge of real biology. They won't be making us jealous and irritated with our own lives for its lack of passion. We can get on with just being at ease. Pleased to be adult and not suffering any more. Grateful that we have found our partners and tied ourselves to them for life. The world full of seriously relieved fully grown people all around the room heaved a collective sigh and went back to ignoring us. Nick and I went back to ignoring what had happened. Except that we couldn't. Not really. It hung between us when we waited to catch the Tube home. It stood full and impudent in front of us when I struggled to get my key from my bag at the front door. It slapped me on my fourteen-year-old face when Andy kissed me in the kitchen.

It hit me harder when Nick kissed Jaine and she laughed to us all over the fresh focaccia that Nick seemed unusually randy for a shopping day. She didn't need to whisper the information – me and Andy and Nick and Jaine have always been very vocal about our sex lives. It's those camping holidays Jaine forced us to go on in the past. Suddenly I didn't think it was funny that Nick had the hots for Jaine. The pheromones were obviously flying because Andy was all over me too, a lustful husband who'd just noticed that my breasts were fantastic, my hair gorgeous, my legs long and lean. Then I knew for definite it was only hormones. I do have a mirror. So I sat in our local Italian restaurant and played teenage girl who flirts with one boy because she wants another to notice her. Flirts with her husband because she wants her best friend's boyfriend to notice her. Orders spaghetti vongole because of the innuendo, even though clams are about my least favourite food and that particular restaurant does a brilliant mushroom risotto. But where's the simulated sex in rice? The fourteen-year-olds flirted and made unnoticed, barbed little comments. They began to grow up. By the end of the evening we were maybe sixteen. Still virgins, though.

Jaine went to call their cab and Andy went for a drunken piss and I took my courage in my hand, swallowed my full glass of wine, leaned across the table littered with beer bottles and wine glasses and coffee cups and stuttering, heart leaping, whispering, told Nick I wanted to fuck him.

He laughed and said, 'I know.'

I accidentally spilt Andy's half-glass of red wine on his new shirt for being such an arrogant bastard, and just as Jaine started to stumble back to the table, he laughed even harder and whispered, 'I know because I want to fuck you too.'

Seventeen and counting.

This is what Nick thinks:
Fuck. God. Brilliant. Fuck.

10

It's hard to play the good wife when inside you're feeling like a bad whore. A good whore. A truly fucking brilliant whore. Not that I had done any actual whoring just at this point, you understand. Technically I was merely whore-in-training. Postulant whore. Simply a lot of hidden kissing and many more phone calls. Mobiles only – the itemized bill is the scourge of the modern adulterer. But the flesh fest was on its determined way. Or safer still, its predetermined way. No responsibility for me. In my previous married-to-the-man mode I'd never felt the need to hide, to be secretive, to keep any thoughts separate from Andy. Perhaps that was part of our problem – my ability, even need, to let my husband know every little thing I thought, felt or intuited. He experienced an entirely lesser desire to reciprocate, but that had been fine – this was about me, not Andy. I'd actually wanted Andy to know my inside out. He knew every pure thought I'd had, and every bad. Knew when I loathed my mother and when I loved my dad. Knew when I despised myself and adored him. And vice versa, though rarely vice versa. He knew I'd had one or two fervent desires beyond the two of us and he knew right down deep in his scrotum that I would never do anything about them. You can't exactly call him complacent – that's what I'd thought too. Seven years of not wanting anyone else, not desiring anyone other than him, seven years of building up that bank account of trust the two of us were based on, low interest but secured deposit. Before the vicious scream of desire grabbed me and turned me inside out into a raging-hormone teenager again.

And so the perfect wife of inner city suburbia became the bitch tart of Brixton. Nothing Andy could do was right, no gesture he made to make things better was wanted or even a little bit necessary. His very presence in our almost perfect house annoyed the hell out of me. Not because he was doing anything wrong, but because I was. Or rather because I wanted to. Because I so badly wanted to do the wrong thing, lusted for the wrong thing, and I hated Andy for being there, in the way. Hated him for being married to me and therefore making wrong what I found myself wanting. Intense flash fights of screamed vicious words and silent nastier thoughts started exploding from me and imploding on our relationship. This was new to us – Andy and I had always been the kind of couple who could go for months without a disagreement. Not for us the huge fight about nothing that starts in the supermarket over carrots and potatoes and forces its way back into the home, where it becomes about the less tangible but far more real you don't love me, you never really loved me. Those fights we happily left to other couples, to Jaine and Nick, so they could tell us about them days later, when the pain had subsided and the bruises were fading and the blush of making up had hidden the mouth-watering scars. Those fights were the ones other couples had so Andy and I could feel hugely relieved that neither of us was that kind of person. But now our previously calm house was too-occasional crucible for my unrequited lust. We had the proverbial bitter fights about nothing – but in our case they never descended from trivia to truth, because I couldn't tell Andy this reality. This truth that wasn't really reality yet. There was a whole week in his life when he honestly thought I cared passionately about the colour of the brick wall at the bottom of our garden. And then, as quickly as my irritation and anger arrived, it would all go away and I'd feel good about Andy again. I wouldn't speak to or see Nick for a couple of days and, love being constant, while in-lust needs the presence of the beloved to feed and thrive, I could see Andy as he really was. I was the good Lisa again, and the pock-plastered walls of our new old house sighed with tangible relief. My days of evil temper would be replaced with a soft week of sorry and good girl and sweetness and light and 'there, there, darling, I don't know what's come over me'. And well-placed fucks halfway up the stairs, in the armchair watching *Newsnight*, in the three a.m. back garden with a delicious do-it-now possibility of the neighbours watching. Until the next time it came. All because I was coming with the wrong man. It wasn't Andy's fault he wasn't Nick. I knew that. It wasn't Andy's fault his body was perfect, lean and fine-muscled and his lips full round, and that I knew all of him just too damn well. Not his fault that he was good and lovely and therefore I should never have been thinking about Nick at all. But part of the reason I was thinking about Nick was that he wasn't good. Was specifically not the good guy. Not Andy's fault that even the strange and exciting sex we were having after the fights and the roses and longer than usual morning kisses – in the good weeks – didn't last and didn't make me really happy and couldn't ever make the itch go away. Not Andy's fault that another evening with Jaine and Nick at the pub followed by the Ritzy and more drinks and maybe a couple of joints back at our place seemed the very worst form of torture, not the easy relaxing weeknight it had used to be. None of it was Andy's fault, but that made no difference. Mine was the pressure-cooker body. Release was imminent.

Nick and I found a way to be potential. We met for a

few secret lunches but my work always needed me back too soon and he could only claim so many lunch-hour auditions. We decided to use our past form and went shopping more often than usual. In the cooler-weather run-up to Christmas this went relatively unnoticed by our football-watching, home improvement spouses – neither of whom jumped at requests to come with us. Requests tentatively offered because Nick and I didn't want them to be accepted, we just wanted to look good. And we did look good – we looked great. We were dressing now not for the spouse who knows every flaw and blemish, but for each other. Dressing for the might be, will be, want to be fucked. So Nick and I were sent off Saturday afternoons and late-night Thursdays, blessed by our partners and free to trawl well-travelled streets for restaurants and bars we didn't know, where we could find moments of dark and promise.

Clocks ticked and time became imperative. I told Andy and my partner Mary that I needed a day at the library for some client research, Nick told Jaine he was workshopping a new play, Andy and Jaine arranged to meet after work for a takeaway and watch the football. I booked an anonymous hotel charting the hypotenuse of Baker and Oxford Streets, gave them my credit card number but told them I'd pay in cash on the day. Taking care of the non-nuptial arrangements was not essentially a classic feminist gesture on my part. Nick is an actor. Great chunks of occasional money for coats or suits or holidays or ludicrously expensive presents for Jaine come his way every now and then, and when they do he's always been very generous. Ready money, however, is not his thing. Ready money, direct debits, standing orders – all left to those of us with proper jobs and four weeks' holiday a year. And all the tedium we can take.

It was done – date set, room booked, perfect clothes purchased.

Seductive but not overtly sexy, nothing demanding too much attention, expressing an excess of expectation. Everything was in order, talking and half touching done. The real adultery was about to begin. All that remained was the sex. Well, that's easy, then.

This is what Jaine thinks:

Nick's having another affair. Or wants to. He lies like shit. There's certainly something going on. I wonder if I should confront him. Maybe I should wait and see what pleasures guilt brings. Maybe I should just go out and have a fling myself. It's been too long, this one-man love, I need a little break. It's obviously what's wrong with Lisa. I've told her before now she ought to have an affair. She's bored, scared of for ever. Everyone's scared of for ever.

Nick had better not fall in love.

11

Of course, everything was so carefully set up something was bound to go wrong. I am well practised in the art of anticipatory dangers, so I wasn't the least bit surprised when I woke up on the morning of the big day with a great fat pus-filled zit in the middle of my chin. Snow White agrees to fuck around and wakes up looking like the Wicked Witch of the West. Ideal. There was also a stomach swollen from my almost-due period, the cramped blood that always wants to come to the party too, and a fierce headache from drinking an excess of nervous vodkas the night before. Brilliant. My first foray into the realms of married adulterers and I go at it like a sixteen-year-old virgin. Worse, at least when I was that youthful virgin I had innocent stupidity to blame my mistakes on. Intentional cupidity didn't let me off the hook quite so well. However, after a degree of pimple-squeezing and the imbibing of two litres of pure spring water with three fat vitamin C pills and half a dozen diuretic tablets, I almost felt normal again. I followed the prima donna beauty regime – scream at myself in the mirror, scream at the bathroom, attack the treacherous chin with fingernails and ten different lotions. Then I further abused my body with a fast, sweaty and bloody long run. Fifty-three minutes in which I persuaded myself I was doing absolutely the right thing feeding this hunger, running away from the frying pan of 'is this all there is' and into the bubbling fat of 'in that case I'll just leap anyway'. Mixed metaphors of guilt and excitement sending me in a leaping arc from maybe to will be to go for it. By mid-morning I was back to almost normal with an under-the-skin ripple of bloody terrified. Which in its own way was cool too. Teenage, pimply and nervous is far from the leaden downward pull of middle-age spread. The Jesus year was progressing rather well, I thought.

The room had been booked, the rehearsed lie prepared.

'Not going to work today, my dearest wife?'

'No, my own true love, we're planning for the conference.'

'But you are still here at home, darling mine.'

'Indeed, beloved. Mary thought we might as well both work from home and then meet up later in the day. Nothing in the office that can't wait and she and I both know we'll get more done if we're not disturbed by the constant ringing of the phone. You know how it is once I'm really into it. And I can't leave my mobile on in the library anyway.'

Perfect lie. Andy would never check with Mary – she irritates him so much he can barely bring himself to wish her good morning if he gets her when he calls me at work. He'd never actually engage her in conversation about my whereabouts just in case she launched into a description of one of her latest straight-out-of-Japanese-MBA techniques. Mary has a history of drink and drug-taking and sleeping as shag-happily as the rest of us, but then two years ago she met Mr Right and translated all her bad habits into good behaviour with the force of his ferociously righteous love, wiping clean both her past slate and her past memories. Mary has remade herself into good girl and doesn't quite understand why the rest of us haven't settled down so well. What used to be a nose for coke and carnival has become a mania for marriage and management training. Though I have never found training quite as fun as she does, it was all right for a while, occasionally great. Then it became normal. Now I like parts of my work and love the cheques I make out to myself. My husband, however, never really got the point. Total quality, performance indicators and thinking outside the box were to him phrases best used by Des Lynam while winking seductively at the camera, not meant for talking about real-flesh human beings. Even though I'd been working in that field for most of our seven years together, and he had not only supported me but actively pushed me to make a career out of it, Andy still didn't understand why a grown man – or woman – earning upwards of a hundred grand a year would feel the need to bond, unite and find the team force hidden deep within his repressed public school psyche alongside forty other similarly wealthy but afflicted blokes. He thought that perhaps a year on the dole might be all the motivational experience they needed. Or a week teaching revised English syllabus to thirty-six fourteen-year-olds. And it's not that I disagreed with him, it's just that my somewhat greater percentage of the mortgage might as well be direct-debited from that as anything else. I did know how to do the job. And training did often take place in rather superior hotels. All of which meant that I not only had the desire to be bad and wicked, I also had the perfect set of lies to facilitate said evil. My work quite often took me away for two or three days at a time. If the adultery turned out to be more than just a one-off, I certainly had the perfect future cover. Fairly good career choice, after all. Clever me.

Sadly my brilliantly constructed lie wasn't even needed. Andy had an urgent call the night before to go into work early – big fat Ofsted trauma looming – so he kissed me sweetly at six thirty on the big morning and departed murmuring that Jaine would be pissed off, he'd got a hell of a day in front of him and he'd probably only just make it to her place in time for the kick-off. Which left me just a little disappointed. There's no point rehearsing and planning your wickedness if you're not given a chance to actually try out your acting ability. Mildly disappointed at seven fifteen, fat and spotty at eight a.m. and itchily unnerved by mid-morning. Ready to call the whole thing off and skulk away to hide in suburban safety. But determined not to do so. Running through all the problems and none of the good bits. Incapable of remembering just what those good bits were. Because there is of course a major problem with pre-planned sex. It's therapy sex really. The kind the better-trained therapists always want you to have – thought out, arranged, considered and dull as fuck. Or not-fuck. Entered into with all the passion and spontaneity of a smear test:

Are you ready for me?

Yes, I believe so.

Then would you like to just hop up here?

Of course, no problem.

And now relax, if you will.

Yes, certainly, with pleasure.

And if you'll just slip off your panties . . . ?

Panties. Any man who says panties is either a doctor or a pervert. They're knickers. The bloody things are knickers. Weirdos.

But back to the sex. Until settling down to the lengthy period of going out with Andy, prior to our marriage, the majority of my sexual experiences, in or out of relationships, had been entered into – as is perfectly usual in the life stories of most of my friends and acquaintances – drunk, horny and ready to fuck. A fair amount of our married sex had been too. Alcohol is meant to lead to sex. It just fits.

Sex ought to be preceded by many other kinds of debauchery. Drinking, drug-taking. Things don't go better with coke – sex goes better with coke. Certainly longer anyway. Which is why, having calmed my qualms enough to persuade myself to get on with the bloody thing, I also made sure to take with me to the central London hotel of anonymous sin one half-bottle of good champagne, one pint bottle of adequate whisky and a couple of lines of cocaine, filched from the thin gram Andy keeps in his bedside table, replenished for special occasions – birthdays, Christmas and a particularly impressive crop of cherry tomatoes we grew in our over-large window boxes in the old flat two summers ago. The plants didn't survive last year's journey from flat to house and garden. Cherry tomato as relationship almanac – it's probably as reliable as matching star signs.

And so on to the juice. I got through my torture run picturing perfect Jaine and loving Andy in tears, in rages, in bed with each other. The latter was by far the more terrifying option. I showered and shaved and exfoliated and dressed framing jealous scenes and fine-scripted angry vitriol. I smothered my body in dangerous lotions and my only really expensive perfume. That is, it wasn't bought at Duty Free. I wondered if the whole world could see the scarlet A branded on my forehead. I tried to dress and discarded five different combinations of clothes before finally settling for what I'd tried on in the first place. I boarded the Tube more fragrant and elegant than anything the Victoria Line had seen since the last time Mary Archer descended on Brixton. I remembered word for word our well-written and ever so carefully not-naff wedding vows, but I wore the perfect black dress and still more perfect Calvin Klein triumphantly sheer black bra and knickers which Andy bought for my last birthday in a fit of passion. And then failed to rip off me in the tedious grip of reality. We got pissed on good whisky and fell asleep in each other's arms on the sofa instead, clambering up to bed cold and stiff at three in the morning. I brought the mood-altering substances, Nick brought his body. I brought desire and boredom and bitterness and interest and desperation, he brought simple passion. I carried an expectation of guilt, he followed through with a choice not to think about Jaine. In the turning throes of the hotel's revolving door I determined to leave my guilt behind me and walked up to Nick full of potential. He asked me what Andy was up to this afternoon. I ignored the question and kissed him. On the cheek. We signed the appropriate forms and received a credit-card-type pass key for the door. Doubly handy, as it happened. It doesn't do to ruin the magnetic strip of your Visa card with Class A drugs. We went to the room, we turned on the telly. *Neighbours*. Perfect. We had two narrow lines of coke each and a big slug of the whisky. The vapours kicked in, masking fast-numbing teeth and I allowed my tight stomach to unclench just a little. I went for a wee – last of the diuretic coffee kicking in – and came back to discover that Nick was already naked and had squealed himself into bed first. Bastard. I opened the champagne, poured us both a full glass, inhaled the last fine line, and bravely, slowly, got naked myself. In bed we drank champagne, touched hands, touched cold and nervous feet and then, deep breath, might as well, that was what we were there for after all, we touched bodies.

Nick and I kissed, sharp and newer coke on my tongue, joining the whisky fumes folding across his breath. His hands on my back were an aperitif. His chest against mine was delicious. He was not Andy. This kissing was different from the stolen kisses. Less real and yet more in the same clammy grasp. It held not only wickedness but also potential. Partly it was also ridiculously funny. We were actually doing it. All the talking, all the planning, and here we were, doing it. Our lips were kissing, as was our flesh. Nick's hands on my back were not Andy's hands, were the aesthete actor hands of someone who prefers his girlfriend to do the garden. I savoured the smooth of his fingers running across the smooth of me, and then the hand turned and bad bitten nails scratched across my fine rubbed skin. We threw more alcohol inside us and chose to be very drunk very fast and even more gratefully drug-induced spontaneous and therefore officially not planned. We were not sober, not intentional and not culpable. He was just there, beside my body, with my body, in clean white sheets in a simple room with London ignoring us completely. New man laid out for me. I forgot the good husband, I forgot the hard-won beautiful house and predetermined life and embarked on a fucking brilliant afternoon. Literally. *Neighbours* finished and, it being a special day for physical activity, a silently open-mouthed Sue Barker looked on in dismay.

12

And so, true lust.

I was discussing team strategy with a group of pleasant enough, if somewhat grey, pharmaceutical company managers. Potential clients. I'd just got to the bit where I tell them how very much my company can make a difference. How we understand their needs and want to help. Not just for the money either, but because we honestly believe in the vital power of change. Which I did. My whole life at the time was a flawless example of that. Not that I'd choose to offer my sex life as a template, but the rush of change happening to me, the joy of the new, was floating around my body like a bliss aura, touching me at unexpected times and sending waves of desire across my skin. I was feeling pretty damn good. At which point the thought of Nick's knee gently grinding my groin infiltrated the picture of five men bonding their way through silly games and kayaking to team spirit and greater profits for all. The carefully structured pitch ending in 'take us on for the job and I promise – we will deliver' faded to a thin whisper as I tried to control the goose bumps shimmering up and down my arms and the independent quiver in my gut. Deep breaths didn't work. Shallow gasping was all my clamped flesh would allow, and I was reduced to delivering my end line on tiptoe, both hands firmly gripping the table, body tight with potential. I guess they took my involuntary shiver for a sign of my commitment to their cause, a new form of Neuro-Linguistic Programming perhaps. Whatever, we got the job.

Andy held me sleeping in the night and I woke from a frantic dream state certain his arms were Nick's. Turned my sleeping self urgently into his arms, his waiting, open mouth. When I woke enough to realize the arms belonged to my husband, I extricated my torso from his hold and slid to the cold side of the bed. I lay awake for an hour imagining I slept beside Nick and that the regular breath, the rise and fall of him, was Nick's mouth kissing the air of my single bedroom. I pictured the impossible dream and didn't for a moment entertain any thoughts of what reality that dream might entail. I was in lust, not therapy.

Reaching for a third tin of special-price plum tomatoes while Saturday morning Sainsburying, I literally had to grab the bars of the trolley to steady myself as my trigger finger itched and scratched to get at my mobile to give me a chance to speak to Nick again. Three calls in one morning should be enough for anyone. Any girl who hasn't time-travelled back to stuttering lust. I wanted to talk to him but had no good reason. Our next meeting place was prearranged, the dates already checked. I wanted to hear his voice but had heard a mocking laugh in his tone the second time I'd called, only an hour after our first conversation of the morning.

'Yes? Did you forget something?'

Only that I already had a husband.

The third time, when he answered. 'And now what?', I should have hung up. Had no real desire to feed his lad arrogance – 'The girl can't help it. She wants me!' Should have hung up, but made seemingly innocuous small talk loaded with only-we-can-understand sexual innuendo. Handed him all my pride, squirming and doing it anyway, only to listen to him give it back bigger and fiercer when, at the end of our half-hour conversation, he whispered, 'Don't go. I don't want you to hang up. I hate it when you hang up.'

Love lifts the phone bill up where it belongs.

I was having a fucking brilliant time. I was paranoid, nervous of seeming either too eager or not eager enough, wanting to look fantastic whether shopping or showering, and then suddenly thinking that perhaps I should tattoo his name on my arm with a compass. Well and truly sixteen-year-old hit, bitten, smitten. And the Lord will smite thee for thy wrongdoing. Yes, of course he will, that's his job. The whole point of the Lord is to strike out wrongdoing and kill the bad guys. Badder girls. For the moment, though, I was happy just to keep playing. For the first time in three years I was actually excited by something a little more heavyweight than the new series of *ER*. Surely God would understand that?

Teenage lust in a woman just clambering through her thirties has some pretty good rewards. Beyond the simple joy of the new fuck and along with the predictable body anxieties – a painful return to 'what can he see in me?' paranoias and my strange desire to sit by the phone any time after four p.m. – there was the major compensation of the soundtrack. The music of our new lust was the songbook of my childhood and early youth, thirteen and counting the love charts. I would drive to work playing songs I hadn't listened to for years. Music I, sanely and with good reason, hadn't wanted to listen to in over a decade. *Start the Week* was slapped off hard and the rambling sound-wave path to my ears became traffic jam full of long-play tapes I'd longer discarded. Admittedly I hadn't listened to most of them for all this time because often they had been so badly recorded on such old equipment from equally trashed second-hand records that the quality was pretty damn poor. Now the scratches and insistence on all treble and no bass became positively endearing. My love was a purple transistor radio on a hot summer Saturday morning. The passenger seat and car floor were littered with early Cure and later Morrissey uncomfortably cosying up to baby Kate Bush and still-breathing Carpenters. Plural. Having to travel long distances to training meetings – middle and senior management tend to think they're not really making the bonding happen unless there's a countryside golf course in the offing – gave me great long stretches of time to singalonga my own infatuation. Nick this and Nick that, and I only managed to shut myself up about half the time. If Andy had any notion of what was going on I was certainly giving him enough ammunition to shoot me down in suspicious flames. But he didn't. Simply couldn't see it. Didn't notice that New Best Friend featured in more than half my topics of conversation. The loving husband missed completely that I was rather more eager than normal to arrive in perfect time for my unusually high workload of meetings. I had all the excuses lined up but never needed to use them. Andy loved me, trusted me. We had seven years of trust for him to count on. No flings, no fancyings beyond tired, semi-imaginative glances at passing potentials, nothing in our past which might lead him to suspect. I had been the good girl for so long, and done so out of choice and desire – now I was cashing in on that trust and reaping the interest. Andy didn't ask what was going on because it didn't affect him, and what doesn't hurt us we tend not to see too clearly. Because my secrets with Nick were actually making me want Andy more, not less. Weird, I know. True all the same.

The would-be Catholic guilts were manifesting themselves in unusual forms. Instead of turning me in against myself or vitriolically against Andy, the passionfuck dalliance with Nick was making me see my husband in an altogether new light. I liked my husband. I wasn't bored with him. Because I no longer required him to make all my problems better, I didn't have to blame him for failing to fix me. It was all working out fucking great with Nick and, astonishingly, so very fortunately, much better than I could ever deserve, it was pretty damn good with Andy too. I'd had the trauma of too many years beginning with three and a too-tidy life and, against the odds, had turned my despair around on itself and back into something good. My life was working out. I'd gone past the initial time of hating Andy for not being Nick, had got to where I had both Andy and Nick – I could enjoy his difference. I could do this. I really could have it all. Winter was closing in, a fat, open-armed welcome to the season of fake snow and real festivities and long night parties and still more reasons for shopping and more chances to dress up and yet more cause to rub fuck-fantastic against Nick in a crowded room and exciting and loving and all things were possible and God, what had I ever done to deserve having it this good?

Nothing. But it was happening anyway.

This is what Andy thinks:

She's happy. Which is great, a huge relief to have her happy, to not need to be the saviour, but there's an edge.

I don't know what it is, something I'm missing, not quite in focus. I like her happy, love her like this, excited and wanting me, like we were at the beginning. I do like it. But it doesn't feel safe, I cannot predict the future.

And after all this time, I prefer safety to the new. Perhaps I've always preferred safety.

13

There is a moment when the imagined theoretical that has been longed for and longer envisioned becomes actual flesh, an instant of transubstantive pleasure. A flash forward into real time when the body absorbs knowledge of another and responds to that intelligence as if there had been no past, no preparation, as if this event had come into being of its own volition. As if it had not been minutely engineered, created solely out of will and desire. Nick was all my present. Nick and not Nick. In some ways, he could probably have been anyman, anyfuck, anyone with whom I was brave enough to make that leap. However, because Nick was my partner in transgression, it was therefore his thin lips that I loved, his hidden body I touched, his close-chewed nails I bit on, his black eyes that drew electric wanting in my skin. I made him the object of my affections and he happily took them. He became the representative of all that Andy was not, turning Nick into the priest of my pleasure. The alternative priest of my pleasure, because Andy was still there, stable and strong and loving and constant. I was a duotheist of desire.

Even in the moment of beginning, though, I knew that what I called having an affair with Nick was simply receiving the magic knowing of another. Nick was a new and willing anyone, and as such he was able to reach me. I allowed him access to my wanting self. Not needy girl, seeking succour and solace, but the craving, craven Lisa. A Lisa of desire and sweat and cold-furred black-cat satisfaction. Nick probably thought my gratification was down to him. I knew it was my own indulgence feeding from without.

Do you want this?

Will this be good?

Can I do this to you?

Oh yes, any and all of it.

No please and no thank you, and less words and no talking. Just do it.

Early evening fucking Nick. He supposedly at a play reading, me at a long-arranged meeting with clients. My meeting was real, not excuse, and I had cancelled it at the last moment, begging mercy from Mary, pleading too much to prepare for the next day's training and getting her to step in for me with half an hour to spare. She was not happy, but then my thoughts were not on pleasuring Mary. Nick and I instead half naked on the bed. Beatles' *White Album* playing. His hand heavy on my left thigh. Gentle and insistent pressure for fifteen minutes, turning down ten, five, four, three. Modified into half-balled fist pummelling at the so carefully exercised flesh. Nick might have bruised me, marked me, made it possible for Andy to see where he had been. And that would have been good too. I could not say this aloud, least of all to myself, but it is clear the danger was as much part of the excitement as our fuck. We had done with talking, Nick and I. We limited conversations to new fashions in outerwear and day shoes, coffee and chocolate. Then cotton sheets hit my skin and all words fell away. I was two lines of cocaine down, he half a bottle of wine through. I refused the rest of the wine, he stayed away from the coke, though nostrils flared. We were experimenting. If I took the Class A and he rejected the AA, which one of us had the better time? Who came first? Brief interruption as we saw a double-moment flash of the woman between us, the one we forced out, crushing our bodies together. My brain, more sensible than my good-buddy soul, would not permit images of Jaine and she was swept up and away, in a quick batting of eyelashes that flirted with open-mouth edge of kiss. Nick's long fingers in my mouth were nicotine-stained, residue tobacco bittersweet on my tongue. He lay at my side, mouth lighting on my collar bone, butterfly kiss to the neck. An expert in polarities, his practiced hand rested in the small flesh hollow between hip and pubic bone and I double-time body-creased along a diagonal line. This was my old friend, but I did not relate to him as such. This was my new fuck, and I knew him too well. Understood that even as he soft-palmed my skin, part of him was movie-image remaking this. I knew Nick viewed his life in a series of film stills. I was starring in his MTV video, and all the more gorgeous for the grainy black and white.

We were using each other and knew that and delighted in it, and between us, beside us, inside us, we were having a fucking good time.

Playing with Nick became both the alchemistry and physics of my new biology. All scientific knowledge rolled into one glorious fuck. Several glorious fucks. Andy was my husband, good man, nice man, kind man, and Nick became my obsession. I thought about him too much and also not enough. Remembered him constantly but not whole. I pictured Nick dismembered – a leg, an arm, the curl of hair at the nape of his neck. Thought about him in pieces, in places, in pieces of me. I went about my day and worked and achieved and completed and was the good wife, great partner, inspirational trainer, and all the while I focused on Nick's heavy back. I remembered Nick's eyes and then turned my gaze fast to the hand of my husband caressing me. I held Andy tight instead of washing my hair when I dragged him into the shower and pictured Nick doing the same to me. He was in my head constantly and not a little captured in my flesh. I thought of Nick not as all man, but as pieces of man. He was my collage lover, created from the found materials of thieving moments.

This is what Nick thinks:

Lisa doesn't know. Doesn't know how delicious she is. Doesn't know how gorgeous she is. Doesn't know how wanted she is. I have been waiting for this to happen to her.

Jaine and I have often discussed how weird it is that she hasn't had an affair yet, not one in seven years. Jaine told me a while ago that she didn't think Andy and Lisa could survive on Lisa's good-girl diet.

I'm surprised that I am the one it happened with. And very pleased. And a bit smug too.

14

Nick and I went to Leicester. It was hardly Paris or Prague, but then perhaps that was part of the point. It wasn't London, it was far enough from home to be safe, distant enough to begin to be interesting. I was working, he came along for the ride. Two-hour double-sided journey – one slow sixty minutes through London, clogged shut until the M1, and then the rush joy of the sexiest sign in Britain – THE NORTH. Turning off at Junction 21 was hard – I could have kept going far into the morning. Long, too-fast driving on up that three-track road, to the real north and beyond, where grey mountains take over the sky and then spill into a cold Scottish sea. But I was working. That was the point. I was not only working, I was working for Mary – making up for the last missed meeting, and the one before that, and the fact that my mind had been far removed from the job for the past couple of weeks. I was guilt-offering myself up for one of her more tedious tasks to allow her a few nights at home with Tim. That she jumped at my suggestion and that she cheerily handed over the files didn't stop her staring hard at me when I made the offer in the first place.

'You want to go to Leicester?'

'No. I don't want to, it's not that. I just think I owe you.'

'You know you do. I've been pretty much carrying us

for the past month or so. It's time you got back into it.'

'Yeah, right. So I'll go. You do something nice with Tim instead.'

I didn't exactly want to get into a discussion of why I hadn't been dedicated one hundred per cent to the cause so I brought her husband into the equation. I wasn't sure what something nice with Tim might involve. I didn't want to think about it for too long, I hadn't yet had lunch, but I knew it would get Mary on side and off my case.

'You will do it, though, won't you?'

Hell, yes, that was the whole point.

'Do what?'

'The job. You will take the job seriously? We need this one, Lisa. These guys could be good for us.'

'Don't worry, Mare. I'll have them eating out of my hand.'

'Just signing us up will do.'

'Mmm. That too.'

We turned right and gave up on the magic of North. Stopped at Leicester. A morning of meetings and pre-arranged business lunch, then a whole afternoon and evening to play together. Able to walk streets holding hands and kiss in corners with no fear of reprisal. I had told Andy I would be away that night. For the first time he seemed uncertain. Too sure of myself perhaps, not taking enough care.

'I thought this was just a meeting day?'

'Oh yeah, but, you know . . .'

'What?'

Quick, make the lie come into my head. 'Well, it was meant to be just the day . . .'

'And shouldn't it be Mary's job to sign them up anyway?'

Too many questions, not enough preparation, so close to caught out.

'Yeah, it is, but then she . . . I . . . she wants some time, with Tim.'

'Lucky her.'

Thank fuck, common ground. If Andy finds it hard to talk to Mary, he finds conversation with Tim excruciating beyond definition. Andy is good and straight and ordinary and wants a happy life. And he likes to drink too much and take coke on special occasions and fuck like a drunken boy when the mood takes him. Tim thinks Andy lives the life of a rebel. He also thinks he ought to get a job where he can earn more money and take a bit more care of the darling wife. Me. But Andy likes me to go to work and bring home the bulk of the bacon. He's happy to make the sandwiches. He and Tim have little to say to each other.

'Yeah, well, no accounting for taste. But anyway, she wants to take him out for dinner or something and they've got some big boss they need me to meet in Leicester and he's not coming in until the next morning, so I have to stay over.'

'Right.'

Warming to my lie, getting into the details of the story.

'And anyway, it's probably better that it's me because I'd have to meet the boss before the actual training. It's all hierarchical stuff they want to deal with, so it saves time in the long run.'

'Yeah. Good.'

He doesn't believe me. What does he know? What can he know? How do I make it clear that there is nothing for him to know? Andy doesn't say anything. Lying beside me in our bed. He's angry and I can't tell why. I put my unworthy faith in his trust and my head on his chest.

'What's wrong?'

'Nothing, really. I just feel like I've hardly seen you properly for ages. I want us to go out for dinner. I want to play with you. I think I've probably seen more of Jaine than I have of you in the last few weeks.'

'Do you want to swap wives? At least she likes football.'

I laugh. He laughs. This is funny.

'Yeah, and she's a damn sight better at DIY than you, too.'

'And thinner.'

Andy strokes my back, my soft-skinned legs. 'Good thing I didn't say that.'

'Yeah, it bloody well is.'

Andy likes this game. He holds me closer, his irritation passed now.

'I suppose if I had Jaine, you'd have to have Nick.'

Stomach freezes, voice catches, trying to stay light, comes out half strangled. 'Nah, he gets too angry too easily. I'd irritate him too much.'

'Maybe. I think he only really gets pissed off with Jaine. Saves his fury for the one he loves most.'

Ouch.

'And you and Nick could always go shopping together.'

'We already do that.'

'I have noticed.'

Fucking hell, does he know what he's doing?

'No, Andy, wives should never go shopping with their husbands.'

'Why not?'

'It doesn't pay to let your loved one see you in the throes of shopping trauma. Too much privileged information.'

'Yes, well, you never want to give too much away.'

Bloody right you don't. I've had enough of this. We're moving away from words as quickly as possible.

'Anyway, Nick's lips are too thin.'

'Mine aren't.'

'No. Yours are just right.'

'All the better to kiss you with.'

We kiss. It is slow and quiet. Kiss against a fat background of so many other kisses, seven years of them, his full lips to mine, his broad body holding me. Push our lips, push ourselves slowly through touch and tender into fast and fucking. We fall asleep and Andy whispers to me, 'I love you. I wish you weren't going away.'

I love him too. And go away anyway.

Nick and I played in the little city. Cold, out-of-London winter, the real thing not tempered by the breath of car-fuming millions. Easy to be there anyway. A long walk past Georgian houses, squat museum spread out behind weathered trees, bare branches reaching into thinner air above. Brief afternoon of clear light, cold from crisp blue sky and slow coffees in places no one knew us. No need to hide our desire to touch. Unvoiced public display of affection so reminiscent of the teenage tension. I want to hold your hand. I want to talk to you. I want to kiss you. I don't know how to do it so I'll just stand here, in the cold at the bus stop beside you. Maybe you'll notice me, maybe you'll talk to me, maybe you'll touch me. Both halves of the new couple, tied up in youth and fear, waiting for permission to get on with it, but not knowing who to ask. Nick and I had permission to get on with it, we picked up our permits as we left London behind. But the chance to act as if we weren't adults, the opportunity to touch in the open air was too tempting. We played young lovers in our thirties in someone else's circle-enclosed city.

We discovered a scarily brilliant restaurant, running through late streets. Walked through the front door into an ordinary Indian restaurant, nothing unusual from the street, but inside the open foyer turned into a long corridor with Orient Express booths on either side, small tables for two or four, each one partitioned off with thin walls to the ceiling, red and pink ribbon wallpaper and a thick curtain as entrance. We were ushered into a private compartment, given menus and shown the dimmer switch to romantic-lower the lights and a button to call the waiter. In a cubicle of 1970s tawdry gloriousness, we were brought wine and food, and left in perfect privacy to feed each other, feed from each other. Slowly ate our shared meal listening to the low murmur of unseen couples equally excited by the tacky opulence of surprise privacy. We took hours over dinner because we could. Because we weren't stealing just an afternoon or a few tight-minuted hours, because we had the whole night to play in, stay awake in. We ate too little and drank too much, expecting Monsieur Poirot to expose us every time the waiter quietly knocked and then pulled back the curtain. Nick and I sat giggling in fear of the truth, though no one could have known we weren't a legitimate couple. It was part of the enjoyment. We stole extra after-dinner mints as we left the perfect place and short-walked through a cold night, starred sky to our newly painted B&B.

That night I fed him chocolates and me. He was hungry. In the morning we slept until the last minute and then went dishevelled downstairs to breakfast like any other happy couple, shared healthy wholemeal toast and sugar-free muesli, and I soaked up too much coffee and watched while he went on to devour a full English breakfast, extra fried bread to make up for the muesli. We were the only guests in a B&B half closed for the wrong season. The manager let us take our time and we were the close comfort with each other that follows hand-holding through a night's sleep. Like any other couple on holiday, it was extra easy for us to be together in a place that wasn't our usual environment, our usual way of being. I liked Nick more there than at any other time. He was softer, missing his usual edge of bitch. He wasn't quite so funny but he was a hell of a lot nicer. And therefore still more desirable. Shrugging off his overcoat of London cynicism, he was sweeter to the touch, the tongue. I was so happy with him that morning. I may well have fallen in love with him that morning, but I was too scared to look at it, kept him in the space of just lust. So much safer than the real thing.

I acknowledged that my feelings were changing and did not say so. Would not say so because even in that soft place I could not definitely predict his reaction. But I knew Nick well enough to guess what it might be and did not want to spoil the moment. I knew for almost certain that talking to him about how I felt would ruin things. I knew for damn near definite that telling Nick my truth would turn him straight back into sharp bastard, cruel comedy tongue and worse, maybe even remind him of who we were and what we were really doing. Nick didn't want feelings, he wanted an affair. So did I, but I was less practised at it than he. I was not practised at it at all. Neither of us intended to leave our partners for the other, neither of us wanted to hurt our partners. We were simply playing. We'd said so often enough, it must be true. I knew that as long as I did not define the mute feelings with actual words, description solidifying truth, I would be OK. If I didn't say the big words to Nick, didn't rock any of our model sailing boats, we could keep on just as we were. If I didn't say the big words to myself I really wasn't being that bad. It was just sex, it wasn't anything more. Keeping my mouth shut meant that I was able to have the playtime, hold the unreal unmelting in my mouth as long as possible. Could not tell Nick and could not tell myself either. I took the truth and put it away in a silver box with velvet lining, hid it at the back of my hopes cupboard, pretending that if I didn't look at it too closely, it wouldn't spoil anything else. We had a charmed time, easy moments of bliss and grace, and I didn't want any intrusion of reality to illuminate the problems of truth and lies.

That B&B breakfast was no more our real world than

when Andy and I go on holiday and are able to be solely with each other with no telephone or fax or work or friends interrupting us. We are able to give ourselves to each other in a way we never can while at home. It is not real life, it is very pleasant. That is the reason for the holy days of holiday – to remember why you love the person you live with. So you can bear the next fifty weeks. I was starting to learn that the affair is simply a concentrated version of the marriage. I had one easy night with my lover to carry over into our next fifty stolen half-hours. Nick and I never went away again.

This is what Nick thinks:

When is it right to announce that lust is bleeding over into love?

15

Andy and I lay in bed at night and discussed us. Discussed our relationship, after the house, the new-move rows, the layer upon layer of things poured into the well of 'what next' draining out to leave yet another gap. A hole that had to be filled as soon as possible if we were to avoid the question of can this ever be enough. Lay in bed, hand-holding, legs entwined, husband and wife friends, easy with each other, easy to talk. He was in love with me all over again. I was fucking Nick and through that had become more lovable, desirable. In Andy's head it had now been worth buying the house. Those months searching for the perfect home, the false starts and aborted possibilities with broken chains and shattered estate agent promises. After the age of endless renovations we had our safe nest made nice and finished for the early-year months, the darkest of winter, and then there would be promised summer and the blister-hand garden and sweet marinade barbecues and long warm evenings to look forward to. Andy told me the work troubles and I soothed him. Believed in him, loved him in the dark, loved the light of maybe future. He laughed with me at the client complaints, at Mary's enthusiasm for the pretend important task of changing the business world. We made small talk and big talk and were just comfortable. The flash fights were over for a while. I was satisfied, blossoming. False spring.

One cool night, t-shirts beating out winter chill and floors creaking in dark rooms beneath us, we lay in the clean-sheet marital bed and talked the big one. The baby discussion. We had been referring to it as potential for years and now suddenly Andy wanted to talk about it seriously. Make plans. Create possibilities. More surprisingly, I did too. I, who had pushed away the permanence of this potential for years, found that I wanted to at least have the discussion. Wanted it in that moment anyway. Somehow the lust for Nick, which was still creating its own smaller degree of knock-on pheromone activity with Andy, was also setting my ovaries up for baby love. The reproductive organs are blind. We had the house, his career groundwork was starting to bear fruit, we were beginning to see money coming in that was not necessarily eaten up immediately in trauma payments, and, of course, I was getting more sex than I'd had in years. I was happy and fulfilled and bloody fit. All that running and sneaky hiding and fat-passion sex was doing wonders for the unwanted gravitational pull on my three-decade flesh. Of course my body thought it was time something settled deep into my uterus. Something other than progesterone-slated sperm.

I had the conversation with Andy holding me in long arms, kissing me with his soft lips, full lips. We discussed years, times, how we could do it and how we would educate it and what to call it and if just one he or she would be joined some years later and turn into them and where would we live and did we even want to move and if not then maybe we could do the loft conversion thing. Andy had always wanted a bird's eye view of suburban Brixton. His certainty neutralized my fear and calmed it enough for me to rosy-glow the future too. At four in the morning we made love again, made love that was not sex and not flesh-eating passion but soft and quiet and an easy tumble in the dreaming bed. Yes we could and yes we would and we fell asleep with close warm bodies.

In the morning I woke aware of some foreboding, questioning my dark-night promises, terrified of the potential constant that had seemed so possible in the middle of the night. I woke to blood on my sheets and went downstairs, slow-start period pains beginning their gradual two-day hold. First an infant's fist of pain, sharp and gnawing in the deep low-down, then the gradual spread of nausea, tiny fist turning to giant hand, steel band spread around my lower stomach and fat fingers piercing my back. My brain might be easily conned with a picture of pretty security – place a baby in the what now gap and ignore the problem of 'is this it?' for another five, ten, fifteen years – my body was less easily fooled. I sat with hot sweet tea and waited for the ibuprofen to take effect, looked out to our winter garden. Gradually the vice grip came away from the rest of me, confined itself to the uterus, eased a little, and meanwhile the morning began. Sharp-angled, winter sun began to tint cool light on slate tiles, planes flew overhead, leaving Heathrow for sunshine and difference. Next door's cat climbed over the fence, and I remembered again that I should have dead-headed the roses properly months ago. I could see that the cat had something in its mouth, I thought a mouse at first and then was relieved to see it was just a feather. Black feather but no bird, no blood. The ten-year-old cat played for twenty minutes with the feather, chasing it around our small lawn like a kitten. Half cute, half vicious. It was playing, but it would have been mauling fresh meat if it could. I finished my tea and took my scratchy, little-sleep eyes upstairs to wash and then to cry under the hot shower.

I knew I was not ready as Andy was for a baby, no matter how easy it might have felt in the night. Knew that I would run to my phone to call Nick as soon as I could, jump scared from the permanence of planned birth and into the welcome uncertainty of lust. Andy scared me with his predestined truths. After all these years of me looking after us, me making the sacrifices for his career, I wasn't yet ready to make the next big offer. I wanted more time, wondered if perhaps I might always want more time. Later, as we left for work together, he watched while I swilled down more pain relief and smiled in a complicity of future plans, the nine months when my ritual forty-eight hours of ten Nurofen a day would be unnecessary. I smiled back, thinking that while Andy probably was unselfish enough to give up the next twenty years of our lives on simply the strength of one big conversation in the cold bedroom, I had an unselfishness of my own. Perhaps my only one, but there all the same. 'Because I want to' might just about suffice as a weak justification for having the affair with Nick, but that same 'because I want to' didn't necessarily follow as good grounds for making another human being. The fact that the world had been procreating without thought for ever was neither here nor there. In the cool light of morning I was hoping for a reason to make a new human being that was a little more substantial than mere biological desire. And perhaps even a better future than just the same old 'and this is what we do next'. Or if not better, then at least different. The terror of stasis is hard to ignore.

This is what Andy thinks:

Lisa is happy. Now is the time to discuss the baby, make real what lies between silences. The child will bind us better than thin wedding bands. Genetic links are forceful where love is not. And for ever.

She is happy and I know I am not responsible for her current state of being. But when she smiles, I can see our future in her.

I don't need to question the source.

16

After the bliss of running away to Leicester, the central London hotel room occasion quickly became too easy, too ready. Too naff. Obviously we couldn't keep going out of town, delightful though the running away was, but we did need to keep pushing at the boundaries. I was aware that first friendship and now an easy lust with Nick held the implicit threat of just turning back into another version of married. Too good too quickly and so too easy to fall into just another pattern. And while I was scared of in lust mutating into in love, I was more scared of it fading to normal. We opted instead for the added risk, added stupidity of the discovery threat that was my house, his house. I diverted my treacherous inclination away from tedium and to the much safer dangerlust. Fucked in the bed my husband carried up heavy stairs on his breaking house mover's back, fucked in the bed Jaine created the perfect housewife quilt for. This was what I had been yearning for but had not known I wanted. This passion and excitement and stomach churning possibility. Having chosen to turn from untrustworthy gentleness and given in to the enticing temptation to blame basic lust and emotions too strong to bear, I easily allowed myself the further luxury of addictive desire. I do not know what excuses Nick gave himself. I didn't ask. We had given up small talk. My good friend had become my better lover. The concomitant loss of a shopping partner to chatter with was not great. I did have a husband for conversation.

And a lover for phone sex when I couldn't see him.

'Where are you?'

'At home, in the kitchen.'

'Where's Andy?'

'Supermarket. Where's Jaine?'

'In the garden. I want to fuck you.'

I'm toying with my toast, squirming at the kitchen table.

'That's good. Now?'

'Yeah, right now. What are you eating?'

'Toast and honey. The honey is dripping on to my hand – the toast is too hot for it.'

'I could lick your fingers clean.'

'Yes.'

'I could feed you hot toast and honey and drip honey on to your face and lick it clean, on to your stomach and wash it off with my mouth.'

'Yes.'

Not squirming now, rocking slowly on the chair, backwards and forwards, feet just touching the ground, just not. Looking out into the garden, wondering what Jaine was doing, wondering if I could come from just listening to him, thinking that Andy would be home any minute, thinking how could I get to see Nick today, thinking of the hot blood throbbing through me.

Licking my sticky fingers. 'Nick?'

'Yeah?'

'Tell me about the honey. Tell me slowly.'

'OK. It's Sunday morning. You and I have stayed together, in a hotel—'

'By the sea.'

'Wales. Overlooking an empty beach. The room service waiter brings in a trolley, tea and toast.'

'And papaya.'

'Mango too.'

'God, yes, mango. I'll feed it to you, peel the skin off and feed it to you.'

'From your own mouth?'

'Where else?'

'Well, if you want details . . .'

I can hear him smiling, feel his slow grin spreading. And then it stops.

'No, don't actually. Jaine's coming back in.'

'Then go into another room.'

'I can't. Look, I've got to go, OK?'

'No.'

'I'll call you later. I'll go out for a walk.'

'Andy will be in later. Walk now.'

'No. Sorry. Got to go. Bye.'

The line went dead and I was left cold in the kitchen. Switched off my phone. He could leave a message when – if – he called back. I wasn't going to run to answer him. I was furious with him for calling at all, for starting what he couldn't finish. Furious with myself for minding. For wanting what I hadn't even been thinking about ten minutes earlier. Then Andy opened the front door and I went to help with the too-many bags, and we argued about how he always spends too much on the shopping, we never need all that food, our cupboards are overflowing as it is. Not so, but my anger had to be vented somehow, and Nick wasn't around to get it. Andy slammed the last cupboard shut and stormed upstairs to get on with some work. I sat in the kitchen, drinking tepid tea and crying. An hour later the husband who can never be angry with me for too long came downstairs and apologized. I was sorry too, good girl in response. We ate lunch. I offered a massage for his hard-working shoulders, a massage for my uneasy conscience, and then the oiled touch turned to kiss, to fuck. We half slept together for an hour and then I left him to go to my mobile again. There was a message from Nick.

'I'm sorry. That was crap. I'll make it up to you. See you Wednesday – I'll bring the honey. Organic, expensive and very runny. Do you think that's why Pooh and Piglet were such good friends?'

Nick made me laugh, and I took tea and toast upstairs to wake Andy, asked him what he thought of Christopher Robin.

After two months of the new fuck, the appeal of the wicked was no longer. It was no longer wicked. It was just what I did, what we did. I was a married woman having an affair. Like so very many others before me. By then the excitement was far less in the fact that we were doing something supposedly wrong than in the possibility of detection. I was no longer running simply on the joy of being bad, I was instead feeding from the pleasure of change. My attitude to work was altered because now I used it as a cover and a place of deception. I told Andy I had to work late and told Mary I would be leaving early to meet clients and trusted they would never converse enough to know I was working, not on the newest account, but on Nick. I was a less conscientious businesswoman and a far more attentive lover. My home had become different because I was looking at it with different eyes, from safe nest through filthy fight-ring into place of desire. Double desire, honest and illicit. The days when I knew there was absolutely no possibility of Andy running home for a forgotten folder or textbook were also some of the days I took Nick back to my house. Our house turned into my house the minute I invited him through the door. Made a fuck-crucible of what had been our cool kitchen. Sated my hunger on the Habitat table. Joy in the pleasure and perverted passion in my own home and sweet glee in the fast shiver of thinking that maybe, just maybe, the grate of squeaking gate was Andy home after all and not the postman lunch-time late on a particularly wet day. And when I was there alone it was still special and different and new. Because my flesh was new, because I smelt different.

The simple act of fucking this anyman, everyman rolled into one beautiful lover had twisted my life round and made it all better. Nick was my spoonful of sugar and the medicine itself tasted honey sweet. I was beating 'is this all there is?', facing it down and fighting it off with Nick. I was perfect wife and lover, happy bunny, and ran the same streets in the dark evenings and didn't mind now when Andy called for me to be careful as I left the house and didn't sneer when Nick said the same on my mobile. There were no more uncurtained windows for me to smash into and I ran laughing through that winter in the dark and the cold. Winter is no season in which to leave your curtains open to the night world. Now there were no tears on my face and no lines of future fret and no problems to weigh down my sprint into the next day. Lucky girl and lucky me, and Jesus striding the wind-rushed waves of Galilee couldn't have been happier with his lot.

17

But even Lot couldn't have everything. Given freedom from destruction and an easy first-class ticket out of Gomorrah he still lost his one true love, handing his wife over to her burning desire to have it all, see it all. Salt of the earth, that woman.

Time passed. Not much of it, but enough for me to find a pattern in what I was doing, enough for it to look like becoming settled. Which might have been fine, unsettled in happy marriage but easily settled into the married adulterer coupling. Loving Andy and getting all the fun from Nick and using the new lust to spice up my home life. Eventually, however, I lost some enjoyment in the just-discovered ease with Andy because, even in the moment of the soft-lip kiss, I knew all too well where that ease was coming from. The new joy in my husband was directly linked to the newer joy in Nick. Should have been plenty for anyone. Anyone who didn't question themselves overmuch, but I was incapable of having too much fun for more than three days without conducting a MORI poll in my head about my actions. In all the excitement I had managed to keep any really serious guilt well out of sight at first, but by the time I eased my way into a third month of seeing Nick, the semi-Catholic poor-girl residue started to rear its ugly head.

I'm lying in Andy's arms. It's easy, quiet here. The cocoon

of his skin on mine will butterfly us both. I have been safe in this place before. It is repetitive no-strain – we know each other well. There is comfort in the return to normality, even a warm desire for the pleasure hidden in the same. Here there is no pressure, no possibility of unwanted needs, no demand for any form of politeness. Occasionally during the afternoon fuck Nick and I scratch at each other's half-open eyes with an unexpected 'Do you mind?', a sweet 'Shall I?'. None of that in the practice of married. We are seven years past asking permission. Andy is taller than me, wider, his body easily encompasses mine. His short, sharp crop stops where my hair, never cut without fuss and tears, takes over the unironed pillowcase. Our arms are crossed with each other's, my left hand holding his right. Andy rolls over, disentangles himself from my Velcro limbs, scratches his balls, half opens his mouth to let out a sigh of incoherent sleep-talk, and makes himself comfortable against my yielding body. He has made himself comfortable against, inside, around, under, over this body for seven years. The flesh that was same flesh for seven years and is now different. Still understands his skin, though. He does it well. I do it well. We matched then and though we mismatch somewhat now, our joint comfort takes only a little effort to achieve. We are falling into a relaxed and genial sleep.

And then I am not falling asleep any more. Andy has plummeted to dream state and is gone, I lie awake alone in the bed. The weight of his head grows heavier on my penitent shoulder, his regular breath ruffles a hank of my night-tangling hair, he twitches his nose against a stray curl, turns away from me, snuffles himself into the three pillows he needs for ease and drops further to an even deeper slumber. A big quiet man – the long limbs he works to perfection every second day weakly welcome this chance to relax, to sink into the luxury-orthopaedic hand-made mattress. Andy will stay quiet there until the morning now, and he will wake slowly and drag himself with difficulty from the dream state and open his eyes with love for me. Because it's what he does every day, because he is not the one who has changed. I have changed, am remaking myself in the light of what I now know I want. I am remodelling both the Lisa and the marriage, and Andy, who only knows I am happy again, simply sees that mostly I have sloughed off my old skin of hag wife, cannot but be glad, sleep relieved. If any part of him questions my about-face, my newer, nicer Lisa, he does not voice that concern aloud, would not provoke the sleeping dog. Sleeping bitch.

I am definitely not falling asleep now. My body lies flat out and still, cold hands and feet for once ditching the attempt to find solace against Andy's centrally heated torso. I wait passive and chilled and let the troubles wash over me. Why am I doing this? How can I do this to Andy? Andy loves me, he is my husband, he has always loved me. We went at it incredibly fast from that first night on the roof of Simon's will-be-beautiful house and no one said don't, whispered that at only just over the quarter-century we might be too young, intimated that perhaps we didn't know what we were letting ourselves in for. Andy and I were just right. He was beautiful and nice and lovely to me – and he was my best fuck ever. Yet. Until then. I had no intention of losing that. We were meant to be and always together and everyone else knew it and I understood his eyes straight away and our wedding day is the one that all our friends still talk about. The most fun wedding. The most beautiful wedding. The most touching and the silliest and the grooviest wedding, big weekend of partying to honour us and amuse the parents and play with the friends, and not a ruffle of ivory silk in sight. Ivory is not my colour. I had no intention of spending my wedding day washed out by the force of meringue dress. I chose a cooler blue, interesting and a little bit different but not too brave. Story of my life. Andy wore a kilt because his dead father wanted it, and though we danced for hours, his dad would have danced for longer. Andy and I have a shared history formed out of our should-be-togetherness. And I do love him. Both the real Andy and what he stands for. Our house, our life, our friends. In the safety of this perfect bed I even love our future. Yet it will only end in tears, I cannot possibly hope to carry on with my present course of action and get away with it. I know that, understand the law of cause and effect, karmic inevitability.

It is dark, quiet but for the hum of night drivers and Andy's alarm clock, ticking until the morning rush of traffic beyond our newly red-painted door and single-glazed original sash windows. Original but restored to within an inch of their lives and well beyond the last excess of our house-fixing budget. We will continue to pay for the windows for the next year or so, no matter what else happens. The overrun costs of our just-made-it house are one constancy I can rely on. I turn and cover my husband's exposed back with my naked body. I hold him tight into sleep and am safe as the protector. I will save him from myself and from my excessive desires. I will tell Nick this has to stop. I will do it tomorrow, make the phone calls, do the right thing. I do not want to lie awake at night, tired and worried. I want to sleep the pastel dreams of a Stepford Wife, sweet-pea-shaded. I choose to ignore the fact that I lay just as troubled before I found Nick. I continue with my litany of what will be, sending a bidding prayer into the dark – I will put away my unwanted desires and yearn no more and be a proper adult and earn my right to have the baby conversation and I will place my undivided attention firmly where it belongs – on the flesh, in the heart, twisted into the sinews of my marriage.

And as I fell asleep I knew that I wasn't being honest. I

wouldn't close up the three-layer chocolate box without a final nibble, couldn't bear to refuse myself the last few sickening bites. My stomach craved more even as my unwilling teeth rebelled in my mouth. I hadn't had my fill. I was still hungry, still wanting. I wasn't quite ready to graduate to self-denial and delayed gratification. Not just yet.

18

And then, with chilly daylight, it didn't seem so painful. The adultery, the deceit. Six hours of disturbed sleep had left me itchy-eyed, restless and, all dark-night promises to the contrary, still wanting the other man. Even at a sharp-alarmed seven in the morning, mess-haired and sleep-mouthed, Nick had managed to find his way in to me. Desire was firmly lodged somewhere between my breast and my cunt. I was hoping it wasn't in the heart. By then, I knew it would be safer if it wasn't in the heart. In the cold light of wet London waking, late-for-work traffic already damming the road outside our house, I didn't feel like such a bitch. I wasn't going to give up on Nick simply because it was wrong by most people's standards, double or otherwise. Nor, less simply, would I give him up because of my love for Andy. I no longer felt like I had the option of giving up. As I said, I didn't set out to be bad, bedded, but once I'd realised how much more enjoyable it was, I was no longer prepared to concentrate every fibre of my soul on being the good girl either. I went along with the new path I was making because it was easier than arguing with myself. And because I knew it was what I really wanted. Nick, part-time and belonging to Jaine, but sort of mine all the same. That was what I wanted. And Andy. And my home. And my friend Jaine. All the good things my life had been up until then. And Nick too. I wanted it all. It was that simple. It was that much of a mess.

Nick called. I was on my way to work. Sitting on a bus, watching wet London pass alongside, the phone rang. I fished in my too-full bag, pulled out the glowing mobile. It read Nick 1. Pushed the yes button.

Definitely yes.

'Hello?'

He always spoke with a slight rising inflection, but not for any regional reasons. I think it was the smile in his voice, the almost-smirk because he knew I would never fail to answer him.

'Where are you?'

On the other end of a silent phone, waiting for the moment you call.

'Bus. I'm on my way to work.'

'Don't go.'

I ignored his words, half plea, half command.

'Where are you?'

'In bed.'

Ah.

'Don't go to work, come out with me.'

Out? What about in?

'Where?'

'There's a funfair on Clapham Common.'

'It's pissing down with rain.'

'Then it won't be busy.'

'I can't. I've got to go in this morning. We've got a new client coming to meet us.'

'Tell Mary you're sick.'

'I can't. I've done too much of that recently. She's really pissed off with me.'

'How long is the meeting?'

'No idea. It won't go past lunch.'

'Then take the afternoon off. Meet me at Clapham. We

can have a drink and go to the fair. Go on . . .' He pauses I can hear the thin-lipped smile, creasing right up to his black-ringed eyes. 'You know you want to.'

I did. I have always loved funfairs. Love the rides, the terror uncertainty and the stomach-twisting rise and fall. Nick loved fairs too. Andy and Jaine didn't. It's another couple divide when we're away together. We went to Blackpool once. They spent the afternoon in the pub, watching some important sporting fixture, we went to the pier and played. Back in the old days when time spent alone with Nick was not yet precious and vital. All that time when I didn't realize that a couple of hours alone with him was all I would think about. I regularly kicked myself for not noticing I wanted him years earlier. Of course I wanted to go. But then I wasn't an actor, still in bed and nothing else to do except fret about the non-existence of my next job.

'I don't know, Nick . . . I suppose I could tell Mary I need to go through some stuff at home.'

'Yes.'

'After the meeting.'

'If you must.'

'And I could take my notes away with me, then I could do some work this evening. Andy wouldn't mind.'

'You could.'

'So I'd go in with something done tomorrow. She wouldn't know what I'd done with my afternoon.'

'No one would.'

'No. But . . . oh, I don't know, Nick . . . what should I do?'

Handing the decision-making power over to him. Freeing myself from responsibility. Not my fault. Not my choice. Only following orders.

'You should do as I tell you.'

Yes please.

I went into the office, got through the morning meeting,

ran away with a briefcase full of notes and files and a hive of active worker bees swarming in my stomach. Plea, please, pleasure – the three-time step, a hop skip and jump from begging to purring satisfaction.

I met Nick three hours later at Clapham Common Tube. It was still pissing down, thick sheets of rain clouding our way to the bright lights on the green. We started with the rides that were at least a little sheltered. Dodgems, the waltzer, the horror house, that spinning, flying thing with the little round covers over each of the cars. By then, though, some centrifugal force had thrown half the rain in London in our direction and we were soaked through anyway. So then it didn't matter. Ferris wheel in the rain. No view except of Nick's eyes, nose, mouth, teeth, tongue. Stupid kids loving the ride so much we did it again. Three more times. Wet-mouth kissing, wetter face, my hair in rain-spun rats' tails. He bought me candy floss, the wind sprang up again, and then I had sweet pink rain-spun rats' tails. He wanted a burger but turned down the grey slab of meat on BSE grounds, ate browned onions and cheese slice in a fat-buttered bun. We giggled silly and then, vomit-denying, took our places in the round barrel of the big spinner. Lying flat, arms above our heads, hand-holding, facing the wet earth, facing the dark sky, facing each other, skin and flesh pulled by gravity. Skin and flesh pulled by lust.

We caught a cab back to my place, threw ourselves into the shower, too cold and wet for it to be sex, just hot and fast and goose-pimpled skin easing back to itself with the force of hot water, clean soap. We dressed giggling in thick white robes. Andy's and mine – fresh smelling and new-towelling, bought for ourselves as Christmas presents. Went downstairs to the kitchen where I hung our clothes up to dry, snuggled ourselves into big coffee mugs and laughed at the lunacy of adulthood. Laughed so much we didn't hear Andy's keys in the front door.

'Hi! What are you two doing here?'

I scrabbled round in my chair. Hot coffee spilled on to my exposed thigh. Ran to the sink, poured the coffee away, doused red skin with cold water, too carefully covering me, not sure who I was supposed to be hiding my body from.

Then Andy and I spoke, both at the same time. 'Why aren't you at work?'

His classes had revision periods for mocks coming up. He'd taken the chance to come home and get on with some other work. I told the truth but in my head it sounded like a lie.

'Nick called me on my way to work this morning. Asked me to go to the funfair with him.'

'Fair? It's been bucketing down all day.'

'Yeah, that's what I said.'

It sounded feeble, I sounded feeble. I had no reason for the face-flushing guilt, but I stuttered anyway. We hadn't done anything that day. Well, kissing, wanting, but nothing real. No official adultery. Only imagined sin, naked wet skin. Skin and wonder.

I made more coffee. Andy made himself a sandwich. Nick and I weren't hungry. I explained about the candy floss and the no-burger burger. Nick took his things upstairs, dressed in damp clothes. Andy said he didn't have to but Nick wanted to go. Wanted to get home to make dinner for Jaine. Jaine would have had a hard day – she was working on a difficult campaign, it was raining, she'd have a crap journey home. He wanted to be there for her. I didn't want him to go, to leave me alone with Andy. I saw him to the door, begging eyes, pleading for a little more time, another half-hour, but Nick played the just-good-friends far better than I did. He had to rush. His gorgeous girlfriend would be home soon and he loved her so much that he'd rather go home in wet clothes than wait here with Andy and me until he would be more comfortable. He loved Jaine that much.

I closed the front door behind him, turned up the thermostat. I was chilled. Crossed Andy as he went upstairs, bag on his shoulder, tray with sandwich and coffee. He smiled at me, was normal. I didn't know how to be. In that instant, that tiny moment of crossing his path in the hallway, I decided I would tell him if he asked. If he wanted to know, I was going to tell him the truth. I couldn't go through that tension again, the nearly-caught delirium. I prefer my adrenalin rush in white powder form. And perhaps I wanted to tell him the truth, get it all out in the open, be honest. Be forgiven. Or be kicked out. Be dumped. I didn't know what I wanted, I didn't know what he was going to say. I didn't know how to be. All I knew was that this was a moment of reckoning, a stench of truth solid in the air between us. I took my cue from him. 'I've got loads to do, Lise, you get your own dinner. I'll probably be working on this most of the evening.'

'Oh, right. OK.'

Moment passed, door to redemption slammed shut in my face. I was both hugely relieved and terribly, achingly disappointed. Andy was upstairs, working, thinking God knows what. Not giving anything away. Maybe he did know nothing. He's never liked fairs. It's not so odd that Nick and I should have gone together. Nick was at home with Jaine, being lovely to her, making their dinner, pouring the wine. They were eating happily, warm and comfortable in their perfect white, Sunday supplement flat. And I sat watching dull TV alone with a Marmite sandwich, feeling cold and tired and sorry for myself. One minute wanting to dash upstairs to Andy and tell all, the next convincing myself that what was going on with Nick didn't really matter – it was only lust, not real love, it wasn't worth throwing my marriage away for. Of course it wasn't. Not yet, not now, maybe never. Maybe tomorrow. I sat alone and dazed, wondering what the hell I was doing, wishing I had never started this, wishing it would all go away, leaving me back where I began, happy enough and just getting by, no reason to question.

Until I remembered Nick's mouth and the rain and the Ferris wheel and my stomach flipped from more than gravity.

19 ʃ

The next night and I was playing happy wife again. I always hated acting at school – the enforced jollity of end-of-term plays, the idiocy of pretending to be a whole other human being, the stupid arrogance of putting it on for show. I had no idea who I was at sixteen, let alone the ability to persuade a critical audience that I could be someone else. Somehow, growing up gave me acting skills. I had become adept at dissembling, cheating and lying – mostly to myself. A mistress of the art of truthful economics as long as I could pull the blackout curtains tight against the image of Nick. Not thinking about him, not talking to him, not allowing Andy to mention Nick or Jaine if at all possible – these were the ways I managed to get through. And it was possible to have a good time with Andy. He made no reference to the afternoon before other than expressing a hope that Nick and I wouldn't get colds from being out in such crap weather. I changed the subject almost immediately. Concentrated on the husband, on the life I was living in that moment. Screwed up my eyes to give me tunnel vision focused solely on the nice life in the nice house with the nice man, telescopic vision microscoped down to gingerbread life. Almost possible, nearly achieved – a whole day passed with being good at work and enjoying Mary's company and then being nice to each other at home and getting through.

Easy to convince myself that yesterday didn't matter, that no part of me was still craving Nick. Huge sighs of relief all round. Little Red Riding Hood makes it all the way through the woods safe and sound. Oh no she doesn't.

'Lisa, it's Jaine. We have to talk. Meet me tomorrow. Lunch. One o'clock. Call if you can't make it, otherwise I'll see you there.'

This was not an unusual message from Jaine. She had always tended towards the short and dramatic in her telecommunications. But at that precise moment I wasn't expecting her to come along and burst my precarious bubble. I'd come in after a rare night out with Andy – not rare because we had gone out together, that happened with appropriately married frequency, but rare because we'd gone out with his work colleagues for his boss's birthday dinner and I'd enjoyed myself. After a long dinner and good food and better wine, with a couple of surprise family guests who turned out to be great drinkers and fine storytellers, we came back to our little home laughing and a bit pissed and really quite tired and ready to settle down to the taped episode of *ER* with a final whisky each and then a good night's rest for two hard-working, hard-playing, modern individuals. Perfect happy couple, perfectly happy. Until I heard Jaine's message.

Then time telescoped into the tight fist slamming my gut and I was warp-rushed forward into a lunch from hell where my best friend denounced me as an adulterous slut to the whole of my second-favourite restaurant, crowded to its stripped brick walls with most of the people I know – shamefaced Nick, stricken Andy, my bitter mother, Andy's pissed brother, Jaine's smug little sister, and Mary, looking suitably shocked even before the announcement was made. How I made it through *ER* I don't know, but the blood and gore on the hand-held camera was nothing compared to the motion sickness I was generating for myself, viewing scene after scene of my recent life through the distorted lens of Jaine's righteous fury and my own guilty fear. Terror into impure anger and back into shame. The old emotional patterns are always the best.

Andy slept his usual undisturbed seven hours, and by the time I rose for a punishing cold shower I was certain of my sad and lonely future. The three hours of troubled sleep had done nothing to ease my nerves – dreams of discovering yourself denounced from the pulpit of betrayed innocence rarely do. I tried to call Nick and find out what was going on but his mobile was turned off. He had probably already left for his day shoot in Ireland, flying out first thing in the morning and not expected back until very late that night, if not the morning after. I'd have to brave it alone and take whatever was coming. It's always more fun to solo-panic whenever possible – it adds to the head drama. I dressed for my funeral in a suitably demure black pinafore and white cotton shirt, swathed myself in a long dark coat in case any slut curves should show, and scraped my hair back from my face. I did contemplate the complete Audrey Hepburn and considered going without make-up entirely, but I figured mascara lines streaming down a well-slapped face would look more penitent than eyes swollen and faded to non-existent red. I've always been more of a Black Narcissist anyway. I kissed Andy goodbye. He didn't notice my especially quiet state, but then conversation before ten isn't his strong suit – he'll never achieve his ambitions of promotion until he learns to say actual words in the morning staff meeting. Not that his future was any concern of mine. Not any more. I held tight to my vivid imaginings until I had to leave and when I could put it off no longer I descended to the Victoria Line. Three pomegranate pips later I'd promised myself to the dark. I was feeling so bad I'd have travelled on the Northern Line if I'd thought it could have made amends in any way, saved me from the doom to come. I trudged through three hours of pointless business in the morning, far too much sudden-granted sense of perspective on what really mattered to take seriously the plans for yet another future-themed sales conference. Far too soon I was seated at the back table, good bread and smooth red placed before me. I sipped the water. Tried a small piece of crust – too dry without butter. Ate it anyway, felt it rip at my oesophagus and asked God to help. Help me choke to death before Jaine arrived.

Then she walked through the door, body buoyed up with the big-named bags hanging off her arms, face a dark pink flush with chill wind and excitement and a big smile for the waiter and a bigger smile for the barman and her biggest, loveliest smile for me. Threw herself into the chair opposite, beaming joy and thrills and not wearing the usual face of a woman badly wronged. Not unless she was planning to lure me into safe waters before planting a well-placed harpoon.

She beamed a bliss smile at me. 'You will absolutely never guess!'

Evidently not.

'I'm pregnant!'

Shit. Christ. No. Three flavours of panic slapped me in the face. I couldn't help myself and it just came out – 'Fuck!'

Luckily the ubiquitous exclamation of our times can cover all states of mind and Jaine wasn't in any fit state to question mine. 'I know, just so fantastic, isn't it?'

No need to ask if she wanted the baby, then.

'I mean, I just can't believe it. Me! Lisa, me! A mother!'

The two-step from guilt to relieved jealousy is an elegant manoeuvre, best done with half a glass of house red thrown down your throat. I swallowed fast before my mouth opened and betrayed me.

Not fast enough. 'Nick – what does Nick . . . ?'

What does Nick have to do with it?

'Oh, he doesn't know yet. No one does. You're the first!'

Great, then perhaps it's a mistake. Those little sticks of pink and blue are easily mixed up. When you're in a state of heightened tension.

Anticipation. Delirium.

'You've done a test at home?'

'No.' She giggled and laughed and came over all Sally Field. The pregnant flying nun dived into her bag for a crumpled sheet of paper which had authority and bureaucracy and Very Serious Medical Laboratory watermarked into it. 'I wouldn't trust one of those kit things, not with something this important. Look, here, it's official.'

The paper was thrust under my nose smelling of Band-aids and glee.

'I just wanted to tell you first.'

Such privilege.

'Jaine, why me? Why haven't you told Nick?'

'I don't know. It just . . . it just feels like one of those girl things. I wanted you to know. I knew you'd be happy for me.'

Ecstatic.

'And I suppose, if I'm completely honest, I'm not quite as sure of Nick's reaction as I am of yours.'

Oh yeah, you can trust my reaction all right.

'That's why I waited. I'm nearly two months.'

Two months? Time flies when you're fucking around.

'Jaine, how could he not know? What about your period?'

Andy knows every day of my cycle. Because I tell him. Because it's obvious. Because it's there.

'Nick was away. Those days in Holland. His newspaper ad. Then when it didn't come . . . I thought I'd just give myself a bit more time. To be sure. To get used to it.'

'So when are you going to tell him?'

'I'm taking him out to dinner tomorrow night. He's not coming back until the morning now. I've booked that little place round the corner from our flat, where we went for our last anniversary.'

Nick and Jaine date their relationship from their first fuck. They've managed nine happy years so far.

'I've already ordered the champagne. I figured I'd tell him there. He loves that place. We had a brilliant night last time we went.'

'Yeah, I remember you telling me.'

I remembered him telling me.

'Actually, I think I might have conceived that night.'

No, he didn't tell me that. He didn't tell me anything about their sex life, knew I didn't want to know.

'I've got it all arranged, Lise. I know it's not what Nick and I had planned, not that we've really made it to the planning stage actually, not like you and Andy . . .'

What had my husband been telling her?

'But, well, it's happened now and I figure that if I just present it to Nick like I'm really happy – and I am . . .'

No mistaking that.

'. . . well then, he'll have to be fine about it. I just needed time to get used to it myself. Get round it in my own head.'

I knew how she felt. She was looking at me. The pause had gone on too long. I was supposed to say something. Say all the right somethings.

'Wow. Jaine. God. Congratulations. That's amazing.'

My mouth emitted a stumbling polka of appropriate phrases, barely damming up the floodtide of inappropriate ones. Which slimed their way out soon after. 'But haven't you . . . I mean . . .' Guilt, greed, jealousy, alcohol – all limiting my usually capable flow of speech. 'I thought you both wanted to wait for a while?'

'Yeah, we did want to wait. But' – and here she rubbed her stomach in sweet madonna fashion – 'This little thing didn't.'

I was determined to get an answer. 'Haven't you been on the pill for a million years?'

'Feels like it. But you know, even the pill isn't completely and utterly safe. Well, not for me, if you remember rightly.'

I did.

'And we have been fucking like maniacs recently.'

No, Nick hadn't told me that either.

'You have?'

Oh yes, I so very much wanted to hear this. Downed another glass of the blood wine, flapped a shaking hand at the waiter to remind him I needed a fresh bottle yesterday, shoved more bread into my mouth. This time I rich-buttered it like a thin woman who can afford the open heart surgery any time she wants it. In about twenty-five minutes, at the rate mine was beating.

'Yeah, God knows what's going on, but I have to say I really bloody like it. Nick's just been so sexy and attentive, and recently it's been kind of like when we first got together, like he can't get enough of me, like we're . . . like he really . . . oh fuck, Lise . . .' She giggled, laughed a little more, threw her head back and squealed with joy, then coloured the elegant maroon which is her black version of my bright red, and came out with it. 'Nick's just been being a truly fantastic fuck. After all these years, it's just so great when those times come – when you get back to how it was in the beginning. You know what I mean?'

Yep.

Jaine chattered on, past salmon in filo, through pesto-drowned pasta, beyond two reloadings of the bread basket and finally cream-coated Sachertorte, which we usually shared, now devoured by her alone, filling her fine-boned face for two. I limited myself to starter, green salad, no dressing, and a bottle and a half of wine. If I didn't have her really good reason for feeding, I did at least have my own far better logic for making myself completely, rat-arsed, falling-down drunk. Even the thought of her swollen to the full nine months didn't calm my seething heart. I knew just what she'd look like. Tall, long-limbed, perfect smooth skin glowing to motherhood perfection, stretched over the rounded stomach and the full breasts of a true madonna. I'd seen magazine covers with mothers-to-be, three weeks overdue and still managing to look like Aphrodite without the excess seaweed, and I knew that Jaine would probably look better than any of them. Without the body paint. We talked for a couple of hours. I mentioned work in passing, Andy in such passing that the point of the sentence was gone before his name came out of my mouth – none of it was relevant. Baby was all.

I kissed Jaine goodbye at the entrance to the Tube. She wasn't going straight home, she was heading for Mothercare. And Please Mum. And Baby Gap. I watched this woman I had known for fifteen years walking down the street, bags swinging at her sides, and wanted to cry. Half a dozen different emotions fighting for supremacy – jealousy that she was enjoying Nick as much as I was and then guilt that I could even think that. Hating myself for what I'd been doing to her while the baby had already started growing, hating still more what I already knew I intended to keep on doing, despite the bombshell news. Envy that she and Nick were creating for definite what Andy and I were only talking about, what still scared me too much to commit to doing, fear that this would make Andy push even harder. But floating to the top of all these scummy feelings came the saddest one. I'd seen it happen before, knew without a doubt that despite the conversation we'd just had about how she wanted me to be involved in her pregnancy, how much she wanted me with her, knew that even if I hadn't been shagging Nick, she and I were now different kinds of woman. Like when I got married and she stayed just 'living with'. I had the societal stamp of approval on my relationship and she didn't. And now she was doing the big one. Becoming a mother. And no matter how hard we tried, and how well we managed to stay close, there were going to be times in the future when she just didn't want to hear about my work or discuss politics or the finer points of falling down your own front doorstep in a drunken stupor. She would want to talk about pre-natal classes and post-natal classes and sleeping and feed times and baby's first wee, smile, word, walk. And she'd be right to do so. It would change her world. But she wouldn't be the same best friend any more and we would never again be on the same footing until I was a mother too. If I was a mother too.

Fucking Jaine's boyfriend just made me bad, losing her to graduate womanhood made me very sad indeed.

20

I couldn't go back to work. Fabricated a stuttered lie to Mary about the onslaught of a migraine and tried to ignore the cynicism in her weary comment that she imagined it must be really awful to suffer your first migraine. At thirty-three. Instead I went shopping. I didn't know if retail therapy was going to do it – in fact I suspected that the only thing that was likely to do it would be the oblivion of yet another bottle of wine, but I thought I might as well try credit card solace first. I bought some clothes I didn't need and would never wear from a shop assistant who lied through her commission-paid teeth that they suited me down to the ground. Didn't feel any better. I went to a boring afternoon movie about American teenagers in love and despair and lost myself in that half-world of tourists and the sad confused. I was definitely one of the sad confused. When I emerged into the street the daylight had vanished and I was too sober to go home. I took myself out for very little food and much more wine and didn't even bother to take a book from my bag, the one that would save me from being the lonely lady dining alone and at least appear to turn me into the kind of interesting chick who actually likes to eat by herself, savour her meal and enjoy her own company. In fact the only literature my life was featuring that day happened to be the *Little Miss Fun* book

Nick had slipped into my bag when the four of us were at the pub the week before, the innuendo thoughtfully highlighted in luminous green. As I felt rather more like Little Miss Fucked and as eye-burning tears were welling up at even the thought of the next time we'd have to play happy foursomes together – now accompanied by the foetal fifth – I thought I'd save myself the trouble and skip straight from alone-and-interesting-and-a-little-sad-as-well directly to do-not-disturb-you-know-you'll-regret-it. The crazy lady is a fearsome thing. I was mad, looked mad. No one bothered me. The time required to pick at a meal when you're only talking to yourself is fairly brief, but I took the wine as slowly as I dared. Poured pinot noir and jumbled thoughts through my brain. Listened to my own tales of woe – how this news had spoilt it all, how Jaine's pregnancy would whip me right back to where I'd started. I might lose the night-plaguing guilts, but I'd lose Nick with them, and when I lost playing with Nick I'd also lose my new-found joy with Andy. What's more, this would be bound to start Andy on about the baby thing again, push him closer to pushing me, when all I knew for definite was that right now there was no part of my heart or soul that could envision the next twelve months, let alone the next twelve years. And more than that, there was the question of where I would now locate myself with Nick. I didn't even want to look at how the advent of this baby was making me so jealous of Jaine's relationship with him. Everything was going wrong, and it was all Jaine's fault, the baby's fault, Nick's fault, Andy's fault.

Which was certainly a damn sight easier than blaming myself.

That night I walked home from Brixton Tube. Two thirds of a bottle of good dinner red in my veins and a thin spill of powder-room coke spinning round my head. The better to keep me awake. It's not as if falling asleep before you get off at Brixton can take you miles beyond your allotted station. The unceremonious end-of-line passenger dumping takes place there with gorgeous regularity. Falling asleep and dribbling into your cashmere scarf isn't too impressive, though – even when your scarf is merely M&S soft wool pretending to be cashmere like mine. I chose the coke. It wasn't a long walk to our house, not even with winter cold ripping carefully arranged clothes from my body at every third step. Ten minutes, maybe fifteen with crap girl shoes. Having dressed for the terror lunch I was wearing sensible, penitent-but-fucking-groovy-anyway boots. Fast to walk in and high enough to add a couple of less vulnerable inches to my girlie five foot two. Leaving Brixton Tube at eleven thirty it looks like all of London is only just awake, bright-eyed and heading out to party. But I was traipsing home to sleep. Not true, I know. I wasn't going to sleep and they couldn't all have been on their way out to an amazing and action-packed life, but in my head and in the time of then, that's what it felt like. Felt like how did I get here and why me and how did everyone else manage to be so simple and sane. Luckily I was walking alone, so no other sad git had to enjoy my delightful bout of coke and alcohol self-pity.

There is about a third of a mile of interest, the first leg of my journey home, where South London transplants itself to every movie of New Orleans made by New York and decamped to Hollywood – people on the street, music from bars, people less white than British television would have us believe and more variegated strands of homeland-flavoured dialects, plenty of drunken youth to scare off the old sober ones and three men to every one woman. A fear group for any political faction to identify itself with. Or against. Walking the first third of my journey home is an easy MTV video trip of chatty extras from gritty soap opera central casting and smiling minicab drivers pointing to half-illuminated neon above my shaking head. They indicate the signs as if their brilliant ability to sell their wares might also suggest a knowledge of the local street map. As if. Still, even if they have no idea of how to get me home, they do see me as lone girl and they are middle-aged gentlemen with youngish daughters of their own and are therefore sweetly concerned. Not a single A-Z between them, though.

Past the garage people suddenly drop off and you are alone until the train station and the enveloping offers of another swathe of minicab drivers. This is the part where I usually think it might have been more sensible to wait at the cold bus stop for twenty minutes, where I wish for streetlights brighter than broken orange, where I speed up my steps and walk heavier and stronger in my big girl boots. I am not frightened of people, of flashing lights and unknown music, young men in packs do not scare me – dark streets and a single set of footsteps I cannot trace do. But not that night. That night I was guardian-angeled by two lads. Five paces behind me all the way from the Tube, they carried portfolios under their arms and talked in Manchester cadences of girlfriends and creativity and steaks – 'like the French say, *bleu*' – chatted about getting up in time either to work or to watch TV, decided that he should not leave her but that the other one might as well do so. Talked oblivious of me, just five steps ahead of them in fake black fur coat and pale swinging hair. I listened to them talk to each other like girlfriends do – meaningful and life-changing slammed unthinking against potential dinner and probable fuck. The old feminism and the new lad have given these men an entire range of conversation we never expected they would allow themselves to have. Or want to have. It made great eavesdropping and soothed my way and gave me safety until I turned into our road, until I twisted side streets into where suburbia emerges from under the railway bridge and I returned to my home and husband and remembered I wasn't leading the way to their boys' flat, wasn't eating the chips they were buying on the way home, wasn't going in to play old music or watch taped TV, but to creep quietly into my own bedroom so as not to disturb Andy, who has had an early night because of a big day at work tomorrow, to undress in the dark and take my make-up off in the bathroom and climb cold beside him into bed. Blessed safe each step behind me until the junction where they went on to possible and could be and don't know yet because the limits seem too arbitrary and I turned into our street and walked down the hill to set and certain and agreed and minds already made up. And I don't think they were that much younger than me, those lads, and I don't doubt they probably want what I have, want the house too and the proper jobs and maybe even the mortgage and certainly, definitely, the stable, reliable, loving relationship. I know because I heard the louder bloke tell the quieter one that he was waiting for her to be ready. That it was his girlfriend who couldn't commit, wouldn't promise. I pushed back the gate and walked along the path, beside the grass that is always greener, and opened the front door to my life. Andy called out to me, half asleep, dozing but concerned anyway. I went upstairs and kissed him and reassured him of my safety and sent him back to his dreams of security.

I took my make-up off in the silent bathroom and promised the unmasking mirror me that I would keep trying. Following whatever stupid trail I was taking. I knew it was dangerous and destructive. That was half the point. Or more. I wouldn't give in for Andy or Nick or Jaine or learned morals or unlearned fears or any other idea of what should be. I knew I didn't know any more what should be. I was making it up as I went along. And if it was wrong, and certainly it was scary, at least it was also new and definitely it was a pleasure. Which seemed like a purpose of sorts. Seemed like something more than giving in to the expected, than just keeping going because I didn't know what else to do. Seemed like at least I was trying. Knowing I wanted Nick far too much and getting closer to dangerous. Too much feeling, every time I saw him, and unable to stop and no way to get out of it now. Not even if I wanted to.

Tired and not sober and not pregnant and not single and not happily married at one in the morning.

21

By daylight the cold night blues had gone, replaced by itchy eyes, runny nose, a sore throat and leaden weighted head, lolling on my aching neck like a toy dog in the rear window of a car, taking hairpin bends at ninety miles an hour on the winding road down to Monte Carlo.

Constantly bending but sadly not breakable. Suitable penance for a good amount of alcohol, too much coke to take alone and nowhere near enough food. The lazy woman's guide to getting thin. Hardly sufficient punishment for what I planned to spend my afternoon doing, who I planned to spend my late afternoon fucking. There had been a slim chance that after seeing Jaine I would have given up on Nick. A moment where I might have put away the whole idea of him as lover, good experiment, glad to finish early before it got too messy. The right thing to do. A chance that was squandered by my night walk home. I still so much wanted what I had hurried past, craved that seething life in mine. All the lateness and the fast drinking and the dark streets and the potential and the edge. Thirty-three-year-old woman yearning for eighteen. Perhaps that was Jesus's problem too – thought he was immortal, didn't realize it was a mid-life crisis. Mind you, it probably didn't help to have his mother following him all over the place.

And of course I didn't want to be fucking a (virtually)

married man, father-to-be, happy family man in waiting. No. Nothing anywhere near so tacky. I simply wanted to be fucking Nick, playing Nick. And beyond that, past the specifics of person and place, I wanted to be in the affair. In the moment of that which was new and exciting. Doing it, having the danger and desire and passion, letting the excitement slip into and stain the rest of my life. I had started, so I would finish. End the affair when I was ready and not before. I did not want to walk into my quiet house ever again and have nothing to occupy my sheep-counting brain but what was for breakfast in the morning.

My infidelity had been the catalyst for a tangible alchemical reaction throughout my life. People were behaving differently because I was behaving differently. I was fresher and freer and so, touched by my new enthusiasm and energy, they were too. I was feeling sexy and Andy picked up on it, fed his own libido from mine, created an internal combustion of both our new-stoked desires. My house was an occasional haven for my lover and me. That energy lingered in the walls and fed my husband's desire. I felt it, revelled in it. I was weekly guilt-ridden and therefore Jaine had a more attentive and much friendlier best friend. I was having a great time with Nick, so Nick was having a brilliant friendship for his extramarital fuck. All this sex was giving me more desire, more passion – what wasn't used up by my husband and lover was being lavished on my house and garden. I had sparkling windows and perfect lawn and the best-kept winter hanging baskets this side of Kew. Other than my work, which wasn't quite benefitting from the peak of my performance, everyone and everything else in my life was reaping the rewards of my actions. As two-timing adulterous traitors go, I was really very generous. It was too much to give up.

Adrenalin is ice cream. Real, home-made, created from love and desire and want, double cream and finest sugar and long slow hours in a dark freezer. And it's something I can do without. Not necessarily willingly, but I am able to practise abstinence until it is no longer simply denial but mutates into an end in itself. I can choose not to eat ice cream for whole months. I can train myself to have no desire for ice cream, no want, no need. And then, quite suddenly, I do want. All I am is want and need and must have. And one spoonful is never, ever going to be enough. It used to kill me as a child when my mother would be doling out the chilled sweetness scoop by scoop. One normally, two if you were lucky, three for high days and holidays. Just not good enough. The point of ice cream is to eat it all. Not because your man done left you in some crappy approximation of inner city London recreating a would-be American sitcom life, and not because you're just being greedy, but because you can. Because it's there. The whole tub, the cookies-and-cream Everest. There to gorge on the sick richness of it. The abandonment of solo-swallowing the entire bottle of champagne, the bath that uses all the hot water regardless of who is waiting to follow, every last square from the bar of sticky caramel chocolate, none saved for tomorrow because there isn't going to be a war again and we don't need to ration ourselves. Ever. The full tub of ice cream is not for sharing, nor is it for lingering over. It is purely for devouring, for filling your mouth with the cold, teeth-burning bite of it.

So I made the next necessary choice. Although I now had a secret Nick didn't yet know, a confidence which should have made me give him up, give him away, give him back, I decided not do so. Not until I was ready. There are no excuses, and anyway, what I was doing had almost ceased to be viewed as purely good or bad. The action of having an affair was no longer the whole point. This was about living the new life, the life in which original was commonplace and sweet chance of adrenalin the only thing sating my hunger. I could not stop. It wasn't over. And there was also the rising tide of a feeling I was refusing to call love. Playing with Nick was one thing, being in love with him would be another matter entirely. Which was why I wasn't prepared to even begin to think about that one. No matter how much it begged to be examined. At the time I really thought it was up to me.

I left work at four thirty that afternoon, apparently rush running to meet an old client for a drink. Ran to where he was waiting. Found Nick, held Nick, was held by Nick. Bit at his bitten nails and breathed in through my own skin the scent of him, perfumed boy. Went to the tacky little B&B he'd booked and did the kissing and touching and energy recharging on a squeaking bed with orange counterpane and Gideon Bible thoughtfully propping up the uneven legs, fucking to the accompaniment of brake-screaming double-decker buses hurtling past shaky windows, double-glazed to keep the magnified dirt between them. The sex was brief and focused and plotted an orgasm-destined crow-flies course. Nick wasn't saying much, but then neither was I. He didn't know about the baby yet and I certainly wasn't going to be the one to tell him. To give them a ready-made dinner conversation for their intimate restaurant meal four hours later.

'Jaine, darling,' Nick says, nibbling on a mouthful of sweet potato and garlic mash. 'Lisa says you're carrying my child.'

'Yes, I am, sweetie.' Jaine swallows another mouthful of her carbonated water, her refusal of a glass of the full juicy red explained.

'Oh dear, that was supposed to be my surprise. When did she tell you the glorious news, lover mine?'

'I think perhaps it was just after she'd ripped all her clothes off and a moment before she started on mine.'

I knew I couldn't tell Nick anything at all. A simple discourse on the weather would have me sending him off for bootees and Babygros in an instant. But of course, as with any must-never-be-mentioned secrets, all the information wanted to do was slip from between my lips and out into that place where saying the words aloud makes an impossible truth into reality. Scared to say anything in case I gave myself away, I filled my treacherous mouth with Nick's lips and teeth and tongue and vocalized only the non-sense, all-senses noises of sex. All body and nerve endings and no brain and no thought, I met him in bed and stayed there for as long as possible, exhausting myself with a constant flow of movement and undercut stasis, held only until it became too much – edge of a kiss, lips almost touching body, skin nearly meeting his. Took myself to that place where all I could do was want Nick – just the flesh of him – thereby removing any need to converse, to discuss, to be adult human animals and offer just a little more than the mere rutting fuck. I wrenched the two of us out of that ordinary side-street B&B and deep into the space where the only conversation is locked limbs and open mouths and wanting. Then yield. Then take over, take under, begin again. Then done.

We were beyond talking. I was heading for sleep, floating out past words to a nearly-evening ether of sticky skin and crumpled sheets. Made it.

22

The point of possible confession long over, I was falling into a brief nap, cool sex-sated sleep warming my complacency, when Nick decided that it was the perfect moment to jolt me out of my self-imposed exhaustion. You'd have thought he might have been just that little bit sleepy himself.

'Lisa, I've been thinking about something for a while. And this afternoon has just made my mind up for me. You are . . . this is becoming . . . well, I think I'm going to have to tell Jaine what's been going on.'

Fantastic. I exhaust myself physically, sexually, so as not to fuck things up with words and thinking, so I wouldn't tell him about the baby, so I couldn't tell him about me, what I felt, that I'd been thinking too, that I did want him, that I couldn't stop this – and even that excessive care managed to fuck things up anyway.

Until that moment I'd only ever heard one really nasty phrase. Stewart Davidson sent it my way, 'Lisa, I don't love you any more.' He was the initial boy love, the only kiss that had ever made it matter and eventually, sweetly, and so much easier and lovelier than most of my girlfriends had experienced, he was the first sex. I had every reason to adore him, and I did and he knew it. But big boys head off to university and younger girls stay on at school and after the first term away he came home for the holidays and broke my heart. Not that he meant to and not that he was cruel, and he told me so sweetly and softly and lovingly that at first I thought it was just another declaration of love, didn't even hear the 'don't' in the sentence. Eventually, though, the bitterness made its corrosive way through and lovely Stewart who only ever meant to be sincere took my handed-on-a-plate heart and broke it all up anyway. Me aged sixteen and having to run crying home, eat a pint tub of raspberry ripple ice cream, make myself throw up, lose me for a while in the sweet milky vomit and then cut into my thin wrists. Not very deep cuts, you understand, just enough to remind myself that I was in pain. Enough to bring me back from the point of unbearable numbness to hot truth. 'I don't love you any more' never hurt worse than the day it came empty from Stewart's kiss-chapped lips. All subsequent voicings of that particular utterance merely echoed the original smack in the face.

But it couldn't compare to Nick lying beside me, body half swathed in white cotton, legs entwined to smooth upper thighs, bitten lips breathing warm into my loose hair, smell of his perfume and his stroked flesh on my skin. I'd like to think that perhaps time has mellowed my recollections, that I'm not really the kind of girl who thinks her cheating heart being found out is worse than the loss of innocence that accompanies the loss of first love. I'd also like to think that drinking single malt whisky in your morning coffee doesn't indicate a problem, an inability to save the good things for better times at the very least. But then delayed gratification has never been my strong suit. I have always wanted my heaven here and now. The immediacy of hell is also therefore an inevitable part of the deal. 'Lisa, I think I should tell Jaine what's been going on.'

I freeze. The room is arctic-waste white and I am naked on the snow. Then I'm sweating, midsummer in hot Cairo street. Glaring white light shut eyes cannot push away.

My body can't cope – the brain is feeding it fight-or-flight pictures and still all it wants to do is fuck. My body is thinly attached to my brain at the best of times. This isn't one of them. In my movie-theatre head he's already said the words. Time has passed and it's all happened and all I can do is watch my life fade to black before me. Paranoia picture-house spinning out the same old reel. Short-cut shots of might be in vivid Technicolour. Jaine at our house, eight months big, telling Andy the whole sordid story. Him smashing everything in sight. Burning all my diaries and photos – they feed the bonfire but we have no sparklers with which to write our names. Andy throwing his wedding ring down to the Thames from Waterloo Bridge. No, this would not happen. I am romantic about Waterloo Bridge, not Andy. But then I am the one rehearsing the mind script, not my cuckolded spouse. I will lose both my men, my home and job in one fell swoop. I deserve it, this is right, I've broken the boundaries. I know it has happened in their relationship before now. I know plenty of others have wanted Nick in the past and do not assume I am special. I know the stories of my lover's philandering. Jaine has told me all his wickednesses. I have commiserated with her about them. And now here I am, the other woman. It is all my own fault.

Yeah, right, bollocks it was. It was all Nick's fault for being so pathetic, for not being able to handle what we both consciously chose to get into. I took the emotions out, turned the fear into anger and, like any carefully therapied girl of the nineties, well away from myself. Nick's fault for not being careful enough of his virile little sperm. Nick's fault for following a pattern where he plays all he wants and then confesses to Jaine, knowing she will forgive, because that is what she does. Nick's fault for not realizing this was not the same as all the others, for not knowing from the beginning that I was going to matter more. He was forgetting, I knew too much of his story. Of course, it could be said I ought to have known too much to get myself into this in the first place. Could be said, but unlikely that I would have listened. I was itching to smack his television-elegant, ideal-for-selling cornflakes face. My left hand still wanted to smooth his cool flesh while my saner right arm would happily have strangled him. But I didn't. I didn't do either. I was calm and rational and the words came out as if sane. Somehow in the throes of hot sand-cold sweats and the terror images I was conjuring up for myself, a margin of rationality glimmered from the dark.

I nodded. 'Oh. Right. Do you?'

'Yeah, well, sort of. I mean, I think I need to . . .'

I turned into him. 'I don't know, Nick.'

'But this is . . . you know, I want to be with you. But I can't. I mean, we decided . . .'

'This was just playing.'

'Yeah. Exactly. And it is, but . . .'

It wasn't. Not any more. I knew. I felt that too. How the playing had got in deeper and changed with each new round of the game, how it had ceased to be playing weeks ago though neither of us had dared to acknowledge it in words. But I didn't say so aloud, wouldn't allow that feeling anything other than the merest whisper of thought. I knew better than to give it the breath it needed to become flesh.

He tried again. 'I . . . think . . . I feel . . . I love you.'

Said it.

'I know that, Nick.'

Didn't know it, didn't want to hear it. Too soon, too big. Repeated the phrase in my head five times until it sounded like nothing, sounded like saying 'I love you' to his mum, his dad, a friend, any friend. Not me. Nick wasn't saying 'I love you' to me.

I held him. I made it better. I told him I understood. In a North London B&B with a dirty carpet that stuck to my shoes and sandpaper-dry towels, I fixed everything. Recreated an uncertain peace I didn't believe in either, persuaded Nick that it was just lust after all, not love, this wasn't really love. Persuaded him we were fantasy made flesh, not the thing itself, he didn't need to make any big statements, force any changes. I was making the bad thoughts go away and I could think of nothing but sticky mess. My entire body was racked by muscles that wanted to flee. Animal instinct reared its fear head, tried to carry me away. This was not the same animal that led me to desire Nick. That one had been soft and sinewy and fine to the touch. It pulled me behind, running fast on a long leash that I then gave over to Nick so he could tie the two of us together. This newer instinctual beast was brutal and throat-tearing cowed, with sharp pointed teeth clawing through my nausea. I ignored the snarling. I lay steady as if Nick had merely mentioned the quality of the wine. I would not show him my fear. His was more than enough to drown us both. Would not even look at my own terror, question if perhaps his truth might mirror something I wasn't prepared to face. Because if Nick was in love with me, then maybe I was in love with him. And in love was so much worse than just lust. In love made me a real baddie.

He let me tell him how to be, gave in to being weaker than me. And he didn't even know the whole story yet. There were plenty more traps for him to fall into yet.

'Nick, you don't need to say anything to Jaine. This is nothing. We both know that.'

'You don't honestly think so.'

No, but I wasn't going to agree with him. It wasn't yet time for us to Bonnie and Clyde our way into a hail of righteous bullets.

'Yes I do. You can't hurt her just to salve your own conscience. That's not fair. We're just playing.'

'Not true, Lisa. This is dangerous. This is changing our futures.'

He was changing my present. I thought I welcomed change. Obviously only when I was instigating it.

'No, Nick. Neither of us is going anywhere. We don't mean to break up our relationships. You know I love Andy.'

It was true. He did. I did.

'Nick, we're just having a bit of fun.'

I wormed my arms still tighter round him, suggested a hint of Goldie Hawn giggle in my voice to impress on Nick how very enjoyable the whole thing was. Particularly that afternoon. I have always adored near heart attacks, double dose, just a bit of fun. I was doing all this for just a bit of fun, the bored housewife me needing something to get excited about. It was nothing. Really. I could have stopped it all tomorrow. Given him up without the slightest hesitation. Of course I could. That was why I thought of Nick last thing at night and first thing in the morning. And when I touched my naked body in the shower and pictured his hands for mine, double span and longest-fingered, nails bitten to the quick, bitten to be quicker. And when I erased his face from my mind screen so I could kiss Andy. And when I pushed up the interest rate on my credit card another notch, shopping for more clothes because I didn't want Nick to see me in the same outfit twice. A little bit of fun. That was why I'd spent the past month turning myself from adult intelligent woman with a good job and a fine future into a Barbie clone. Why Jaine's pregnancy gave me afternoon sickness. Why I cried for whatever I might have been doing to my marriage and still chose not to stop. I comforted him and soothed him and eventually Nick seemed to believe it might just be all right. And if he didn't actually believe in it, then at least we both decided to collude in the same lie. Telling the truth would hurt our partners. Sure it would.

I told Nick it was all OK, we were doing just fine, we would just keep going as we were. I could have told him about the baby, could have turned it all off and sent him away. Or I could have agreed with him that it had gone too far, I could have admitted I was in love with him too. I could have told Nick what I'd known but not admitted since watching him eat a full English breakfast in Leicester. But how could I tell him what I'd only just been jolted into confessing to myself? I couldn't tell the truth and I wouldn't let him go either. It had gone too far for me to contemplate letting him go. Sweet lust had made a rash leap for freedom and was now free-falling in love.

Nick and I kissed, washed, dressed and parted. I hurried back to Andy who would be on his way home from his Thursday evening planning meeting. Nick caught a bus to Jaine. She would be telling him about the baby in a couple of hours. I didn't know for certain that I had soothed his fears enough for him to make it through the evening, but I couldn't keep him with me any longer, I had to risk letting him walk away with his just-stilled passions. He and I had lives to get on with. I couldn't shake the smell of him from mine.

Home again. Returned to real life. Pretended I wasn't bomb site brain, behaved perfectly civilly to Andy. Got on with it. The good wife cleared up after the quick-eaten supper with better husband. Andy stayed in the sitting room sorting out some term papers for the next morning, I dried dishes to a Carole King accompaniment, louder than was fair in a terraced land of neighbourhood watchers. Putting cups away I felt Nick's hand warm on the small of my back, just resting there, almost holding me. Tying up the rubbish bag and carrying it through to the council-ordained easy-access bin, I knew Nick stood just behind me in the doorway, long body perfectly backlit by the wedded glow of my home. I felt him beside me all that evening, a breathing spirit carcass of him haunting me as I sleepwalked through the rehearsed moves of bathing, cleaning teeth, setting the alarm, kissing goodnight. That night a ghost heaviness of his real flesh settled an aching rut in the bed between Andy and me. I wanted him there and I didn't. I wanted Andy but he wasn't enough. I wanted myself and I wasn't enough. But I knew that the phantom Nick was stronger now, outlines filled in, memory touches turned to blood-warm flesh where he had earlier brushed my skin. This wasn't supposed to happen. Nick's trauma had provoked the truth out of me, slapped me with reality in the cold-shudder middle of the night. My playing wasn't meant to become real. I hadn't meant to fall in love. This was not the answer. But it was what I was left with. In love. Really fallen, grazed knees bleeding and bowed down with the heaviness of what was supposed to be candy-floss light. Couldn't let him go, couldn't keep him. Didn't want to hear the truth, even from my own mouth. Especially not from my own mouth. I knew where that mouth had been.

Dark night. I lay alone with my deep sleep husband and wondered how their dinner had gone. Hoped Nick hadn't told her, assumed Jaine was still blessed ignorant because there had been no fierce knocking on my door, begged then that I'd still be able to have him and was also terrified I might still have him. Lay awake and did not understand, did not know what to do. The pregnancy had changed everything and yet changed nothing at all. I still felt the same about Nick and just couldn't see my next move, couldn't see a way out and didn't think I really wanted one. I begged a no-more-thought, end-the-confusion solution from the three o'clock morning. Asked for help from a God I didn't believe in and a Buddhist universe I'd read the texts for and still didn't comprehend. And I got a reply of sorts.

From the storm of confusion inside my barren head came a bliss-gift response. I did not want to leave Andy, loved

Andy, had home and future with my husband-love. But there was also Nick and Nick was too strong. There was such an overflow of him in my head, under my skin, in the meat of me, and I could not give him up, it was too late for that. Then the idea crept in that perhaps I could dilute him. Water down my craving by choosing to want yet another. I didn't know how I would do this, didn't know if I could add another to my life mess, but I had no better answers. I could only fail, and after all, I wasn't exactly winning right then. I saw no way past the desire. I wanted Nick too much and needed to stop it. But I wasn't going to stop it, had no intention of removing myself from the source of my heat. I couldn't go backwards, have always hated to retrace my steps, even when irretrievably lost. So I would go on. Add not subtract, and hope like hell that I was multiplying solutions not problems. The agony aunts always say you only get over the last love when you begin to love another. That night, it felt like anything was worth a try. Anything that didn't involve breaking completely from Nick.

I was clutching at straws and finding infected needles in the haystack.

23

Have a thought, act on that thought. I've never been one for taking the time to think things through logically. Distrust of delayed gratification again. That and the fact I was too scared to wait. Even more than Nick's, my own love revelation had shocked me into action.

There are few real commands for getting on in business. Mostly the rule-breakers are those who've become incredibly successful while having a fantastic time smashing down traditional barriers, brag to all the business magazines about how they threw away the rule book to become the magnificent person they are and then fine their employees for not dressing down adequately on a Friday. There is, though, one sensible dictate that I've happily stuck to in my career:

Never shag the client.

There's no point in messing up the glossy foyer by shitting on your own doorstep. Not unless you're on really good terms with the cleaner. Or indeed are the cleaner. That was our only real office rule. At least it was the prime precept until Mary did the evil deed herself and then married said client. But over a lunch of wine and pasta and a bit more wine and then just another little bottle of celebratory champagne we decided she wasn't really being too sinful, because by the time she got around to actually telling me what was going on, the edict had been changed to 'Never shag the client unless you intend to marry him, make him yours for ever and thereby ensure continuation of the business contact and contracts'. I'd ordered champagne in honour of her wicked transgression. We put the lot through expenses. And fair enough, I'd have done the same in her position. Though not with Tim. Even my more recent eclectic desires have never extended to accountants, and Tim is the absolute epitome of the archetypal company number-cruncher. That is, he is not one of your hotshot City-boy accountants gorgeous in hand-made suit and finer silk tie, living the good life with perfect girl-chick in some bare boarded riverside loft conversion, a postcard view of Canary Wharf and a hot line to their personal ski resort travel agent. Tim fits the pattern of the more traditional accountant. White shirt, blue tie, grey suit, shoulders dandruff-speckled. Not too hot on interpersonal communication skills either, if I remember correctly the psychological profile he filled out for me. So it's rather fortunate he's married someone who can take care of all that talking thing. And if neither of them is brilliant at listening, I don't suppose the other four-fifths of the population equally stricken will complain too much. As if anyone would listen.

Kim Fitzgerald wasn't strictly a client. More of a contact really. Mary and I first met through a networking organization for business women – my friend Zoe's annual birthday piss-up in her suntrap garden for a like-minded group of women, followed by a truly extravagant and drunken dinner in the tiny part of Soho that convinces tourists we actually have an American-style Chinatown in London, stopping at a different restaurant for each of the five courses – though every one with an equally annoyed team of waiters. It's one way of celebrating future liver spots and crow's-feet. Mary and I hadn't encountered each other before, met on a coke run to Zoe's bathroom, discovered we were both freelancing in the same area and thought, five sea breezes to the wind, that setting up a joint office had to be more enjoyable than working from our respective kitchen tables. It was. And when we were sober we realized how very clever our drunken selves had been – not only was working together more fun, it was also a damn sight more lucrative. Trust a trainer to know what skills they're lacking. While we both work in training and teach similar versions of various management skills, Mary is far better than I am on the selling side, the actual process of getting the work in the door. I prefer the talking, meeting people, working out the methods that will deal with their problems. If they decide to use them. We analysed our current market forces situation, created a problem solving template and actioned the solution. Then we shared a bottle of cheap wine at the local pub. And an even more daring king-size bar of fruit and nut. Galaxy. Particularly smooth and creamy, girlie chocolate. None of your bitter grownup seventy per cent cocoa solids clever-boy stuff. These days, though, I devour the chocolate alone. Mary has become very proper, a new way of life carbon-dated from her marriage to Tim, which kind of puts her out of the running for appalling gossip or all-night drinking sessions – something marriage to Andy never did to me. Funny that. So now she pretty much runs the office with our part-time secretary Lucy and I take on most of the actual training, with Mary or the occasional freelancer filling in the gaps. Which is where Kim came in – we originally took her on to fill in one of those gaps, but she was so good at it that the client who'd hired her to motivate his sales team then gave her the job of actually running the sales team. Earning the same daily rate she was getting freelance, but on salary and with all the benefits his company could provide. So we lost Kim as a regular employee, changed her position to someone who could work freelance for us if we really needed her and booked her long enough in advance, but better than that, we also gained her as someone who could occasionally employ us. And pay for a longer lunch than either of us could stretch to. Not technically a client, then.

Kim was, however, a woman. And so am I. And I'm a straight one. But only in the purely experiential sense. Rather as a BMW convertible is an exceedingly desirable item, but not all colours are as appealing as British racing green, I would have been with a woman sooner, if only I'd met any I'd really fancied. Or if any of the ones I had fancied had been gay themselves. There was the luscious Megan Albright at college – Barbie-blonde but with better legs and finer breasts – though if I had even hinted to her what I regularly fantasized as I lay three feet away in our first-term shared room, four pints of cider squirming inside me, she'd have run screaming sexual harassment to the campus newspaper in a minute. Sadly she was as excessively homophobic as she was stunningly gorgeous, so I dismissed my desire as a passing phase and got on with the serious educational business of learning how to drink for England. After Megan there were one or two others who made it into the beginning of my fantasies but never quite stayed the course to the end of the dream, usually replaced by Paul Weller or Morrissey. You'd think I'd have noticed something was odd. And I've always had a soft spot for Andy's sister too. But she is his twin sister and, even if I ignored the fact that perhaps I fancy her because she looks an awful lot like the girl version of Andy, there's still the little matter that one isn't often encouraged to shag one's sister-in-law. So though I'll admit to lesbian virginity, it wasn't through want of desire or imagination. My lack of initiation into the other side of sex was simply because at about ninety-three per cent heterosexual I'd taken the more traditional route to self-fulfilment and happiness. Of course I had, which is why I now found myself in love with my best friend's boyfriend.

Married to one man, surprised to be in love with another, of course the only solution was to add in a third. In retrospect, it's clear that sanity wasn't my strong suit just then. But then you never see the horizon in hindsight, and even now I don't intend to live with a permanent crick in my neck. The new lover seemed a just about plausible possibility. In the fierce-light examination of my excess, embarking on another affair in order to dilute the power of the first one seemed almost possible. What's more, I did know she fancied me. Kim had told me so herself on one or two drunken occasions. Years ago she had actually asked me if I was sure I was straight. I'd told her I was. Sure and straight. Now I wasn't sure about anything, didn't want to be, was actively running from the only certainty I knew, the one about wanting Nick beyond where I thought want could lead me, which made Kim a pretty good choice. Unlike when I first kissed Nick, I did at least know she was interested in me. Or had been once. If I was going to be able to water down Nick's potency in my life, I had to hope that she might just fancy me still.

Kim Fitzgerald. Successful, monied, charming, beautiful and gay. I picked a good one – I might have been desperate, but I wasn't stupid.

At least, I didn't think I was stupid then.

24

But how to let a woman know you fancy her? Particularly when you already know she fancies you, when you've rebuffed her twice before. How to bite the bullet of squirming embarrassment and leap into the unknown abyss of possible rejection. To do it so you're not a complete idiot. Or maybe you are but at least it isn't showing to the whole world – just the internal agonies of embarrassment, same as any other day. How to make a move on someone you've known for quite a while, who has known you for that same while and who has always known that you are straight. Which you are. Primarily. So she's not mistaken. But to let her know that what you thought about yourself and what you told her as truth is no longer the only reality. Simply smiling sweetly and batting eyelashes will not do. We have no method of seduction any more, no planned negotiation of yearning. It's all desire and consume. I am all desire and consummation. The twentieth century has stripped us of a known pattern of courtship and left us fumbling in a wasteland of dirty lust tempered with political correctness.

I took the modern-woman option. I talked about sex. Debated the possibilities until they mutated, through the very fact of their open discussion, into tangible realities. Realities simply begging to be taken. We were at a business breakfast. Just Kim and me, breaking our night's fast. At the Ritz. Kim takes her recently extended expense account very seriously. I'd declined the offer of eggs Benedict and a glass of freshly squeezed orange juice, champagne an optional extra, in favour of the more sedate toast and tea. I did manage to stretch to Earl Grey, though. You can take the girl out of the South London council estate, she can educate herself into casual abuse of (other people's) wealth and occasional extreme privilege, but you can't ever really get her to leave behind the feeling that one day she'll be found out and all this nice stuff will be whisked away far faster than it came, hollandaise and egg yolk dripping a telltale smirk behind it. I've also found that staying off the champagne first thing in the morning calms the creeping paranoias just a little. Kim had no such qualms. Obviously a clean conscience. The eggs, the champagne, the juices (blood orange and pink grapefruit, a single colour theme of red stain), enough fresh fruit to send a scurvy-free Captain Cook twice round the world, and two fat croissants: Kim does both acquired privilege and natural thinness very well indeed.

We were eating, she was drinking. I sipped warm tea. We had actually been discussing the business event we were planning, taking our breakfast seriously, doing the job. But, to be completely honest, unless the company I'm working for is a dead loss and really needs to be shaken up from the top down, I find I can usually juggle any number of our training plans and come up with something that will suit the mood of the day. Or I could as long as I was concentrating on the job and not letting thoughts of Nick squander my creative flow. And as the whole point of squaring the triangle with another relationship was specifically to rid myself of those thoughts of Nick, I was trying harder than usual to stick to the apparent point of our meeting, to keep things focused on work. Which meant that by the time I'd finished two slices of unbuttered toast and was just wondering if that evening's run would stretch to a croissant (the run wouldn't, my greed did), we'd planned the workshop and training sessions, agreed on a reasonable fee, and were ready to slam on to the next topic of conversation. Sex in general for me, followed by a few discreet enquiries about Kim's current relationship standing. All delivered in my own carefully honed, elegant prose style.

'God, I don't know what's going on, must be early spring fever or something, but I'm just so horny at the moment. Are you shagging anyone right now?'

Kim laughed. Like me, she doesn't especially enjoy the polite conversations you're usually forced to have when business-breakfasting. Or lunching. In fact at any time in a meal oriented towards the corporate establishment – except near the end of dinner when the wine has been elegantly sipped enough to turn into a guzzle, gratefully removing the enforced need for tiptoeing delicately beneath the glass ceiling. Unlike me, though, Kim does tend to stick to the script. Maybe she has more to lose. But then, she wasn't the one on the prowl, she didn't have to make the first move. And nor, as I rapidly discovered, was she shagging anyone. Anyones.

In the next thirty minutes I heard that she'd broken up with a girlfriend two months earlier but that she wasn't anywhere near heartbroken – the relationship had never been especially serious. Just fun, just playing, nothing heavy. Treated with equal levity on both sides and ended with pleasant amicability. I was fancying this woman more by the sentence – she had all the easy disengagement I'd found surprisingly lacking in myself. She was still pining for the woman who came before just-fun-girlfriend, but that would never have worked anyway and she knew she had to get on with it. Finally, of course, there was her son, who lived weekdays with his father and weekends with Kim, and the fact that most prospective suitors found the idea of a six-year-old weekend chaperone a little more demanding than they bargained for in a new relationship. Something about preferring late nights to night-lights. Basically Kim was looking and wanting but not holding out a whole lot of hope.

While she spoke I very slowly ripped open a warm pain au chocolat. Offered her half. Ate my half as she did hers. Slowly, small bites between bright teeth, around carefully delivered words, soft-melting chocolate on my tongue. There was a crumb on her lip. I leaned over and wiped it away like it didn't matter, like she was my sister, my best friend, my girl friend. Not my girlfriend. Laughed and smiled sympathetically and nodded in all the right places and some of the wrong ones too probably, but above all I was attentive. When my thoughts strayed to her moving mouth, I dragged them back up to her heavy dark eyes. When my hand strayed to her side of the table, I left it there. My fingers on her arm, an understanding warmth holding comfort about the unrequited-love girlfriend. Then I kept my touch there long enough to mean possibly that little bit more. I praised her friendly relationship with the ex-husband, her bravery in breaking up when she knew it couldn't work, her commitment to her son. Kim asked about my home life. I was happy to talk about my husband. Kim already knew about my husband. I didn't mention Nick. The subject of other lovers didn't come up. And I pushed his warm touch to the back of my mind.

When they gave us our coats at the door we walked out into a morning-chilled Piccadilly. I helped Kim pull her hair from the collar of her jacket, held the hank of thick jet hair just that little bit longer than necessary. I hugged her goodbye and told her I'd e-mail the details for the workshops later that week. She said that e-mails were so technical and difficult. She said she'd much rather do this kind of business face to face. She said she'd really enjoyed the morning. She asked me out for lunch. I figured perhaps it had worked. Certainly I had her interested. And I was interested too. As before, I liked the new. But I still had Nick in my head.

This is what Kim thinks:

I don't know why she spent the morning coming on to me. But I'm glad she did. I've always thought Lisa was gorgeous. It'll be interesting to see if she can go through with it. Interesting to see if she really wants to. I know I do. I think I'll like it. Like her. I like to play.

I wonder, why now?

25

With Kim, the new was palpable. Because she wasn't a man she couldn't be compared to either my husband or my lover. Kim was way out there in the separate stakes, somewhere beyond girlfriend and before partner, and the simple fact of her gender lifted her clean out of any race between Andy and Nick. Furthermore, my real best friend was preoccupied with her own vital matters, pregnancy foremost – Kim therefore made an excellent substitute girlfriend as well as lover. The synchronicity of replacing one tall, elegant, lovely black woman with another was an irony not lost on me. Not lost on my educated-into-middle-class guilt either.

Kim's home was a revelation. A riverside warehouse conversion that actually felt like someone lived there rather than being a show home. Perhaps it was because at least one of the bedrooms was scattered with Lego and PlayStation accoutrements and discarded clothes, old sweet wrappers, important pieces of something that looked like so much forgotten junk. Perhaps it was because she must have even greener fingers than Pippa Greenwood, and her originally sparse and white apartment was covered floor to ceiling in a fine reconstruction of the tropical greenhouse at Kew. Or maybe it was just that Kim was not what you'd call especially house-proud. She did not have my husband's desire for smooth surfaces and clean corners, nor did she possess my yearning for tidy drawers and easy-closing cupboards. There were dust-balls furring themselves beneath the hardwood and white linen sofas. The huge windows that fronted the apartment, opening on to a north view of the Thames, were streaked, not merely with Jack's childish pawprints but also with hand, elbow and foot marks from where Kim eased her way on to her late-sun verandah and an evening of slow dinner and slower sunset. There had been just one dinner in the romantic setting of her newly purchased balcony. It was the occasion when she broke up with the girlfriend before the girlfriend before me. The last one to really matter. The dinner took most of the night. It had been in the middle of last summer, and Kim pointed out that at least three of the handprints and one of the footmarks were from that messy occasion. Partly she couldn't be bothered to clean them, but it was also a choice to leave Angela's mark on her window. As a memento. A warning perhaps. I was never sure to whom. Kim's kitchen cupboards were super-stocked and overflowing on to the once pristine tiled floor. The sauce-splattered glass tile walls were a fine testament to her love of cooking and disregard for cleaning. This was the woman who got up at a quarter to six in the morning, ran for half an hour on her home treadmill while scanning the terrestrial and cable channels for City news, put in a minimum ten hours at the office, ate a full and satisfying business lunch daily, regularly brought home piles of work, spent three out of four weekends learning the intricacies of her son's relationship with Lara Croft, and still managed to look like she'd just stepped out of a page from *Vogue*. French *Vogue* where the women are always sleek and refined and perfect. And the slice of wholemeal walnut toast she munched for her breakfast was cut from the loaf she baked herself on Sunday morning. Kim was nothing if not contradictory. I liked to hide in Kim's world because it was running away.

Kim's home was a new continent – there were no reminders of Nick with her.

Playing with Kim was extraordinary and incredibly exciting. Not, as might have been expected, as I had naively expected, because the sex was so amazing, because the fashionable lesbian event had finally arrived in my life and I had come home, come to my senses, or merely come. None of those cliches proffered by the trashy new-woman novels I had devoured in my late teens and early twenties, now being visualized as even trashier TV. The sex was good, great sometimes, brilliant at others. But actually it was also not that different. It was just sex. Kim was a good lover and an inventive, attentive one. In some ways the sex with Kim was actually easier than with Nick – I wasn't in love with Kim, sex with Kim didn't leave me lying shattered beside her, crippled with the passion and the supreme effort of holding my real feelings in check. And in addition to the relief it gave me from the Nick trauma, there were added incentives to the new relationship. The absence of delicious and painful and ultimately futile extreme desire was replaced with an alternative excess. In this affair there was even more subterfuge and secrets and lying. More need for care, more whispered confidences, more danger. I had gone from simple adulterer to subterfuge superlative. They say power is a great aphrodisiac. Maybe so, but risk is a far better fuck.

I was having an affair with a woman who wasn't out. Didn't intend to be out. Had less political opinions on gay rights than my mother. I had discussed the whole outing thing once with Kim, long before we lurched from good acquaintance into the more revealing phase of our friendship, and had been told in no uncertain terms that her decisions about her sex life had nothing to do with me. She was right, but I was still interested. Once we were officially lovers I was even more interested, and I did at least have the right to say so now that it had a little to do with me. I tried again. In bed. Post-sex. Fresh coffee, scent of season-expensive strawberries and our perfumed, still-ready bodies in the air. 'Kim, haven't you ever wanted to be honest about your sexuality?'

A sigh, a raised eyebrow and a terse, 'No.'

'Does no one in your family know?'

Another sigh, turned bare back turning a little further away from me. 'I think they all know. I assume they know. I'm thirty-five. I lived with Jack's dad for three years, eighteen months either side of the birth. Tried it, didn't succeed. Women before him and women after him. If anything, he was the real surprise to my family. And when it didn't work out I just went right on back to not bringing up the subject. They long ago stopped asking if there were any new men in my life.'

'But you haven't talked about it?'

High brick walls of her riverside home loom down. The words hang over us, Tuesday afternoon sunshine slipping down winter-early at the silvered bend in the Thames. Turned back turned back to me, Kim, wearing a look of blind resignation, wearily trotted out her usual line.

'Do you talk to your mother about your sex life with Andy?'

'Hardly.'

'Have you told her about anyone else?'

I took the leap and went with the lie. 'There hasn't been anyone else. Not since I got married.'

It was easier than telling the truth. Lies so often are. Kim didn't notice my momentary lapse of concentration, went right on with her lecture.

'Fine. So if you're not prepared to discuss your sex life with your family, why do you want me to?'

No good answer to that one, but I am politically correct enough to know that gay people are supposed to be out –

that's what we're all meant to want. A society where it's all OK, and everyone can be who they are and no one has to hide or pretend or lie. All this I know. I also knew that I'd become fairly damn stunning at lying myself.

Kim went on. 'Look, Lisa, I'm black.'

I kissed her proffered arm. 'I noticed.'

'I've managed to do quite well—'

'Oh yeah, I think a new BMW every year and this flat—'

'Apartment.'

'Apartment, and a big fat bonus on top of your big fat salary and seven weeks' holiday a year is doing pretty well.'

Kim smiled smugly and nodded about the room at her life of fine possessions. 'Right. And we both know I have all this despite being black in a society where an even distribution of dark-toned melanin isn't the first thing an employer looks for in his prospective employee.'

'Could be that the employer is a woman. Or even black herself.'

'Could be, but I live in the real world, babe.'

'So you think that coming out would hamper your chances of success at work?'

'Hamper, Lisa, is one way of putting it.'

'But there are successful gays everywhere—'

'Oh yeah, of course there are. I forgot. One in the Cabinet, one or two others in Parliament, maybe three in the City. Lisa, there are queers in public life, but I think you'll find that most of them are men.'

I was warming to my subject now, no real expectation of winning, but the juice of heated debate has always been for me a fine precursor to other, less elevated passions. I launched in. 'That's just because there are still more men running things. But that's changing.'

Lying in bed with my first girl, my only girl, all caught up in the post-sex, pre-sex glow of sisterhood naiveté.

'Fine. Then I'll come out later. Maybe. I'm not a campaigner, Lisa. I live my life, I am successful, I am black. I can't fail to be out about that. But I don't have to be out about my sexuality.'

I didn't really want a lecture, not one that interrupted mine. I got it anyway.

'Being gay is part of who I am, not all of what I am, and sure, I do see that other people have been out and achieved in spite of it. I also know it's harder.'

'Yes, of course, but . . .'

'Shut it, and listen.'

I did.

'I just don't choose to make things still more difficult. Very occasionally in my life, it has been positively beneficial to be black in a white business world. I can't see where in that world it would do me any good to be also known as gay. One token might be an occasional entry ticket. If you're very lucky. Two tokens in one and you're heading for the exit.'

I knew I'd started this and I also knew there were cogent arguments against her proposition, but it was clear that most of them involved me telling Kim what she should do with her life. Naked with warm feet tangled isn't the best position for getting on one's high horse. Kim turned on me. 'Anyway, why is it my job to save the world? Are you going to tell your mother about me?'

Now there's a new thought.

'I don't know. Maybe. Probably not.'

Definitely not. Whatever her views on gay sex, I rather think my mother believes it should at least stay in gay relationships, not in the sleepy afternoons of my marriage.

Kim grinned her delicious smile full at me. 'I think my point has been made by your silence.'

I could have told her that as I intended to stay with my husband coming out would be hypocritical. I could have added that as I was also in love with another man, that kind of placed me somewhat closer to the straighter-than-Julie-Burchill end of the occasional lesbian spectrum. Instead I decided we'd done politics for long enough. I kissed her forehead, eyes, nose, lips, breathed in her body, tasted the scent of her in my mouth. Held black skin, gay skin, with my white skin, straight skin, and decided talking was all very well but there were far better things to be done in the brief hour we had left together. If I couldn't convince Kim of the importance of coming out, I would at least give her a damn good reason for staying in.

And in doing so I would stop dreaming about Nick, stop worrying about Andy, just stop. Which I did. For a while.

I had no illusions about my affair with Kim. I was a diversion in her life. She had prioritized it all – child and work and gym and her own family and a small circle of select and fast-silenced friends. Kim did not need me. She wanted me. I was the chosen one who would provide distraction from motherhood and making it and having it all with a career to work yourself into the ground for. And I was allowed to be this diversion on her terms. Which was fine with me. I was juggling enough distractions of my own at the time. And being wanted, albeit on a very occasional basis, was delicious. It tasted different to loving Andy, to Nick desiring me, to my own perilous yearning for him. Being wanted myself was a new blessing, one I welcomed, luxuriating in the ravenous touch of need.

I was happy simply to pass time, ignore everything else with Kim. We talked little about work, still less about world affairs or mutual friends. And never about Andy. She made it very clear right from the beginning that she didn't want to get to know my husband any better than as the passing acquaintance, spouse-of-colleague that he already was. Not in reality and not through my stories about him. Suited me perfectly. I also took her attitude as an indication that I didn't need to bring up Nick either. We talked about ourselves. Long discussions I hadn't had since I was about sixteen and just working out who I wanted to be, sitting late in Heather's kitchen, listening to whatever LPs we could beg from her brother. Long discussions I'd rarely had with my husband since we'd concreted over our relationship with the pressing concerns of the everyday and our conversations became crowded with the more vital matters of house and garden and just when does the local authority collect the empty bottles for recycling. Discussions I used to have with Nick until sex overtook our need for conversation, and my excess desire kept my telltale mouth tight shut. And it wasn't that the sex with Kim didn't take over sometimes too, but because we still had to get to know each other properly, because she wasn't Nick whom I'd known intimately for years, because she wasn't my best friend, we actually took the time to grow to like each other too. We didn't have years of friendship to fall back on – so we were interesting to each other. The past still held delights. We talked about ourselves and we went to galleries and movies and then she went back to work and I went back to my life. Kim was totally demanding in the time I was with her, and totally absent the rest of the time. She never invaded any part of my privacy, though I suspect I might have wanted her to. She never asked me to be with her when I had arranged things with Andy. If I had organized something with Nick and she wanted to see me, she happily took whatever excuse I offered as fact. And I was quite prepared to have her on a limited time-share basis too. At the time it seemed ideal that she was so detached from me. I couldn't have asked for a better third partner.

But then, I never expected to need more from her.

26

Kim and I went out – very late afternoons only, when she wasn't working, when I could sneak away from the office or plead an early start the next day and needing time at home to prepare. Where Nick and I had become all fast desire and the glorious anguish of impossibility, with Kim it was light and frothy and easy. A post-work happy hour of silly cocktails instead of a night on expensive single malt. With an unexpected enlightenment thrown in for good measure. A lunch at the Tate one day, early evening at the Hayward the next – Kim saw it as her job to educate me in the finer points of artistic endeavour. Though even with Kim explaining to me just why the bloke at the ICA saw razoring his arms and bleeding on to a plastic sheet as a perfect expression of his inner beauty, I have to admit that I was certain I wasn't interested in understanding that particular art form. But I liked seeing it with her. I liked going out with her. Playing with Kim was easy. I wasn't enjoying ease with Nick, I was indulging in tortured longing – undeniably pleasant in its own way, but not quite as simple to turn off after a couple of hours together on a rainy afternoon. Spending time with Kim was an end in itself. It didn't spill over into the rest of my life, staining my happy home life with the indelible dye of 'what am I doing?'. Instead I partied with Kim, did girl lunches, went to galleries, the occasional early-evening movie and while my cunning plan of desire dilution was working to a degree, in that she did manage to take my mind off Nick, it was only successful for the time I was with her. The wanting Nick didn't go away.

Once Jaine had told him about the baby there were a few exceptionally unpleasant phone calls, a couple of horrid, rushed meetings. He was furious that I'd slept with him once I knew Jaine was pregnant. Then he was sorry, he understood I owed it to Jaine to let her tell him. And then he was really very unhappy indeed. What were we going to do? We couldn't see each other. We had to see each other. He still wanted to tell her. How could he possibly tell her now? He was a bastard. I was evil and manipulative. He was soft and sorry, and I was perfect, beautiful, and his only solace. It was a mess. The sex that followed these tearful exchanges did nothing to make either of us less confused, less agonized. But then again, the thought of ending it and saving ourselves from the guilt-purgatory wasn't something we seriously contemplated either. Wedged tight between a rock and a hard place – and choosing to stay there.

After another fraught fuck and fight and reconciliation – all accomplished in less than two hours – I told Nick that we ought to spend a little less time together, that he needed to adjust to the baby thing, work out what he wanted with Jaine. Persuaded him that this was about what he should do, sort out his baby/mother/lover priorities. He agreed it might be useful if we saw a little less of each other, took some breathing space. I don't think either of us believed it for a minute. But I took a deep breath myself and played on with Kim anyway, waiting for the moment when the overlapping desires would overtake my wanting him. It hadn't happened yet, but I was working hard towards it. Nick and I rationed our time together to our usual foursome gatherings and tried to cut back on our phone calls and grabbed hours. On the occasions when I would have met Nick, I used what now felt like spare time to see Kim and enjoyed the relief of not having to be with him, feeling what I knew I shouldn't feel – the jealousy, the anger, the bitter wanting, and the overriding, fuck-me desire. I was a very busy bunny and filled my time up with lovers and husband, squeezing work into the kind of fourth place that doesn't merit a mention on the honours board. Mary wasn't happy.

'And where are you going now?'

Out for lunch with Nick actually. We were seeing less of each other, not nothing of each other. And of course the concept of less just meant I wanted him more when I did allow myself to see him. He'd asked for somewhere dark and quiet and secret enough to exchange fast-lip kisses. I expected to come back hungry. My body was getting thinner by the lover-used hour.

I smiled, ignored the blackboard-scraping irritation in her voice. 'For lunch. Do you want me to pick up something for you?'

Mary the aptly named martyr sighed, bit a chunk of dead skin from the side of her thumbnail. Obviously peckish.

'A sandwich? Bagel?'

'Lunch? Lisa, we have until five o'clock today to get this proposal in!'

Mary was speaking slowly, in cartoon capitals, convinced of my workshy imbecility. Five o'clock was four hours away. Nick was waiting three streets distant. I hadn't seen him except in our happy foursome for over a week, which with Jaine blooming prettily and Nick playing best-in-the-world-dad-to-be had not been a brilliant time. Not for me anyway. This lunch was to be just the two of us and I was craving that space with him. I looked at my watch. I was already five minutes late.

'Oh God, Mary . . .'

'Yes. See?'

She countered joyfully, certain that now I had realized just how late it was, finally understood the terrible position we were in, I would throw myself back at my desk and knuckle down in the self-same head girl manner she had spent the morning perfecting. Sadly I was destined to disappoint.

'Sorry. I have to go out.'

'You can't!'

I stood there looking at her for an interminably long five seconds. She was right. I should stay. She needed me to help her with the proposal. The job we were hoping to get would really make a difference to our finances, and it would be bound to lead to other contracts as well. I'm better at proposals than Mary and I had promised her I'd work on this one and I had meant to. And then Nick had called this morning, as I was walking to the Tube. My mobile read 'Nick' and my skin swooned. We weren't due to meet for another three days but he had to see me, he needed some time with me, he needed to be alone with me because all this happy foursome pretence was driving him crazy. I knew the baby thing was scaring him more than he cared to admit and in many ways I was his only link to the old responsibility-free life. He needed me and I loved that so much. When he needed me, I wasn't the only wicked one, the only idiot. When Nick wanted me I was less concerned about the excesses of my own passions – at least when they were reciprocated I didn't throw myself into the panic of unequal desires. My job or my lover. No contest.

'Well?'

My five seconds thinking time was up.

'I'm sorry. I'll be back as soon as I can.'

I left the office with Mary spiralling poison into my irresponsible spine. The nature of my appetite for Nick meant that I didn't think about work at all when we were together. I was so full of him that I really was able to shut off from any nastiness – until I walked back into the office. That I walked back in just after three didn't help Mary's mood any. I did finish off the proposal and we did get it delivered in time but it took her until the next week to get around to talking to me civilly. My attitude of super-penitence didn't help a great deal. Nor did the fact that a week later we heard we'd been shortlisted but hadn't actually won the contract. Mary punished me by insisting I take on the delightful job of five days' training would-be supermarket managers way out in the wilds of Middlesex. I took my medicine like a tamed wild child. Andy would never contest an occasional late return home when I had the M25 to deal with.

But even potential canned goods supremos need their rest, so on day three I gave my charges a well-deserved bonding break. An afternoon off to recharge their team batteries with tenpin bowling and as much plastic pizza as they could endure at the local leisure arena – all mod cons and happy family conveniences, conveniently located at a seven league carpark within easy lead-inhaling distance of the throbbing motorway. That they would no doubt decamp to the nearest pub immediately following my departure was irrelevant. I know enough about training to know that quite often the best bonding is done semi-inebriated. My husband and I have always thought so anyway.

I drove down the A1 for a spot of in-house training myself – a late-afternoon movie in North London with Kim. Subtitled films aren't exactly in the first rank of my ten most fun things to do on a day out – if I'm reading for pleasure, I'd prefer it to be an actual book, rather than the kind of too-small, over-close screen reserved for dusty films in black and white. I like my movies to come with giant popcorn and a bladder-bursting amount of Diet Coke, not decaff coffee and a chunk of dry carrot cake. But I did want to be with Kim. And Kim wanted me to see the great film. So there I was, seeing the great film.

Not surprisingly I don't remember much about the obscure little Polish number she'd picked out for my further education, but I do remember the sixteen different qualities of grey light illuminating her beautiful face, the warmth of her arm against mine, her long thigh pressing against my shorter leg in the dark, the touch of her narrow fingers holding my hand in the tearful bit. I remember being grateful that I was there with her. I remember knowing I was happy in that moment, no other thoughts to distract me, no unruly longing to knife me from inside. I remember the joy of stealing a kiss when the theatre was at its darkest, least lit by the screen because our long-suffering heroine had at last retreated to an abandoned monastery to live out the rest of her days in bitter silence. I think the chapel wall with its velvet-shrouded crucifix was a metaphor for the hopeful girl hidden in the now cold-hearted woman. I think Kim's hand on mine told the same story better.

And I also remember the hot flush of terror when Kim and I bumped into Jaine as we were leaving. I had run into the loo and was just coming out of one cubicle when I practically knocked Jaine over as she tried to get into the second one. Very trendy arthouse cinemas tend not to waste a lot of room on anything quite so prosaic as the girls' toilets.

'Lisa! What are you doing here?'

'Jaine! Hi! I was just . . . well, you know, the movie . . . it was . . . good . . . wasn't it?'

Jaine laughed. 'Yeah, it was great, but I wouldn't have thought it was your kind of thing.'

I washed my hands. Thoroughly. Paid a lot of attention to just how much chemical-scented luminous pink soap I could get out of the dispenser.

How hot the water would run before it really started to burn.

'No. Not usually . . .'

Stall her. Think of an answer and stall her. No answers came so I went with questions myself.

'Shouldn't you be working?'

Jaine smiled and patted her stomach. 'Yeah, but pregnancy's a great thing if you want an afternoon skiving. I took the day off to get on with doing the baby's room, then the paint fumes started making me nauseous so I decided I needed a break. Nick's going to have to do the job by himself, after all. He's going to be well pissed off.'

We laughed together then, just as we might have done months ago, before all this started, knowing just how much Nick would hate being landed with the paint job.

Jaine went into the cubicle and I dried my hands. She shouted over the noise of the dryer. 'Are you heading home now or do you want to get a coffee?'

I snarled at myself in the mirror and shouted back to her, 'No. I can't. I'm here with someone. A friend. Kim. I think you probably know her. She did some work for Mary and me? A while ago. We're working on a project together. Just needed a bit of a break from it. So we came out. Here.'

Too much detail. Far too much detail. Jaine came out of the cubicle, washed her hands. We're very clean, my friend and I.

'Oh, you must have been the two sitting near the back.'

Brilliant. Too-small bloody cinemas where there's only five of you watching the movie at any one time. Hardly ideal for hiding in a crowd.

'I'd have come and sat with you if I'd known.'

I wonder if she came in before or after I put my hand over Kim's in the opening credits.

'Yeah, you should have.'

Jaine shook the excess water from her hands. She hates hot-air driers.

'Kim. Black girl? The one with the flash job?'

'Yeah, that's her.'

'Right. But I thought you were out in Middlesex?'

Oh fuck. Shoot me now. Then Kim pushed the door open, calling for me as she came in. 'Lisa, what's taking you so long?'

She looked sicker than I felt when she saw what was keeping me.

'Oh, hi. Jaine, isn't it?'

We exchanged stilted pleasantries in a too-hot ladies' toilet in Hampstead and eventually I was able to get all three of us out of there on the pretext of Kim's pressing need to pick her son up from the childminder. Obviously I was dropping her off so wouldn't be able to take Jaine home too. Completely different directions. Central London traffic being what it was at that time of the day it would take Jaine twice as long as the Tube journey, even on the Northern Line. We parted without Jaine mentioning Middlesex again. I dropped Kim off as I had said I would and then hurried home to manufacture a semi-truth for both Andy and Nick just in case Jaine mentioned our accidental meeting any time within the next fifty years. Snail-crawled away through the choking snarl of traffic, wishing I could run to a cold Polish monastery of my own. The solitude of the velvet-draped crucifix seemed deliciously appealing for an hour or two.

This is what Jaine thinks:

What the hell was all that about? She was so weird.

No. Surely not? Lisa's never even had a fling in all the time she's been with Andy. Nah . . . couldn't be.

Lisa should definitely have an affair, though. She needs something.

They're too settled with each other. They need something to shake them up before it's too late.

27

When February arrived it brought with it a particularly welcome form of pretend spring, breeding virulent yellow and violet crocuses out of every corner in the garden, shovelling great clumps of daffodils up from the wet earth. Each new flower blooming in uncertain ignorance of the fake season, sure that it was already late March. Andy and I hadn't yet had a complete year in our joint house and the new-season miracle of cherry blossom return was still pretty damn impressive. Part fresh passion and part serious appreciation of Mother Nature's offspring – I thrilled to every new bulb breaking green from the cold dirt. Their timing was impeccable. And foolish. March frosts were inevitable.

On a Saturday afternoon in the middle of the mildest February on record, I took myself for a rare daylight run. Exercise as a way out of my brain. I'd booked Kim into my later afternoon. She was unusually available and I was happy to accept her offer of weekend time. Anything to distract me from thoughts of Nick, which now inevitably came with sticky-sucker attached thoughts of Jaine and the baby. We were still meeting regularly as a foursome but I was finding it harder and harder to be with Nick when he was playing happy dad-to-be, which he did brilliantly. Because now that he'd got used to the idea, he was looking forward to the baby, was as excited about it as Jaine was. Which was great and fine and dandy for the two of them and knife-turning sharp for me to listen to. It also sat pretty uncomfortably with Nick's continued declarations of love for me whenever we were alone. I didn't blame him for having the temerity to hold two contradicting emotions at once – I was pretty brilliant at doing the same thing myself. But the fact that I understood he could be excited about his future with Jaine and the baby and still want to think about having a future with me didn't make it any easier to cope with. Comprehension does not necessarily breed acceptance. I knew I shouldn't keep holding back that part of my heart I had reserved for my beloved, but it was becoming less and less feasible that Nick would ever claim it, no matter what he whispered in cool sheets, dark rooms. Self-analysis wasn't working, there was no one to talk to, and exercise was the only thing that really got me out of my want/can't have stupor. And in a crap girl-magazine corner of my mind I knew that exercising to get Nick out of my head was also exercising to make me more gorgeous. More appealing. I didn't bother asking myself more appealing to whom. I knew the answer wouldn't be worth the saliva it was spat out with.

The park was available, overcrowded with kids and small yapping dogs running dangerously free, but available all the same. Saffron-bright crocuses and the grey squirrel colonists, nearly blooming daffodils and narcissi threatened to overtake every inch of grassed playing space. Little children were wading toe high through haphazard floristry and warm sun fell on my back, making a myth of winter. I played loud love ballads on my runner's sweaty hand-held Walkman and allowed the music to fill me up until I cried into the soft breeze, overpowered with the warmth and the plenty and the possibility of so much more. Overpowered with what I was creating. In love with the joy and agony in the thrill of my own life. Gone in a spin of exercise endorphins from irritation and boredom and despair to excitement and change and my days spiralling out of control in winter sunshine. Certainly it made Lou Reed into an esoteric philosopher *par excellence*.

The park was stunning that day, despite the preponderance of dogs and their stupid owners who couldn't or wouldn't read the Dogs Must Be Kept on Leashes signs. With winter having arrived and the trees stripped of their straggling leaves, I discovered I could run and view a not-too-distant Big Ben and the Houses of Parliament and the BT Tower and that still more famous London landmark, the Battersea power station. There are days when it is possible for even a London sixties council estate to look beautiful, and this was one of them. I was so full of yearning-enhanced desire, the white concrete housing monoliths in the near distance looked positively Mediterranean to me. There could have been an azure sea just about where Stockwell meets what were once the lush Zoological Gardens of Vauxhall. Could have been, wasn't.

I ran on, a third long lap around the park, and my head was turning from the lazy morning in a slow bed with Andy to my afternoon and evening promised to Kim. Andy and Jaine were making one of their infrequent but terribly important footballing expeditions and could be relied on to stay out at least until ten in the evening, when I expected Andy to return pissed and, depending on the state of the match, either up for a late dinner and more drinking and a funny, fumbling, drunken shag, or a long night's sleep with a big hangover for Sunday lunch. Kim's son was spending the weekend with his father and so I had in front of me an afternoon in which I could expect a frenetic array of diversions to turn my head from the true object of my affections. If the time spent with Kim wasn't managing to wrench my heart away from Nick, it was at least well filled.

Good wine and a fine body, sparkling conversation and a still more glittering lust. I was enjoying the planned image too much for a fourth lap and far too much for any more of moaning Lou. I snapped the music off and ran the downhill slope home. Fast. Turned the corner to our little terrace, and raced the last hundred yards to my squeaking gate, keys in hand for the door. The fifteen-year-old girl with the freesias looked set to win the hundred metres at this year's South London Olympics. Pulled up short just before the tape – sprained ankle, ripped hamstring, out of the race with the end in sight. Nick was standing on our doorstep. Waiting for me. And suddenly the sunshine was long gone and thoughtless tower blocks became again paradise for crack dealers and idiots. Like the stupid early blooming flowers, I was in for a first sharp hit of unexpected frost.

Sweat falling from my face, hair scraped back in a hedgerow of free falling tangle, grubby track-suit bottoms and a shapeless t-shirt are not the attire I'd usually wear to greet my lover. Still less when what I actually had planned was no greeting at all but a double-fast shower, five minutes to slather my body in patchouli-overtoned Chaos, fifteen minutes to dress studied casual, followed by a pleasant late afternoon and evening in the company of my new girlfriend. The choice of perfume was vital, evocation of a particular scent for each of the three helping me to stay with the person I was seeing at the time, rather than letting my mind wander to one of the others. Chaos for Kim, CK One for Nick and Eternity for Andy – three relationships on the go at once stretched my toiletry resources somewhat further than the realms of Duty Free, but didn't extend to anything that could make me smell sweet after a forty-five-minute run. Nick was on my doorstep as aware as I was that our respective spouses were spending a long-booked afternoon together at Stamford Bridge. I'd been running mock-spring-happy and looking forward to the three hours I had safe with Kim, and now there was Nick smiling down at sweaty, red-faced me. Pink roses in one hand, bottle of chilled Cava in the other and gleeful expectation written all over his face. I'm not especially fond of being seen in my running gear, I hate surprises, and I really loathe having my in-control feelings ripped away from me by love's own dream. But of all that I loathe, pink roses in crackly cellophane must be well up there in the top ten. He wasn't doing too well in his role of one true one.

Which at least meant I didn't feel the need to rip out my tongue to stop me declaring my undying love and desperate adulation. Small mercies, little blessing.

28

I was hardly the classic warm and welcoming hostess.

'Oh. Hi.'

I was exactly nothing but seriously pissed off. Nick has known me for ages, should have picked up on my mood – even if we hadn't been lovers he ought to have felt the cool. Or actually noticed that my baby-blue eyes were glaring Amazonian daggers from beneath my sweaty brow. But no, he had the wine in one hand, he had the unwanted pink roses in the other, and he wanted his girl clasped somewhere between the two. Rose thorns and icy bottle. The ideal hug.

He laughed, smiled indulgently. 'It's OK, Lise. I'm sure you're delighted for me to see you looking all hot and sweaty. I know I would be. I'll give you time to change.'

Great. Not only did I not want him there, had been relieved not to have any actual reasons to think about him at all that day, was pleased to be let off the hook I'd speared myself on and had been looking forward to some peace of mind for a few hours, but he also thought I looked like shit. His condescension ought to have helped my 'must stop Nick mattering so much' campaign. Unfortunately not. I wanted to displace him by my own choice, not because he was fucking me off. I didn't want him to fuck me off, I wanted him to fuck me. My lust has always been more powerful than my reason. Even when sweaty and not so cute. I wittered some pointless words of unwelcome and got on with dealing with the joy of the unexpected.

'Yes, no, it's not that, not what I'm wearing. Oh, whatever. Come in.'

I was the original 'Beware Dorothy' doormat. I unlocked the door, turned off our paranoia burglar alarm, pushed him towards the kitchen.

'We can't nip upstairs for a quick one?'

'No we fucking can't. I smell like shit.'

Elegant phrasing is not my strong suit in moments of stress. Not when I really want to scream 'Hell, yes!' but don't trust myself to offer any more than angry bad-mood face. I pushed him away and flung myself into the bath, hoping that ten minutes of hot running water via the most expensive shower attachment Andy could buy would help my brain to come up with a good reason to get rid of him. Somehow I just knew that 'Go home, darling, I'm supposed to be meeting my other lover in an hour' wouldn't quite cut it. Especially when what I really meant was my other other lover. When maybe I didn't want him to go anyway.

I was covered in soap and ultra-intensive conditioner and right in the middle of the tricky process of removing fine pale hairs from my shinbone with a brand-new razor, when the shower curtain was pulled back and Nick climbed in beside me, delighted with himself and his brilliant idea, naked but for the two glasses of bubbly he held against his chest. Soap flicked up into my left eye, my hand slipped and cut a sharp bloody chunk out of my leg. For a moment there he'd nearly beaten down my badly built defences, but the bloody laceration razored me to my senses. I winced in pain, shouted as Nick pushed me back under the running water and the conditioner rinsed down my face. As I struck out to wipe my blinded eyes I knocked a glass from Nick's hand and sent it flying across our clean, fluffy white towels. At least the wine wasn't red, but I was in no mood for a quick blessing count. I had my first ever fight with shopping buddy, great lover, fine fantasy and the keeper of clearly reserved heart space.

'What the fuck?' From both of us.

'Oh shit.' Him.

'For Christ's sake.' Me.

And then a whole lot more me.

'Bloody hell, Nick, what do you think you're playing at? Why did you do this? You can't just come over with no warning, I wasn't ready for you, I need some time . . . for fuck's sake!'

'Calm down, Lise, it's just an accident.'

'It's Lisa.'

'What?'

'My name.'

'Bollocks. Everyone calls you Lise.'

Not everyone. Not Kim.

'Not when they're shouting at me.'

'I wasn't shouting.'

'Whatever. You can't call me Lise when I'm pissed off with you.'

He laughed at me. Actually laughed.

'Have you thought of mentioning this to a therapist?'

How to really cheer me up.

'I just don't like it.'

'Why not?'

'Lise is for when people are being nice to me.'

'I am being nice to you.'

I didn't want him being nice to me. I wanted to fight. I wanted to clear the air and clear my head of him. I wanted big screaming argument and slamming doors. I wanted to send him away never to come back again and I wanted to keep him there for ever. Just too crap.

'Then stop shouting. Anyway, it's irrelevant, you can't be here, in my bathroom. You just can't.'

'Why not?'

'What if Andy comes home?'

'He won't. Chelsea are losing two – nil. Andy's still clinging to Jaine for dear life and hoping for a miracle.'

Water running over my face, more rinsing conditioner in my eyes, cut shinbone bleeding down the plughole and stinging sharp.

'You don't know that for definite.'

'Yes I do, the game's been rubbish all afternoon. They haven't got a chance. They're going to lose and then the two of them will have to spend a couple of hours in the pub getting over it. We've got ages.'

'Yeah, well, maybe,' lifting myself gingerly from the bath, 'but anyway, that's not the point. You can't just get into the bloody shower with me whenever you feel like it. I do need some privacy.'

Nick quite rightly looked at me like I was talking absolute crap. I was. I am hardly the world's most private woman. We've often had showers together. At his place, at hotels, at B&Bs. He said so too. 'Lisa, this isn't the first time . . .'

I cut him off. I didn't need my irrationality questioned. Especially when I wasn't being irrational. Just surprised and concerned and irritated and deceitful, so it looked irrational. 'Look, Nick, I'm sorry. I wasn't expecting you, that's all. You threw me, turning up like that. I only just got in from my run—'

'I know, and I have to say you smell a damn sight sweeter now.'

Bad move. Seriously bad move. Nick tried to hold me. My shin was stinging and dripping a small but constant flow of fresh red on to the nice white bath mat, my shoulders were slippery with conditioner that seemed to think it could do more good there than on my hair, the rest of me was sticky with the Cava, and I had forty minutes to get dressed and on my way to Kim's. I pushed him away, made him wait outside and got back under the water – an average-sized bath masquerading as a reservoir-draining power shower is hardly designed for ideal passion anyway. I rinsed the blood and other gunge from my body, gave up on the shinbone and left it half shaved. When I was finally ready, had mopped the bathroom floor and dumped all the soaking towels in the washing machine, I went in search of Nick, who had sloped off somewhere to sulk. I had exactly ten minutes to get rid of him before I was over half an hour late for Kim and therefore fifteen minutes too late to blame it on the Tube. I went after him veiled in white towels and nun-like contrition.

I found him pouting in front of the telly. He was right. Chelsea had just gone down in flames.

'I thought you'd like a surprise.'

'Sorry.'

'I knew they were both out and I thought we could have a nice time. Here. We're never here really. Not for any amount of time. I thought it would be exciting.'

'I'm sorry.'

'We're almost always out somewhere. I thought it might be good. To be here. You know, properly, with time. Take our time.'

'I know. I'm sorry.'

I've been married too long not to know how best to placate the party that believes itself to be most injured. No matter that my privacy had been invaded. No matter that I wanted to hold him, to kiss him, to fuck him then. No matter that my shin would need plastic surgery before it could be bared to the summer beach-going world. If I said sorry Nick would feel better and that way I could get him to do what I wanted, what I had decided I ought to want. I was charming and apologetic and semi-naked, a little wet and a lot kissy. I apologized again. I explained about the prior engagement with an old girlfriend-workmate.

Completely true. Explained that I really needed some time with neither of my men. Also true. And far safer. Explained my girlie squeamishness about being seen to be not quite perfect. Not really true at all, but living as he does with the glamour doll of the western world, Nick believed that one most easily. And then he was ready to go and apologizing himself. There was just one awkward moment when I came back downstairs all dressed and made-up perfect, a vision created in a record nine and a half minutes. Nick bent down to kiss me and pulled away surprised. 'New perfume?'

'Oh, yeah, Mary brought this back last time she was in the States. Thought I'd try it out. Like it?'

'Yeah. It's good.'

He kissed my neck to breathe it in better. I wanted him to stay there.

'It's different, kind of sexy and clean at the same time.' One last kiss.

'But I think I prefer the one you usually wear.'

'That's good, because that's the perfume I save for you.'

I sorried and niced Nick all the way to our parting Tube lines and arrived only twenty minutes late for Kim. Smelling sexy and clean at the same time, apparently.

This is what Nick thinks:

Well, this is fucking brilliant. Now I get to spend an evening in the tedious realm of football despair instead. What's her problem? Jaine always loves surprises. Lisa loves surprises. She certainly loves pink fizz. She's Lisa, it's alcohol. I thought she'd be elated. I hope she isn't going off it, this, us. I hope it's not because of the baby. Fuck it. It's all too messy. I have to do something about the baby, have to make a decision about Lisa, have to work out what I'm going to do. But I don't want it to stop. Fuck. Shit. Cunting fucking shit.

29

I saw a little less of Nick alone, a little more of Kim with me. Tried to calm Mary by squeezing my lovers into that after-school time of day when I could feasibly have been meeting clients, and attempted to placate my husband by being good, better, best wife when I was with him. Life chopped into four overlapping and almost manageable lines, only needing a soft half-breath to blow them all together again. Bravely facing down the guilt demons, then simply ignoring them whenever they threatened to take me over, forcing me to give up that which was both exhilarating and bliss-terrifying at the same time. However, while I could take control of the times alone with Nick or Kim, there was nothing I could do about our regular foursome meetings. I couldn't suddenly claim lack of interest in those Tuesday nights of drinking and movies, made even more fraught now that each week brought pregnancy revelations, baby scan pictures to look at, a new change in Jaine's body to exclaim over in the ladies' loos. I would watch Nick with Jaine, holding her hand, rubbing her stomach, drinking for two now she was not drinking for one, all the while cursing myself and my illegal jealousy and my undeviating deviant desire. But continuing to desire anyway. Continuing anyway.

For the past six years the four of us had been to Brighton

for Jaine's birthday dinner. Pisces woman, she demanded watery pleasures for her natal day. Brighton has never managed a Pacific bequest of roaring ocean and crashing waves, but it was technically close to London and within evening driving distance. Obviously the vagaries of those gorgeous choking roads out of London and then the M25-A23 torture axis meant time-keeping was a less important point of the excursion than simply being on the road. Jack Kerouac wouldn't have been quite so eager to witter on about travelling free if the road he'd been on was heading out of London at six in the evening. The cones hot line – it's why England produced Pam Ayres instead of the beat generation.

The four of us would climb into the car of the one designated no drinking, lots-less-fun driver and join the lemming-led commuters leaving London and heading for their idyllic countryside and coastal retreats. Join them in their stilted crawl down the Purley Way, the glorious exit from London past the Ikea and B&Q and Homebase megastores that line the entrance to lives lived beyond the swelter of the inner city. Outer city, green belt, M25 and then, as the company cars and business managers sloped off to their mock-happy wives and mocked-happier children, we were left in the thin stream of drivers heading down to the sea. We usually arrived late for our dinner reservation, hot from the bother of negotiating the traffic despite the chill of a March evening, and more than ready to start throwing wine down our throats. Those of us, that is, who hadn't already joined Jaine in the minimum one bottle of champagne she opened during the journey.

I had hoped to avoid the occasion altogether, thinking that the impending baby might bring something of a halt to the usual proceedings, but while Jaine's pregnancy precluded her drinking as many bottles of champagne as she would have liked – or indeed any – she insisted we still make the pilgrimage to the sea. The only change would be that as the one carrying the foetus, she would also be the one to carry us all there and back. We three would be allowed to drink as much as we liked. We had, after all, enabled her to do the same over the past years. And very generous it was of us too.

While I had endured our regular Tuesday evenings, the couple of Christmas parties, the huge New Year do we four had been to – endured and only just made it through the evenings without revealing all, guilty mouth wanting always to speak what cheating heart understands better in silence – I had managed to get through those nights with no major traumas. No outwardly obvious ones anyway. Jealousy, pained silences when left alone with Nick, constant on-edge nerves tingling – these emotions were inevitable in my situation, though I managed to hide them pretty damn successfully. I had not, however, had to deal with anything quite so close as cosying up in a small car, just the four of us. On the drive down to Brighton there would be no loud music, no extraneous people or movie extras to look at, no dinner to shove down my truth-craving mouth – nothing to distract me from the proximity of my husband, my lover and his pregnant girlfriend. I was nervous, to say the least. So I chose to deal with the situation in the only way I knew how. Years of being a teenager – well into my late twenties – had taught me that the best way to cope with feeling nervous and worried and positively petrified about what could be to come was to fill my body with whatever cocktail of drink and drugs I could lay my hands on and pretend I was having a good time anyway. Not particularly good for the heart, brain, liver or kidneys. Works, though.

I got into the back of the car and snuggled up beside Nick. Jaine decreed the seating arrangements because then she and Andy could listen to the football on the radio and I could chat to Nick. Very generous. The two lemon vodkas in my stomach were really looking forward to a three-hour journey in the back of their two-door car. The several lines of coke trickling down the back of my throat were ecstatically enjoying the paranoia invoked by my nearness to Nick's well-dressed flesh. He didn't look too damn elated about it all either. I arranged my studiedly nonchalant frame in the back seat and Jaine drove off.

Her birthday fell on a Saturday, so we were able to miss the traditional road-crowded journey down – no frantic commuters desperate to get out of town in time for a last hour of daylight, thereby making their purchase of a non-London abode so very worthwhile. We got the Saturday home improvers instead. We weren't able to miss the match, though, in fact we were leaving especially early so the football fantasists could listen to the whole thing on the radio. We were eating earlier than usual anyway because Jaine's pregnant stomach seemed unable to digest well after about eight thirty at night, so we'd had to bribe the restaurant to seat us two hours early with promises of big meals eaten and lots of wine drunk. It wasn't a promise we were likely to break. And we had to leave with even more time to spare because Andy didn't want to watch one half of the match on television and listen to the second half in the car. Something about how difficult it is to concentrate on a match if you have to adjust from visual to aural sensation. Very clear about his football protocols, my husband.

Nick opened the champagne, handed me a full plastic glass – the better to spill most of it down my newly purchased dress – gave one to Andy and poured the last one for himself. Jaine smiled the resigned-mother grin she was planning to perfect in about twenty years and sipped her mineral water. Andy, Nick and I sang happy birthday in perfect harmony to our friend and lover and then reverted to type. Andy and Jaine launched into a pre-match free-fall covering the Chelsea Italians, David Mellor and the relative merits of Ken

Bates. Like were there any. The match started and their discussion evolved from erudite argument about the evils of electric fencing to the various oohs, aahs and yeeeses necessary to the complete enjoyment of a radio-relayed match. They didn't care about the two of us in the back at all, knowing from past experience that we were beyond uninterested in the game and that we would quite happily finish off the champagne and keep ourselves amused as the M25 gave way to the South Downs.

Nick stretched out his arms, reached one hand around my shoulders, pulled my head next to his.

'Don't do that,' I hissed as the star Chelsea striker missed his second easy chance in ten minutes and the front-seat footballers filled the car with their groaning dismay.

Nick, for some reason, was not quite as guilty as me. Much less drunk and still less Class A-induced paranoid possibly. He didn't understand my problem. We had often travelled like this. Holidays as a foursome, these birthday outings, plenty of evenings when my head had fallen against his in sleep or in laughter, or even ended the night with my drunken out-for-the-count face in his welcoming, innocent lap.

He smiled a sly grin and inched towards me, whispered close to my ear, 'What's wrong? Am I distracting you from the game? You want to play something else?'

My stomach flipped and I hated him for knowing me too well.

His hand was stroking my hair, my neck. Andy turned round and smiled at us. Jaine looked at me in the rear-view mirror, caught my eye and winked. The wink was meant to mean, 'Thanks, I appreciate your taking care of Nick so I can enjoy myself with Andy'. That's what the wink had meant for years, from the time I first looked after Nick, taking him out so Jaine could watch first-round Davis Cup matches with Andy. It was an unspoken girl gesture that acknowledged our past, how far we had come, that what had once been an unselfish gesture on my part, had mutated into a good solution for us all. Four happy people and no irritated half-couple feeling left out. That's what the wink used to mean. Before Nick. Before my indiscretion. Before the winkee started fucking the boyfriend of the winker. And in fact, that's what the wink might have meant even then, had I been a little more sober than I was. As it was, it meant nothing of the sort. I saw Jaine watching me and decided she must have known. Couldn't not know. That the whole evening, this ludicrous charade of travelling the vast distance to Brighton to celebrate her birthday when she couldn't even have so much as a glass of champagne for herself, had all been arranged to do me in. Seemingly beaten paranoias have a way of repeating themselves with alarming regularity – especially if the behaviour that engendered them in the first place is allowed to continue unabated. Nick had, of course, confessed the whole truth the minute Jaine told him she was pregnant, and they were just waiting to see how long I would continue with lying and cheating. And everything was about to be revealed. OK, so I would do it, beat them to it. I would tell the truth.

Luckily Chelsea scored just as I opened my mouth to make a complete tit of myself and in the resulting yells of delighted excitement Nick took the opportunity to smile at me, honestly and openly, as if he really liked me, loved me, reciprocated it all. The brain chemical paranoias lifted for a moment and I remembered what was really going on, noted that travelling down the motorway at eighty miles an hour probably wasn't the best time to tell the pregnant driver that I was having an affair with her man, and returned Nick's smile with open relief. I joined heartily in my husband's prayer of gratitude for the young Czech who'd only joined the team a couple of months ago and was obviously well worth double what they'd paid for him. Just fifty minutes in the car and I'd already been through a major crisis of conscience. We turned on to the A23 and I realized I was in for a bloody long night. I've never prayed for another goal quite so much in my life.

This is what Jaine thinks:

I'm so glad these people are my friends, will humour me, year after year. This is my last birthday as a not-mother. It will be different after this, always different.

I'm lucky I have Andy to play with, that Lisa puts up with the football. Just as Nick is lucky that I put up with his shit. Your daddy's such a tosser sometimes, little bump. Such an arsehole.

I don't know who she is. But I have an idea. I will pleasure myself tonight. I will watch them, drinking and partying for my birthday. I will enjoy their enjoyment, stay sober, be the good mother. And watch.

30

'Go on, my son! Want it, want it! Yes, yes, in there, come on, get in there!'

My husband was shouting directions from the front of the car, while my lover was quietly threatening to carry out his orders in the back. Jaine slowed down, moved into the left lane, the better to concentrate her own thoughts on the match. She was paying little attention to her loved one. I was looking after him for her.

'Oh no, oh, come on!'

'We're going to lose him.'

A moment of tense held breath.

'Yeah, that's it. What did I say? Stupid tosser.'

'Bloody brilliant.'

'That's the last thing you want to do when you're playing away from home!'

Jaine brought the speed down to a sedate fifty-five, Andy shook his head in disbelief, Nick and I grinned, complicit adulterers in the back seat.

The four-way conversation continued between Jaine and Andy and the two radio commentators. Hopeless has-beens who were quite obviously complete idiots and knew nothing whatsoever about football. Unlike Jaine and Andy who, listening to the match as they were, had a far better picture of what was really going on. Neither of them bothered to look in the rear-view mirror.

Down goes the keeper. My hand follows the line of Nick's spine to the curve at the base of his back. They're taking up very good positions here – he's made space for it on the left. I hold Nick's hand, the one still wrapped around my shoulders. Oh, that was very good, he manoeuvred himself into a position where he could go right or he could go left. Bring Nick's fingers to my mouth, carefully, quietly, nibble at the edge of one of his barely existent fingernails, place the hand back on the relative safety of my distant upper arm. They're coming up quick, playing it forward. Nick crosses his left leg over my right. He tries to turn, tries to hold it in the area. I slowly increase the pressure of my hand against Nick's skin, his back bending to my touch. This is lovely, you can tell they're not scared to go one on one. Nick holds his gaze level on the back of his wife's head, I enjoy the passing scenery, we move in, millimetres closer to each other. Now with his head, down the centre. Nick's arm on my shoulder is heavy and warm. He's very comfortable in that position, really uses it to its best advantage. Nick tangles his fingers into the thin strands at the nape of my neck. He's created the space for it and gone right in up front. My stomach ripples inside as Nick pulls on my hair, cranial osteopathy for my craving. He's by far their most innovative player, this boy. My lips want to kiss his. I nod my eager head towards the radio instead. Yes, he's playing for it, yes, he's got it. I could fuck him now. With Andy in front and Jaine shouting at the radio, oblivious to us. Could, don't. They might be able to squeeze a second winning goal out of this one. Can he pull it back? I lean my head into Nick's, warm my body towards him, close my eyes. Hold it. We could be anywhere at all. The relationship quadrangle melts, new angles form in an unseen instant, Nick brushes his lips against my forehead, unwitting kiss, easily missed, ignored from the front. Result!

Chelsea won and so did I. Two – one. Unintentional. Not at all planned.

But fucking brilliant anyway. Both of them.

I'd had no intention of doing anything with Nick that night. I was the virgin queen married to the best man in the world, Little House on the Prairie and Mrs Walton just moved in, rocking chair on the verandah. I would be perfect friend and wife, nice girl, good girl. I would talk breast-feeding and NCT classes and be neither jealous that the conversation was not really mine nor terrified by the potential repercussions the motherhood concept had on my own life. No part of my being could be called into question, there would be no reason for guilt or reprimand, and one bout of repetitive paranoia was enough for the day. But dinner was very good, the football had its own cheery outcome, Jaine and Andy were happily ensconced in their post-match analysis world, and Nick and I were left to our own devices. For far too long.

It started with a classic move. Jaine reliving the Chelsea striker's move up front, my lower right leg inched closer to Nick's. Andy finished his first glass of the Australian Chardonnay, I poured another each for Nick and me of the less stringent claret. Jaine turned down a third glass of mineral water and gave the strained-smiling waiter her order. 'No dressing on the salad, thanks, no raw eggs in anything, and can I have the tuna steak well done, positively no blood?'

My leg had moved perceptibly closer to Nick's – wicked leg, moving all of its own volition – and while his left hand stayed tight on his glass, his under the table hand was doing a little more than usual. Jaine broke off from her diatribe against the radio commentators long enough to apologize briefly to me for the fact that she was monopolizing my husband.

'Don't be stupid, Jaine, it's your birthday. You can do what you want. It's fine, really. I'd be silly to complain. I mean, it's not like I want to spend the evening discussing the match with Andy. You're doing me a favour.'

She was doing me a favour. Football talk meant there was less baby talk. Football talk meant I didn't have to squirm in my seat in a combination of fear and envy. The keeper's abilities deflected my twin attackers of despair and guilt. Football talk meant Nick was allowed to direct his attention towards me instead of the never-ending future he and Jaine were building. It meant I got to ignore the truth. Jaine smiled in gratitude and went back to the matter in hand. So did I. According to Andy, the afternoon's greatest break was building a very fine side around our central defence. Nick's was shot to pieces. Or maybe he'd given up on defending. Either way, with Jaine and Andy debating the pros and cons of the last minutes of the match, they certainly weren't paying enough attention to us. Rather like the Arsenal goalkeeper. It's not that I don't pay attention to football, I just much prefer it as a metaphor for life.

Dinner arrived, the match dissection ended and we returned to the main purpose of the evening. Celebrating Jaine's birthday with her nearest and dearest and enjoying the company of our closest friends. We were by the sea, there was an R in the month and half a dozen oysters on my plate. I fed them to my husband and he fed me his. We swallowed them slowly, playfully, like we really enjoyed feeding them to each other. We did. It was both a show for ourselves and for our friends. For us it was the easy might-be sex of the long married, a flirting that acknowledges the shared past and constant knowing but decides to behave as if you've just met anyway. When Andy and I behave like that, we know we've got a good night ahead of us. Joined in playing rather than simply in mortgage and joint accounts. And it didn't hurt for me to make Nick just that teeny bit more interested either. They were also bloody good oysters. Jaine turned her head from us in mock disgust, really only pissed off because she wouldn't allow herself the small risk of raw seafood – and because Andy and I were unashamedly taunting her with her second-favourite birthday treat. Her first being the champagne we'd downed in the car. She directed her attention steadfastly through the plate-glass window to the illuminated seafront, Andy and I oohed and aahed and slurped our way through a plate of pearl-shaded finest, and Nick kept his eyes on me. I wasn't watching. My own eyes were locked to my husband's. I could feel it, though. The pressure of Nick's leg against mine, the pressure of his gaze. Jaine thought I was enjoying the oysters so much to tease her, Andy assumed it was all for him. They both had it only partly right. Nick understood that I was really playing up for him as well and he was perfectly happy to enjoy the solo half of my two-hander show. I ordered asparagus to go with the salmon for my main course, teeth-cloying rich chocolate raspberry torte for dessert. After the excess of the oysters and asparagus, the thick gooey centre of the cake was too much for me and I had to share it with Nick. Andy and Jaine don't much care for chocolate. I knew that when I ordered. We drank more, ever faster. Jaine was having a good night too, despite the safe food and the no alcohol – she and Andy had moved from fantasy Chelsea management on to just how best to remodel the spare room for the baby. I scraped the last of the excessive dark chocolate from the plate, Nick licked the remains from my spoon, and I gave it my best shot.

'Do either of you boys fancy coming to the unisex loo?'

Andy looked at me, momentarily puzzled, and then a big smile crossed his face. 'You didn't?'

'It's Jaine's birthday. I think we should do everything she can't just in case she feels, in any way, that things haven't quite changed completely. Got to get her used to reality.'

Jaine laughed. 'You're such a bitch.'

'Yep.'

She couldn't possibly know how much.

Then my darling husband picked up on my offer and proved just how right I was to marry him in the first place.

'Look, why don't you go with Nick? I'll stay with Jaine for a bit. Might have some a little later so I can stay awake and keep her company for the drive home. But don't be too long.'

'We won't.'

I stood up, took Nick's hand and dragged the speechless one from the table. As soon as we were out of earshot he turned to me in shock, 'How did you know Andy would say he didn't want to?'

'I didn't. But I figured that even if he did come with me for this line, I could always take you for the next.'

'You're amazing.'

'I thank you. God knows I try.'

Nick and I shared a fat and fast three lines in the spacious disabled toilet downstairs on the ground floor of the restaurant, safely at the back of the building and away from prying eyes. We then shared a still-faster fuck, especially useful wall-mounted chrome handles to hold for added safety as we took five minutes to burn off the built-up pressure of an entire afternoon and evening's anticipation. Nick returned to the table a couple of minutes before me. I did the usual girl thing of reapplying my make-up before I went back to sit down. Retouching the kissed-off lipstick, brushing the pulled hair, massaging down the wall-fucked thighs. I had another line for good measure and returned to our table especially bright-eyed and bushy-tailed. I paid for the meal, part birthday present, part thank you, part big guilt, and Andy went for a little walk to the loo himself before we drove home, enabling him to stay wide awake and chat to Jaine the whole return journey while I quite legitimately fell asleep in Nick's back-seat arms. I'd had a long day.

I woke up when we got back to our place – decaff coffee for Jaine, brandies and a joint for the boys, a little more coke for me, and birthday cake for us all. Six eggs and fine-ground almonds and half a pound of butter blended into a light and delicate concoction covered with more than its fair share of fresh amaretto cream. Made with my very own fair hands. When Nick and Jaine finally fell into their car at three in the morning, Andy and I left the coffee cups and smudged glasses and cream-smeared plates scattered across our lounge floor and stumbled upstairs, threw ourselves fuck-ready into our willing bed.

'I thought you were incredibly sexy tonight, Lise.'

'That's lucky. I was trying to be.' I didn't have to tell him the whole of the why. 'Do you think Jaine had a good time?'

'More or less. I mean she did miss out on a bit, but it was a bloody good match and that put her in a great mood all afternoon. And it was her choice to go out. She knows you and Nick, she knows neither of you is likely to hold yourself back just because she can't partake.'

Very true. Then my husband and I fucked ourselves into easy sleep, four arms holding two well-matched bodies.

I fell asleep, my flesh printed all over with the sense-memory touch of both Andy and Nick, body taking back time in sleep to reacquaint itself with my own skin boundaries. I lay still before rest, amazed at my evening, stunned by my bravery. I hadn't known for definite that Andy would suggest I went for a line with Nick. How could I? We had imbibed far too much alcohol for the usual markers of spousal behaviours to be that obvious. And in truth I didn't really mind what the outcome was to be when I let my offer fall into the middle of the dinner table. I would have been perfectly happy to have been with Andy instead. For most of the evening I had even managed to still the double-barbed pangs of jealousy and guilt that came every time Nick and Jaine mentioned the baby, talked about their threesome future. Every time Jaine encouraged Andy and me just to get on and have a baby too, told us that we should just stop thinking about it and go for it. And she did so every half-hour. But even her insistence that making another human being was the simplest thing in the world and something we should jump at didn't annoy me as much as it usually did. It was Jaine's birthday, she was smiling, and I understood more than at any other time that she had no reason at all to understand my reservations.

In the moment before giving in to calm I realized the only thing missing from my otherwise delightful day was a goodnight kiss from Kim. For a whole few hours I actually felt like I was getting most of what I wanted most of the time. I didn't know how long it would last, and the question of my excessive yearning for Nick, added to whether I actually deserved such pleasure, was impossible even to think about, let alone answer. But I was pleased to be in that time and place. I fell asleep, knowing that for that night, at least, I was happy. I was content.

This is what Andy thinks:

She is amazing and brave and beautiful and audacious. I love her. And I think maybe something else is happening. I am scared to touch on it, to ask her. I'm not sure if truth is what I want to hear. I would rather enjoy the moments of bliss. She is scaring me.

This is what Nick thinks:

She is amazing and brave and beautiful and audacious. This will have to end very soon. And I love her.

31

It went on. Managing the three. Always wanting Nick more, too much. Loving Andy and knowing I couldn't hurt him. Friends and lovers with Kim and not knowing how to stop even if I wanted to and wondering if I would ever feel like I wanted to. And scared too. Scared of being found out and scared of going on too long. Scared of it stopping, terrified of being tied down, tied up, running from planned years and no more surprises. So fearful of the future inevitable.

Spinning plates, high on thin poles, holding three, four, five of them up at once and two on my head and one on my foot and another just keeping going on each hand. Spinning plates that when my back was turned would chance a perilous escape, try to come crashing down, fling themselves on to the hard concrete floor where I danced below. Except my tensed spine always sensed just when they would fall, willed itself into a dervish twist of defiant body to make the saving lunge, reached out to rescue the flying crockery from their kamikaze fate, grabbed the spiralling death wish in midair and flicked it high back on to the narrow place of moment. I was spinning plates in the air, didn't expect it to last for ever. I just wanted to see how long I could go on, blood running the tainted voodoo of wouldn't you if you could. Working my own miracles.

I was throwing myself from one love to the other. Three

nights of wedded bliss with Andy, happy families and old friends for dinner and showing off the delicious imperfections of the freshly decorated house. Our hand-decorated house. The unintended nooks and architect-horror crannies and the live plaster years old and too expensive to fix, slowly and inexorably falling down our London walls, my fair lady. We had completed the project, the place was ours, was home and had made us one. United the untied. We were idyllic country cottagers in the heart of rural Brixton. Just like all the others.

Where Andy and I were happily settled, with Nick I was frantic, frenetic. As Jaine's pregnancy became more advanced, more real, he became more excited about fatherhood. At the same time he was fearing the nameless terrors of pregnancy and childbirth far more than Jaine, was running scared from parenthood and sleepless nights and the next twenty years planned of necessity and crashing headlong, right into my open-armed desire. I had not reconciled the wickedness of wanting him. There was no reconciliation. I chose instead to ignore it whenever I was with Jaine. Dichotomy brain, triptych chick. Simply switched off the truth and went into easy-girl mode. How big and how much and which scan and which dress. Vitamin E for her stretch marks, Vitamin D for their bones, Vitamin A for the blind eye I was turning to what I was really doing. It wasn't hard. Jaine was full up with baby and overflowing with baby talk. She was having a blessed nausea-free pregnancy and blooming in full Renaissance madonna glory. It was easy to sit in Jaine's glow and bask in reflected motherhood. Easy to sit with her and kid myself into planning my own perfect pregnancy. Life passed her by, tinted with a placenta-hued rosy glow, just as it did for her baby, and all was right with the world. Who was I to tell her the truth? Or Nick for that matter. What she didn't know couldn't hurt. And plenty of other assorted cliches that let us off the hook and into the bedroom. We liked our being together, Nick and I. Our fucking was in no danger of becoming usual, mutating months after we had begun into the still more inventive and playful. We were absolutely not married. Our games were far advanced from Mr and Mrs. And even in the bliss laughter of it all I knew he still mattered far too much. We hurled our fine bone china plates high into the sky and knew they would fly.

With Kim I had new delights. There were none of the guilts accompanying her knowing my husband or me being friends with her wife. None of the worry of being spotted. No concern that she might find out about Nick. She was the third level of my magic, claiming a clear space of her own in the uneven universe of my affections, beyond gravity, laws of physics superseded by the purely physical. We met only for safe, virginal business lunches and equally safe, slag-happy sex. If the love and friendship of one is delightful, that of three is bliss cubed. The only risk with Kim was of personal exposure, giving too much to her, when I knew she would never be prepared to give as much back to me.

Three plates spinning high in the air. Just about holding it together, just about letting it all go. Dervish girl tap-dancing on a knife-edge, and every time I turned I felt the delicious blade kiss-hot against my throat.

My body was changing. Not in reality perhaps, but in how I saw it, what it felt like to wear myself. My flesh had become even more other than usual. Lisa desire, Lisa mind and Lisa body – trinity of three wilful selves and no unifying god to hold them together. Despite the certainty that I was creating this for my own pleasure, when I looked in the mirror what I saw was not my own reflection, but how my body seemed to them. Three affairs and three other bodies and not one of those bodies really my own. Or maybe all, theirs and mine, maybe it was all too real, a confusion of too much flesh. The constant corporeal. It was certainly becoming harder to tell where I stopped and they began. Not with that in-love rush that comes with first desire when you honestly do not want to believe that the body of the loved one can be separate from yours, but in an altogether more prosaic fashion. My legs and arms were simply so used to being entwined in the limbs of another, one other, any of the others, so accustomed to being touched, that they became empty when I was alone. My long blond hair had become the hair that other people held and kissed and touched. The hair Kim pulled tight in her fist, the hair Andy bent his head to smell while it was still wet from the shower, the hair Nick pushed back from my face all the better to kiss my eyes.

This was a self-created demolition and reconstruction job on my own flesh. Not the body obsession fanned by the flames of glossy magazines or billboards. Now there was constant re-creation initiated by my own actions and continued because I actively wanted to. Trinitarian torso with no mind attached. The well-wrought body was the part of me that I parcelled up for my husband, the me that held Nick in strong arms and then, maybe only hours later, made love to Kim. Bent my head to Nick's bare neck, kissed soft along Andy's jawbone line from earlobe to lip, touched Kim's tattooed left shoulder with my right hand, each movement silently expressing the fine polarities of repeated coupling. I stepped back from myself and watched, marvelling. Astonished at this malleable Lisa body that could change not only its abilities but also its desires. Go directly from hard kisses to soft kisses to fast fuck to gentle love. The easy body so simply satisfied. My wanton body that needed merely anyflesh to hold it quiet and calm its wants. Cheap body.

Not so my mind, where the dissatisfied spirit continued to hunt elusive possibilities. I was still running. From one lover to the other, but also for the sake of exercise. In search of the infinitely satisfying end-in-itself. Daily, the sweating grind through streets that were falling ever later into night, spring stealing half-light minutes from the evening hours of dark. Stalking the elusive flesh perfection, the perfect bonding of body and spirit. I was running towards a distant point at which my being might feel peace. The push through to where it didn't matter what I wanted, what I was or wasn't getting, what I maybe would never have. To where I could simply be in the one time, neither past nor future, with no longing. Trying to find a place of being by myself that was in the same league as the time of pure sex. That abandon, fast freedom, given over to single-thought sensation and being. There were moments where I nearly reached through to the ease of self-satisfaction. In lying half asleep with my husband, morning sunlight filtering through deep red curtains, in fast-panting fuck with Kim before she had to run to pick up her son, in laughing for three hours with Nick and then adding the long kiss that turned our old friendship into new desire – each time a chance to lose the rasping irritation of thought. The sex pre-eminent, the mind turning purely physical, or the end of the fifty-minute run – these were the few hours when I was rid briefly of the constant hunger that pushed me forwards in search of the never quite there, never quite mine.

I knew Nick wouldn't fix it, couldn't make me better. I knew now that Kim couldn't fix the yearning for Nick. But they had become my addictive Turkish delight. I couldn't stop myself finishing the box and every morning it was miracle full again. And I still hoped that somewhere in all the tangle of loving Andy and needing Nick and wanting Kim I would find a way out to the other side. The easy shore where I could give in and it would be enough.

This is what Jaine thinks:

I can smell the lies on her skin.

32

When the phone call came, I was sitting on a train returning from a day in Derbyshire with Kim, cool dark England sweeping past me on an overcrowded and haltingly late return journey to the exalted metropolis, the mouths of half the passengers turning down in uncontrollable sneers as cool countryside made way for the gravel-grey sidings and industrial wastelands that welcomed them back to London, the other half heaving sighs of relief at exactly the same sight. I was caught in the sigh, tired and fairly comfortable and just settling into a warm near-sleep, passing rain tattooing the window. Even the giggling pissed girls at the table opposite couldn't dent my cosy glow. I was not ready.

It had been a very successful day. In a placatory bid to ease Mary's simmering anger I'd taken on a supreme-martyr task, one of the outdoorsy kind of jobs both of us liked least. She wasn't very grateful, accurately sensing a motive behind my offer, but at the same time she wasn't prepared to look this particular gift horse in the mouth. The task was to organize a day-long training course for overworked banking executives, specialists in ethical investment all. I figured the actual training could be taken by Kim, which had Mary raising half a finely plucked eyebrow in my direction, but no more. While her instinct told her she was right to be suspicious, her far stronger sense of Tim-taught propriety told her that to think that anything was going on between Kim and me was plainly ludicrous. The perfect marriage had wiped clean away all the memories of her own juicy past and left Mary with little to build suspicions on – the unexpected blessings of born-again middle-class nicety.

I borrowed Kim on a couple of day's loan from her real job. The reasons were twofold. One was that the company had recently come up with a corporate policy on multiracial staffing. That is, it had finally occurred to them it was possible to promote the occasional black or Asian employee. They hadn't yet made it to considering women especially necessary for the management team, but I was sure that would come eventually. Given the appropriate promises of EU subsidy. The five white male heads of division had talked it over with me and I'd suggested drafting in Kim. Who agreed to play altruistic stalking-horse for the hopes of a fairer future for all. And double her usual freelance fee. The second reason was because I'd get to spend some time with Kim away from the city. And it occurred to me that a bracing walk in the country with my colleague might be a very pleasant thing indeed. I'd travelled up the night before and put in a little ethical investment of my own, with some special heart-of-the-country guilty shopping for Andy. And for Nick. The three way nature of my desires was playing havoc with my already costly gift-buying nature. I think Andy and Nick just assumed I was feeling unusually lovely. That too.

I had dinner with two of the bosses, who had arrived early to ensure that everything would be perfect for the next day and that their hard-earned money was going to be put to good use. I confirmed for them that tomorrow's team involvement and corporate image extension modules would result in direct down-line actioning of quality principles throughout the company, in-team confidence and an overall upturn in management benchmarking stakes. People would work harder and they'd make more money. I employed all the long-winded and marketing-speak phrases I could find in my jaded brain to impress on them the seriousness with which I took their company ethos and they nodded their heads sagely at my excellent command of business jargon, terms which they only came to understand last month, having invented them the month before that. We then retired to the bar the better to resource the in-house facilities. We drank rather a lot. I quickly talked through the day to come and set Kim up as the saviour of all their woes, then retired to my lonely bed before either of them could get drunk enough to give me his room number. The bliss of sleeping alone, mobile turned off, country quiet outside, safe in clean white sheets washed and ironed by someone else, can never be over rated. Certainly not when you've got three lovers on the go and mattress, base and duvet take on a quality not often associated with actual rest. I had a fantastic night's sleep. Perhaps I should have left my phone on that night.

Kim arrived at seven in the morning. I introduced her to the biggest boss, who inwardly congratulated himself once again on his bravery for allowing a black woman to run the day. It would do wonders for the company image when he published the course photos on the cover of the in-house magazine. This did not go unnoticed by Kim, who marked him down as one to assign to the most difficult group later. We then all trooped off to meet the twenty nice but nervous men who had just parked their unnecessarily large, latest-registration company cars, and were milling in the hallway like so many first years waiting to find out who their new form teacher was. They looked new-kid uncomfortable in their fresh uniforms too – a regulation relaxed look of new jeans and clean white socks and checked shirts and cable sweaters, all ironed to within an inch of their lives. After a hearty breakfast of traditional English cholesterol, the men followed Kim through to the meeting room – a formal dining room turned into business event chamber for the morning – with tables laid out in a long rectangle and laden down with just the right amount of orange juice and sparkling water and stale mints to make them feel at home and safe and like this was exactly the same as every other work-related training they'd ever attended. Kim did some talking, a little more listening and then revealed her bombshell. She threw open the French doors on to a moderately warm morning, sun doing its best to break through the early spring haze, and outlined the details of their work to come – a four-part group exercise designed to test their communication, leadership and interpretive skills in a tense outdoor battle between two randomly selected teams. It was also supposed to be fun. Best of all, the whole activity was meant to last three hours, completely unsupervised. As a planned part of the workshop both Kim and I were deliberately making ourselves unavailable to them until after lunch. There was a little moaning about new shoes ruined by wet grass, a good deal of self-congratulation on the part of the human resources manager, who viewed our impending departure as a brave new breakthrough in training etiquette, and a final burst of jolly enthusiasm from the three or four delegates who knew the workshop was a chance to exhibit their highly motivated team skills. Thereby earning themselves inevitable promotion. And perhaps even a company car that didn't look like all the others. The bosses loved them already. Kim left the men to get to grips with their pieces of red and blue plastic sheeting, varied lengths of yellow nylon rope, paint guns and pretend money, and we borrowed an Ordnance Survey map from reception, climbed into her rented car and made our way to the remotest place we could find. Giggling like truant schoolgirls all the way. Juliet running away with Romeo's little sister.

Before we could embark on the wilds of Britain, though, we needed to stock up on provisions. Necessary manna for our odyssey. The astonishing coup of Brie and walnut sandwich on sundried tomato bread with an even more celebrated combination of mascarpone and grapes to follow. These two purchased from a truly unlikely petrol station. Then the obligatory medium-price Cava – the fizzy bottles being so much easier to open than those requiring tools that might weigh down one's girlie handbag. And a final necessary chick compromise of low-fat chocolate bar thrown in. To share. Kim was humouring me, humouring my flesh. We then took ourselves off a B road, small enough to require four numbers, on to a worryingly narrow access way, and finally parked with a great primeval rock on one side of us and a glorious vista stretched out on the other. We weren't prepared to cross the stile and walk down the track to the river at the bottom of the hill, though Kim was sure it would make a fantastic – and private – picnic place. Good-girl business suits and better-girl high heels weren't designed for traipsing across this green and pleasant land. Anyway, if we were to attempt a real walk, and of course the vitally important scramble to the top of the primordial rock in order to get a better view of the sweeping valley below, we wouldn't have enough time left over for hire-car shagging. And that would never do.

There is something very sexy about another woman's hand on my thigh. Actually, there is something very sexy about anyone else's hand on my thigh, stroking the skin contained within a mask of Marks & Spencer's thirty-denier black Lycra. When it's a woman's hand, though, there's slightly less chance of a ripped nail or callus snagging the weave, especially compared to Nick's snarl-bitten fingertips. Andy's hands too are not ideal for smooth leg-stroking, tempting. They are the hard working hands of the modern DIY dynasty. Kim's hand on me and just staying there, just moving the slow five, six inches back and forth, a gentle yet defined movement each time, no sense of purpose or destination beyond the flesh of my upper leg itself, no sense of hurry though the car clock ticked silent in front of us and we had to be back to our twenty men in a couple of hours. A bird called from above the rock, I smiled, knowing Andy would have told me what it was. Kim hadn't even heard it. She was kissing me. Face, neck, jawline – my clothes were falling away. Not leaving my body, this was a car after all, but falling back, uncovering my skin. We were carefully dressed to suit the occasion, both to impress the men we are dealing with and for convenience, because we knew we'd only be able to steal an hour or so together. My jacket and shirt had just two buttons each, my skirt a long and quick zip. Kim's hand removed itself from the Lycra and proceeded to skin, no chance of laddering this thin tissue. She climbed down my collar bone to softer flesh, my body offering up willing hand and foot holds. The hire-car fuck was a slow and elongated twenty minutes. Time faded beyond the green hills laid out in front of us, bird call and Kim's call and my call twisted into the rush of wind through new-leafed trees and heightened by the ignored, but not forgotten, ever-present possibility of detection.

Then we ate sandwiches, drank Cava – too much for complete sobriety and too little for it to show. We kissed away the crumbs and dressed again, twentieth century fabrics denying the possibility of telltale creases. Viscose – the fabric choice of the serial adulterer. We replaced wiped-off lipstick, tidied disarrayed hair and arrived back at the country house in time to watch ten men whoop and cry joyously around their very own personally assembled pyramid, dregs of quick-grabbed lunch included, while ten others looked on in an undisguised mix of bitterness and admiration. The leaders had reinvented themselves and Kim now had the delightful task of an afternoon's analysis of their performance. I stayed for the discussion of working methods, afternoon tea enlivened by the presence of a local choir and then, following a quick giggling kiss in a hidden corner of the old house, I waved goodbye to Kim and caught the last train out of the deserted rural retreat, back to my home and husband. And lover. Nick would be picking me up from the station on his way back from filming a breakfast cereal commercial. We'd have a quick drink and then meet Andy and Jaine for dinner. Happy foursome, same old every second Tuesday. There would be no time for kissing Nick, but there was a chance my clothed body might see some innocent caressing action. The journey home was a welcome chance to replenish energy.

I claimed my seat on the train, settled my bags and coat to reserve the empty seat beside me, enjoying the thought of a couple of hours to myself. I was excited about the return to London, had made a decision of sorts. A small resolution, one that hopefully wouldn't cause too many ripples for my karma queen paranoia. I'd thought about it during my one peaceful night alone. I had been wishing for too long that someone else would make the big decisions for me, take control of my fate so I didn't have to be responsible – for good or bad. But that wasn't going to happen. I needed to be brave. I was going to declare my reciprocal love when Nick met me at Euston, tell him I felt it too. Maybe. Probably. I intended to be brave and choose not to deny the truth any more. There was every chance it would be a really stupid thing to do, with the scariest of repercussions, but also maybe it wouldn't. Just possibly easy and cool simply to say it aloud, so at least Nick wasn't whispering 'I love you' alone. I thought about calling him, leaving a message on his mobile, but I wanted to do it right, to his face. I'd decided I would make my mind up when I saw him, see what came out of my mouth and trust in chance. Until then I was going to wait in excited expectation, relax into the few hours of on-train stasis. It felt good, potentially huge, potentially nothing, but coming.

There was little I could do about the woman on the opposite side of the central table, she was on the train before I got on, but as long as she didn't try to start a conversation I would be happy. I cut off her welcoming beam with a quick nod and much tighter smile and sashayed down to the buffet car. Bravely ignoring the tempting sheen of dry Danishes and curled-edge sandwiches, KitKats glistening slut red on cheap silver, I merely purchased a chaste black coffee and returned to the lure of fat and glossy magazine, coffee compromised just a little with my bottom-of-the-bag whisky flask. At the matching table on the other side of the aisle sat an old man. Late seventies, maybe older, he had the look of a High Court judge, an old man who had spent his life handing down severe custodial sentences. I watched him reach into his briefcase, expecting him to extract a red ribbon-bound sheaf of fine-typed notes. He pulled out a tube of fruit pastilles and ate them, one by one, slowly, savouring each Technicolor sugar bite. He ate them like a little boy, and when he had finished the whole roll he carefully screwed up the wrapper and quietly dropped it to the ground, kicking it under the seat in front. He then unfolded his newspaper and started on the *Telegraph* crossword. I smiled at his bent grey head. I was happy and comfortable and waiting, smelt of nearly seeing Nick and thinking of Nick, wanting Nick and remembering Kim and looking forward to home with Andy tonight and past pleasure and near anticipation and the moment of revelation in a couple of hour's time. All good things come to she who reaches out to grab them for herself, and the willing will inherit the soft sweet kisses.

The Virgin Trains InterCity was just announcing a ten-minute delay at Milton Keynes when Andy called. Nick wouldn't be coming to meet me – Andy would be at the station instead. Nick was dead.

33

British Rail trains – no matter who's bought them and poured seemingly easy-earned millions into tidying them up – are not a good place in which to vomit. Nausea has never been an ideal travelling companion for the Grand Tour. There is the long walk from seat to carriage door, the need to clamber over the fat old man cramming the overflow of his too-ample flesh into the edge of your seat. Once in the swaying aisle there is a stumbling negotiation over a minefield of well-travelled Australian backpacks and heavy German overcoats and small children's legs and far-flung handbags, and all the while the train shudders against itself, beating in rough-rhythm syncopation against the harsh pounding of a dozen teenage personal stereos. Outside the toilet itself you find that the self-congratulatory claiming of a seat that cleverly placed you just a short swaying walk to the buffet car now means the toilet odyssey involves negotiating the hungry queue, the stench of overheated burgers oozing from their polystyrene caves and a clutch of angry smokers breathing their last into the between-carriage ether, stubbing out illegal cigarettes whenever the guard makes a surprise reappearance. Enter the chosen cubicle eventually and other people's hair and dirt and piss coat the floor and walls, and you pray for antiseptic or the adult anaesthesia of drunkenness. Even when the toilets have just left their home station, newly cleaned, there is still the taste of overuse and too little space hanging in the tired air. I never go there if I have a choice. I had no choice.

I couldn't speak to Andy, couldn't bring myself to do the how and why. Didn't want to know. He started to tell me what had happened, trying to make sense of the senseless. Helpful husband, knowing this was so hard for me – bad timing, bad placement, bad all round. But that wasn't what I wanted. Explanation was irrelevant, impertinent. I wanted Andy to say he was joking. Bad taste was the least of my worries. I wanted nonsense. It was nonsense to say Nick could be dead. To suggest Nick was over. I didn't want to know how and why, didn't want the explanations that would make the impossible real. I couldn't listen. Told him to call me back, there was a tunnel coming up. Not a lie. There would be one. Eventually. I was heading downwards fast, spiralling into another tunnel, black hole of shock, fuck me, no. No more fuck me. Dead. Impossible. Dead couldn't be. Dead funny. Dead bad joke. I stood up. I didn't know why. Stood up, turned around, sat down, stumbling parody of little children's party game, gazed finally at the irrelevant ceiling, bags suspended with finer precision than Nick's life. Laughter or tears or both churning up, beginning to bubble to the surface. Then I realized I hadn't moved, had tried to stand but the brain-to-legs synapse wasn't working, nothing engaged except stupid mouth, idiot wide. Stood up again, made the connection, legs moved under me, held a little weight and then my knees, understanding sooner than my brain what was going on, buckled and sat me back down anyway. The woman opposite smiled. I didn't. The man who had forced himself into the seat beside me glared. To be asked to move once in a four hour journey was obviously inconvenience enough for him. I sat still. Waited. Nothing happened. The world did not fall apart. The sun did not stop shining. It had already set. The clichés continued. It was a fairly pleasant evening outside, cool, the possibility of warmth and true spring just around the corner. A moon had risen somewhere – there were clouds and breezes and foxes. Probably. A child screamed for its mother, who smacked his legs to shut him up. I waited. Waited for it to be different, waited for something to change, for my phone to ring and Nick to laugh at me. Nick and Andy joking. Not funny. Didn't happen. The woman opposite had stopped smiling, the man beside was no longer there. He had moved to another seat. Deserted my sinking ship, crashing train. The nice lady offered me a handkerchief. I didn't know what she was talking about, looked up and a pool of tears and snot and sobbing dribble fell from my face on to the table stretched between us. From a long distance I heard my moans – sick cow feeling very poorly. The child was screaming for its mother. I was the child. Then the vomit hit. For a split second the woman opposite thought I'd let her off the hook. My moaning stopped. I looked at my watch – ten minutes had passed and Nick was still dead. Finally it got past my head and into my stomach, where all truths reside. I threw myself from the seat of discomfort and trampled irritated strangers in the rush for the loo, got in, half closed the door and gave up my insides to a railway line somewhere in the never-quite-dark countryside between Milton Keynes and Watford. I threw up until I could only vomit bile, and then I stuck my fingers down my throat for the extra release. I cried myself dry in five minutes flat and again vomited what I didn't know was left. I sat on the filthy toilet floor, hugging the hard plastic bowl, wondering if I was going to piss myself as well. Clambered up, grazing knees on other people's shit, hand down on the basin in someone else's leftover dirty soap scum, slammed the part-open door, lifted a useless hand to catch the lock. Shaking hands, trembling arms, shuddering body. Somehow my knickers made it to my ankles, me to the toilet seat. Crying, pissing, throwing up – my body gave up all pretence of businesswoman elegance and took the fastest possible route to safety. Grown woman to mewling, puking infant in three easy steps.

Ten minutes later I woke from my shock trance to the sound of the nice lady knocking on the door. I covered the appropriate parts of my body and opened it a couple of inches. She was offering both my handbag and a very concerned look. She smiled hesitantly, nice lady, then when she saw what I looked like, realizing a smile was pushing stranger concern too far, her face reverted to worry. 'I brought your bag. Your handbag. When you didn't come back. I thought, well, it looked like something must have . . .'

I ran a filthy hand through my filthy hair, 'Thanks.'

'And your phone.' She gave me that too. 'It's been ringing. A lot. I didn't know . . . I mean, I thought . . . maybe I should answer it, but . . .'

'Right, yeah, thanks . . .'

'I hope I haven't . . . it's just that you looked so . . . well, I'm sorry, I should go. Do you . . . is there . . . anything? At all?'

She was so English in her polite concern I could have hugged her. I loved her. For being polite. For being as nice as she could under exceptionally trying circumstances. I neither kissed nor hugged but I did try for reciprocal polite, vomit breath notwithstanding. I took the phone and the handbag and thanked her nicely and quietly closed the door on the waiting, interested world. I can do nice too.

I washed my hands and face. I combed my hair. I brushed my teeth. I am that kind of girl. I carry a BodyShop folding toothbrush and toothpaste with me wherever I go. I carried three small bottles of each of my perfumes. I was having two affairs. It was useful to maintain a clarity of personal hygiene. To keep them separate, lovers and loved. I remembered, I was having only one affair. I started to cry again and, hating it, brought myself to a shuddering halt. Briefly. The bastard tears would have their way. Part of me watched in the badly lit, soap-spattered mirror, entranced as the crying ripped my face back on itself, mouth wider than I'd ever imagined it could go, lips curled back in snarling reverse smile, long slow silent scream, bulging neck muscles, collar bones prominent and sharp, head racked by knowledge too enormous to comprehend. Snow White's stepmother peers in the looking glass and this time the mirror is telling the whole truth.

After another fifteen minutes I managed to achieve a semblance of pulling myself together. Pieces of me strewn willingly across twilight railway tracks heading fast for the city. We were making for Euston, my train companions and I. My husband would be waiting for me. I had at least to get myself out of the toilet and into his arms. He would hold me and look after me and take care of me and make it all better. No he wouldn't. Couldn't. Even in my new stunned state I knew Andy couldn't fix this one. Didn't know enough to even begin to try. But he would give it a go and he would be hurting too and I would hold him and then we would go to Jaine and hold her and hold her baby bump and Jaine would need us, would need me. The revulsion shuddered up from my empty stomach and tried again to make a wailing alien of my face. Nothing doing. I had put that grief firmly where it belonged. For now. Swallowed it down with two huge mouthfuls from the whisky flask at the bottom of my bag. Fished out the dregs of Brighton coke at the back of my wallet and numbed my chattering teeth. I was aiming for numbing me, then remembered instead the last time I'd opened that wrap. Shuddering yowl of tears again. Licked the paper – must be a place of no feeling, no memory to reach somehow. But I'd have to do the helpful and loving best friend thing first. Andy would expect it. Jaine would expect it. Nick wouldn't.

I made up my battered face. Powdered over the fresh cracks. Smoothed the smudged eyeliner. Didn't bother replacing mascara. I'd had enough of zebra mask for one day. Washed my hands again, adjusted my clothes. Left the toilet cubicle looking nothing like I'd found it and staggered to the buffet, bought another couple of whisky miniatures for safe-keeping, safe sleeping, at the bottom of my bag. I looked at my phone. Five unanswered calls. Four from Andy, one from Nick. Double-take, and no understanding why he was calling me, why his name was on my phone. Opened one of the miniatures. The half-swallowed bottle nudged truth towards dawn and I realized Jaine must have called me from his phone. I expect hers was busy. Tied up with the sympathy-flood rings. I hoped she didn't wonder why he had me on a rapid memory dial. It is possible I was being compassionate. Concerned that this was a bad time for her to question our relationship. Their relationship. Her relationship. Aware of my friend's needs and her horribly difficult situation. Half of me was honestly concerned. Paranoid heartbreak fear held stronger sway in the other.

The train finally ground into Euston fifteen minutes late, wrong sort of bile on the tracks. I was exhausted and walked up the small slope into the station as if it were the final ascent to Marathon, only I'd forgotten to light the torch. Walking through heavy darkness and chilled. Andy was waiting white-faced and cold, his arms out to take my bags, my tears, to take me. I fell into him and for that moment it was enough, safe. When he sat me in the car, put the safety belt tight around me and drove off I realized I still didn't even know how Nick had died. Not that I was burning for details. Not yet.

34

I was spared the pain of going straight to Jaine and Nick's. To Jaine's. As Andy said, despite the toothpaste and the perfume, I still smelt like shit. And whisky. No worries about him scenting the perfume in that case. Nick's perfume. The taste of me made up for Nick.

Home instead to remove smudged make-up and cry and shower and cry and wash and cry and slowly dry – no thought of bothering to put on any new face gunge, simply throwing on moisturiser to try to alleviate what would inevitably become a three-day saltwater binge resulting in a break-out of dry skin calluses across my delicate peachy-fresh face flesh. I dressed in old soft jeans and big husband-borrowed jumper. Just enough sanity remaining to understand the importance of comfort clothes. Long-sleeved t-shirt and thick woollen socks underneath. Winter was well gone and the globally warmed south-east climate had slipped into an easy spring masquerading as early summer, but I couldn't stop shaking anyway, teeth clattering against each other, frozen to a shocked core of still-disbelieving pain. Clambered downstairs, hanging on to the bannister like a tired old dowager coming home after yet another hip replacement. Then hot sweet tea, just because that's what you're supposed to have but I don't know if it's ever worked for anyone. Tea with more whisky because at least I know what that does, though Andy wouldn't allow me too much. He jumped straight into caring father mode and sat me down at the kitchen table. Parental caring – the comfort zone of the control freak. Cheese sandwich cut into tiny bite-size pieces and my shaking sleight of hand that couldn't quite get food into my mouth before my body revolted again. Churning stomach decided for me, I was sticking to whisky and the tea, unequal parts for the unequally parted.

It was eight o'clock at night. The day had gone on for ever, divided into three mismatched sections. Separate jigsaw pieces, each one claiming to be part of my life, none of them making any sense. I'd been in the midst of a corporate training event, clever businesswoman, using all her skills and running her work and life with clockwork precision. I'd stopped in the arms of my lover, in the wilds of free England, and pretended that none of the rest of it existed, fucked like there was no clock and the second hand was put to better use. Now teetering on the edge of the pain abyss, no way out but falling in and no chance that I'd find myself in the warm escape of sleep any time soon. There was Jaine to face and comfort first. And before that, there were the forced explanations of death.

'Lise, you're going to have to listen. Jaine needs you to know what happened. She can't keep having to tell people. It's too hard for her to have to say the words. It's best if you already know.'

'Don't want to. Don't tell me. I'll pretend I know. If she doesn't want to talk about it she doesn't have to. I don't want to talk about it. I don't suppose she does either.'

'Yes, but you need to understand . . .'

The difficulty of shutting off my ears had never been so apparent.

Screwed-tight eyes didn't quite do it. I closed them anyway.

'No. Don't say anything.'

Ignorance really is bliss.

'Sweetheart, look, I know how hard this is, I know how close you two are . . . were.'

'No you don't.'

Grief removed the obvious necessity of camouflage – my careful and worried husband could have heard almost anything then and not really listened through all the tears. He was purely in caretaking mode, which meant getting me over to Jaine's place – and with some semblance of coping – at whatever cost. As long as he was looking after he could cope. As long as everything was going according to plan – even an emergency plan – he would get through it himself. Amazing, the lucidity with which Nick's death let me view our coupling. Me horrid, snotty, tear-streaming mess, him cool and tight and in control. Both of us just hanging on. Fuck knows to what.

'OK, whatever. I know Nick and you have been even closer in the past few months, but you're just going to have to be strong now. For Jaine. She needs you.'

Andy's clichés were grief-stumbling hackneyed, but his look of open sympathy wasn't. He meant what his face said, not what his stupid words conveyed. He couldn't help himself. He grew up in the world. So did I. We have only bad words for death, cheap phrases and ignorant silences. We know the words are lies and feel obliged to say them anyway. We are successful in that world and therefore brilliant at the art of talking crap while relying on our eyes and the soundless movements of our tear-ripped faces and crippled arms to get past the words of rubbish and to attempt truthful communication. It was bad, it is bad, it will be bad. Faithful mystery of grief and nothing to make it better or jar me out of my own suffering. I was falling deep into the welcoming selfishness of pain, and unfortunately Nick was the only one who knew enough to give me permission to go there.

Andy tried again. 'Lise, look, you've got to snap out of it. Just for now, for the next couple of hours.'

Liar. He must have known we'd never get away before dawn. Even in my dementia I knew we were in for a very long night.

'You and I can do our grieving at home, we have to cope. Jaine needs you.'

If he told me one more time that she needed me, I would have had to tell him the truth. Jaine didn't need me. Didn't know how much she didn't need me. What Jaine needed was for Nick not to be dead. Me too.

'I can't do it.'

'Yes you can, Lise, I'm with you.'

Cold look to Andy who could only see tear-stained face and the classic grieving good mate, sorry for her girl friend and getting ready to miss her boy buddy. He could not translate my truth through his own pain and concern for my immediate state, couldn't really see anything. He picked up a chunk of sandwich, held it towards my mouth. I retched, reached for the whisky.

'Go on, then, tell me about it, if you really want to.'

Hated him for being the messenger, despised him for lancing truth through to my numbed brain.

'Nick had a stroke.'

'He's too fucking young.'

'Apparently not.'

'What do you mean, he had a stroke?'

'Well, that's what the doctors think so far. Anyway, they're doing the tests now. At least they were going to do them this afternoon. And tomorrow I think. They told Jaine that they expected to know for definite some time later tomorrow.'

'What tests?'

'Autopsy stuff probably.'

Brain not working, too much anger at reality to actually allow comprehension to take place.

'What?'

Calmly. One more time. Holding my hand, stroking it, as if physical pressure could make reality get through where words couldn't. Helen Keller and patient teacher and the death story is water trickling truth through to my closed brain.

'They need to perform an autopsy.'

'Perform? What kind of a word is that?'

I wasn't interested in making it easier for him. I didn't want to know, and if he insisted on telling me then he could put up with whatever shit that engendered. Another flash of illumination. Andy takes, I give. He takes whatever I give. Good or bad. It's what he wants. Or if not what he wants, then it's what he's always done.

Andy sighed, took it. 'Or post-mortem. Do that thing. I don't know what it's called. Whatever, that's not the point. They need to do tests. To find out why he died. What happened to Nick. How Nick died.'

I've seen too much *X-Files*, know too well the sounds accompanying pictures of Scully masked and gowned. Didn't want to hear Nick's name next to the death word, cutting noises whining across the back of my head. The whisky churned up through my stomach and I just made it across to the kitchen sink in time. Brief vomit, more water, more tea, sweeter still this time. More whisky anyway.

'They're cutting him up?'

'I suppose they have to.'

'No they don't, of course they don't. If he's dead, he's dead. They should just leave him. What's going on? Why doesn't Jaine say no?'

How could Jaine let them cut him up? How could she let

them make a mess of him? What was she thinking of? Nick was perfect. How could she let them touch him?

'She's six months pregnant, Lisa. They need to know what happened to the baby's father.'

Baby. Nick's baby. More whisky. More tears. Less tea.

The stupid words wittered around my kitchen and spat in my face with their trite simplicity. One of those things. Not really that uncommon. Andy's uncle's best friend when the uncle was a kid. That bloke off the telly, the one in the soap opera. You read about it. Happens in the movies. You never know. He probably wasn't in pain. Or not for long. Just arrived at work. An ad. Recording an ad for some stupid breakfast cereal. The pathetic banality of it. There were plenty of people there. They did the right things. Tried to do the right things. Same at the hospital. No point. No need. No reason. No sense. Non-sense. These things happen.

'Well, they don't happen to me.'

Not grief but truth. These things didn't happen to me, not in my life. I knew nothing about all this. Not a thing. More tears, more sobbing, more of my face ripping itself off my skull, wailing lips crawling back to tear me open. Andy holding me and crying too and the pair of us sobbing in our kitchen, curtains still open, lights shining out bright into the night garden, illuminating the ignorant narcissi.

'I know, babe, I know, Lise, come on, that's it, just breathe. Yeah, I know.'

Andy did know what he was doing. Had been here. With his own father, with three out of four grandparents in a single nasty, eighteen-month period, with a schoolfriend killed in one of those horrible typical drunk-driving things at baby seventeen. Not me. I only knew about holding him through it. The tears the night before our wedding because his dad wouldn't be there. Sitting up with him late and just holding on to him as the pain spewed out. Stroking his never-going-to-sleep back after the dead-people nightmares. I knew how to look after Andy when he was sad, how to hold him until the morning, how to have no solutions but hang on to him anyway. Knew how to be there for his suffering, to make it, not better, but make it through. I knew nothing. This one was for me, this pain was brand new and vicious, kicking me hard in the face, the stomach, ripping through my guts and out the other side to smack me still harder in the back. Didn't know where I was headed, didn't know anything about the form, the protocol, the processes of grief. I used to think I was lucky and Andy had really suffered. Felt sorry for his contact with such pain. Suddenly I realized that he was luckier than me. He knew what was going on, had built up a few trusty yardsticks. But I was too bloody old to learn a new skill. I had no dead parents, no dead grandparents even. There were no dead siblings, no dead friends, no dead lovers. I was a death virgin. And my first time hurt like fuck.

35

I stopped crying. Gave up the pain long enough to allow my eyes to shrink back to something I could actually see out of. I wasn't terribly interested in viewing all that much anyway. Turned from suffering for a short while and chose instead whisky and the scrubbed-face appearance of coping. For the moment. Andy and I got in the car, bought easy eating and easier drinking provisions on the way, and went to Jaine. There was a long night ahead and it was only nine thirty. Grief process slowing up the span of time, catching speeding clocks in its sticky arms, minutes viewed through tears magnified into hours. I was terrified of what I might have to deal with and heartbroken about what I couldn't tell and we were going to get through this night and I would be good for as long as I could. Fine bone-china plates shattering to the ground all around me.

My husband drove. Fifteen minutes to my dead lover's flat. Big plain building, rescued from sixties ugliness by the cool and groovy, who had taken it to their artistic hearts and now lived inside. I could see it was the cutting edge of contemporary living, understood that it was interesting, millennium modern, Sunday supplement modern. It just still looked like a block of flats to me. A block of flats, and one in particular, floating on the grey of grief. Jaine and Nick's place was full of mourners, those who would be revellers but didn't know what sounds to make for the death of their friend. Later at night and the whisky was flowing a stilted and embarrassed dance, copious cups of tea and coffee pointlessly poured, people coming and going and so many flowers piling up beyond the use of elegant vases and ugly jars. Over it all, the incessant ringing of the mourners' telephone. In the middle of the insanity was Jaine, half the time running around seeing to the crying, the other half stretched out on the sofa. She'd announced very early in the proceedings that their bedroom was available for anyone who needed to stay the night. There was no way she would climb beneath that cover, too scared that lying beside the missing shape of Nick would finally convince her he wasn't coming back. Jaine wasn't going anywhere near their bedroom. Because neither was Nick.

Jaine gave the appearance of being astonishingly sane. People kept telling her to rest, take it easy, think of the baby. They needn't have bothered – the twenty-six-weeks queen mother was doing just that. Taking great care of herself and better care of everyone else. And making the cups of undrunk tea and cutting the fresh ciabatta sandwiches that were left to go stale and sitting down every five minutes to rest her foetus and taking care of everything and everyone. Doing it all like she wasn't the focus of constant covert attention, as if it wasn't her loved one who had just died, like everyone in the whole place wasn't watching her through swollen eyes for the minute she looked like cracking, the second her coping fell into the blood quagmire of pain.

As soon as I walked through the door, she was off the pity couch and over to me. 'Lise, sweetheart, are you OK?'

Was I OK? Was I OK? Where the fuck was she putting the emphasis in that sentence?

'No, I mean, God, of course not, but you, Jaine, it's not about me . . .'

'Yes it is, it's about all of us. Everyone loved him. And you especially. You and Nick, you've been so close lately, spent so much time together, this must be awful . . .'

Awful. For me? Oh yeah, pretty bad.

Jaine was understanding, lovely, soft. Which of course made me feel so very much better. She knew I would be devastated. Nick and I really were best friends. Everyone said so. Everyone knew it. Jaine saw that Andy was in a terrible state. She understood that Nick's big macho bloke brother Mike could barely cope and was never going to get up from his corner on the kitchen floor any time through that long night. Jaine knew everything and was all caring and all seeing and as long as she kept her focus on everyone else's grief she didn't have to bear a single moment alone with her own. Very wise. Very disassociated and only moderately insane. Grief patterns playing out their traditional rhythms and we all knew Jaine should have been trying to take some time for herself and no one could force her to do it. Who's going to argue with the pregnant widow? Not her dead partner's lover, that's for sure.

Eventually there were just six of us left. Nick's brother, passed out on the kitchen floor, had been transferred to their untouched bed. No need then for Jaine to be forced to sleep in it. Or Andy and I. More profound gratitude from inside my crumpled heart. Mike's wife sat beside him in the dark bedroom and stroked his heartbroken, no-tears, big-man's forehead. Andy and I sat with Jaine on the sofa and Jaine's little sister Meg fell asleep in the big armchair. Once she was properly asleep Andy picked her up and carried her into the spare room, the will-be-baby room. He put her fully dressed under the duvet of the narrow single bed, brought from Jaine's childhood home only last week, ready for when the baby would grow from cot to big bed. Ready for all those grannies and grandpas who would need to stay over. Jaine was rooted to her sofa bed. Except she had no intention of actually sleeping there. The terror that crossed her face as each person left the flat, the look of abject horror when Andy suggested she might want to sleep herself – she had no desire to let the day go. To make today into tomorrow. To allow it to be yesterday that Nick had died and not today.

Somewhere close to three in the morning, Andy fell asleep in the armchair vacated by Jaine's sister and I returned from the kitchen with yet another attempt to entice Jaine's taste buds. She was very sensibly requesting food. For the baby. She just couldn't manage to make it go past her lips. I sat on the spread-out sofa bed with my friend and slowly fed her marmite soldiers. Soft, fresh white bread, yellow real butter, all fat, all salt, just like our loving mothers had given us. Jaine ate the food from my hands, managed a whole half a slice before her stomach rebelled against the constraints of pregnancy.

'I can't, Lise. Not any more. That wasn't bad, though, was it?'

'Yeah, babe, you did good.'

'It's odd, isn't it?'

'What?'

'This. I keep expecting him to walk in, half a bottle of wine in one hand and a joint in the other. I keep having to remind myself it's not going to happen. Nick's stopped.'

'Yeah. He has.'

'It's very odd. I don't get it. I don't get death.'

'No. I don't either.'

'I can't believe I'm never going to talk to him again.'

We were quiet then, the lights very low, my husband sleeping not five feet from us.

I pulled the duvet back for her. 'You should get in. You need to sleep.'

'I'm not tired. Or I'm too tired. Fuck it, I don't know what I'm feeling.'

'You're in shock.'

'I thought the horrible sweet tea was supposed to deal with that.'

'It might have if you'd actually drunk any of the cups we've been trying to pour down you.'

'Sorry.'

'You don't have to apologize. It doesn't matter.'

'No. I know it doesn't. Lise, I'll get into bed if you will.'

'Do you want me to go?'

Half of me so ecstatic to be let off, to be allowed to run away from this house of pain, where I couldn't bear standing so close to my unvoiced truth. Half of me terrified that I would have to leave, wouldn't be allowed to stay in that place where Nick's things were, the only place where Nick still was.

'No. I didn't mean go home. I don't want you to go. Andy's asleep anyway. Stay here, Lise. Sleep with me. I don't want to sleep by myself.'

Of course she didn't. I didn't want to sleep by myself either. I wanted to do what Jaine wanted to do. I wanted to sleep with Nick. With Nick's warm body and Nick's long legs beside mine and Nick's arm heavy across my back.

'Hang on a second.'

Jaine got up and came back a few minutes later with a t-shirt for me to sleep in. She was my friend. This wasn't the first time we had shared nightshirts. But she wasn't giving me her t-shirt.

'Do you mind?'

'What?'

'It's Nick's. You don't have to. But it smells of him. It was in the washing basket. I mean, it's not dirty or anything – he was wearing it yesterday, just around the flat. Anna and Mike are fast asleep in there, I don't think they even heard me come in. I turned the light off. I don't think I disturbed them. I put a blanket on them. You should put a blanket over Andy too, look – there's one in that cupboard in the hall, it gets cold in this room at night and he won't be very comfortable, but the t-shirt, this – please Lisa, don't think I'm strange, I just . . . I'm sorry . . . I want . . .'

The rapid stuttering words finally stopped and she started to cry, arms shaking, holding the t-shirt out to me. Silent tears racking her mouth into the howl mask I'd seen on my own face hours earlier. The brief time of a single working day was all it had taken to shatter everything. I sat her down on the sofa bed, 'Jaine, it's fine. I know you need him. It's OK. I'd like to wear it. It's OK. Really. I promise I'll hold you, all right? You can go to sleep. I'll hold you. Come on, honey, come on now.'

I was nice to her, kept my voice low and gentle. I held her and coaxed her into the bed. I covered Andy and pushed a cushion under his head. Then I took my clothes off and put on Nick's t-shirt. It did smell of him, it was like wearing him. I never wanted to take it off. I held Jaine as big as I could until she fell asleep, wet head on my shoulder, face buried in the material covering my body.

I lay in the dark and wore Nick's t-shirt, smelt my lover, felt him there. Listened to my husband's sleeping breath, heard the half-night cries of my wounded friend, injured and wishing it was fatal. I fell asleep pretending to be him holding her. Pretending to be him holding me.

36

I am falling asleep. My legs jerk a few times as the muscles rescind their rampant tension, that which has held me together for the past half a day. I lie beside Jaine and turn away from thoughts of pain into the welcoming nothing. Travel there too fast – already there is a dream waiting for me. I am scared to go into it, half awake but body given up, unable to move away, to wake myself enough to cut off the dream. I do not want to dream. I am scared of what I might see. Fight it for as long as I can but inevitable grief narcosis overwhelms eventually. And it might be good. I might dream of him. Dream of him then. Not now.

I am wide awake, cold and bright. We are skating. Ice-skating. Broadgate ice rink, small circular site, open to faded stars, crammed about with over-tall buildings, but it is outdoors and it does have the best of what Londoners refer to as fresh air. The air rises off the ice and smells cold, good. They are all there with me. We are at a party or a picnic – Andy and Nick and Kim. All skating. Everyone skates really well, not the stumbling and laughing we manage in real life and not double quads or triple toe loops either, but smooth and elegant, easy waltz time to silent music, backwards and forwards, arms linked and solo splendour. Jaine is watching us from the seats around the rink. She is the only other person there. And the baby is near her. The baby is a little boy – soft brown skin, long curly hair, his dad's black eyes. Jaine and the baby are in sunshine, warm sunshine, though it must be winter and there are stars in the night sky anyway. Jaine calls the child to her and they leave us, waving goodbye. They are all smiles. Jaine does not look back though the little boy tries to.

Kim skates backward in front of me, in perfect counterpoint to my forward motion, each backward leg in union with mine. She kisses me and it is soft. Her lips are cold like the ice but soft anyway. My body warms to her, bends forward to her. She pulls away from me and now it is Jaine I am kissing, Kim walking away with the little boy holding on to her hand. I am surprised to be kissing Jaine but don't stop, don't want to stop. Kissing in rhythm with our feet, one and two and one and two, and it is fast, getting faster. Jaine is not as tall as Kim but I still need to stretch up anyway. I wonder if she is standing on something and bend my head away from hers to look down. Her skates are enormous, huge glinting blades cutting into the ice, each one buckled on to her real skating boots. She glides off, laughing at me over her shoulder. I know I should leave, that it is time to go, the sun has gone away with Kim and the little boy, I need to pack, to tidy up. I know beyond a shadow of a doubt that I should leave now, but we are laughing, having fun.

Jaine is gone now too. It is just me and Andy and Nick. We are holding hands, arms linked, the three of us. The rink is much wider. We cross from one side to the other. I can hear a church bell somewhere. Andy's hand and Nick's hand cross in front of me. They are holding each other and holding me. Between them I have perfect balance – it is as if the ice glides beneath me, not me over it. When Nick leans in to kiss me I am terrified that Andy will see, try to push him away, but he insists. Face close to mine, eyes caught into my blue, I try to turn away, make it a kiss on the cheek, the forehead, a hug, anything but what I know is coming.

We are still skating but now Nick and I are kissing, holding on to Andy's hands, carrying him along with us, the kiss a virtual fuck, skating over the ice faster than before. The bell is tolling louder and I can hear our skates slashing the ice. Water is splashing me, my feet are getting wet. I can't keep up the pace. I don't want Andy to know what is happening half a foot to his left. Nick pulls me away and throws me down to the ground. It is practically a paddling pool now, wet and dirty. Andy skates on, around us, his head always averted from the kiss, the nearly-fuck. I can't see any stars now, just the tall buildings, crowding in, crushing behind Nick's face. His hands are on me, all over me. I am still trying to push him away. Trying to send him away and welcome him at the same time. I know he is dead, I so want his life, need him to hold me, want this kiss, this fuck, want it so that I am prepared to risk anyway. Trust that Andy will keep skating, skating clear over eight inches of water. I am soaking wet, it is freezing, Nick is on top of me. I squeeze my face out from under his kissing mouth and see that Kim and Jaine and Andy and the little boy are all there, the four of them skating around us. They are just watching, not shocked, not amused, interested. I cannot fuck him now, but he won't listen. I am trying to push him away but he is too strong, too heavy, and I am fighting Nick off me, hitting out at him. He keeps kissing me, tongue in my mouth, hands on my breasts, my stomach, pushing my legs apart, holding me in that cold and dirty water. Nick is not interested in the fact that this is not a good time. This is what Nick wants. And it is what I want. But not like this.

I open my eyes to scream and his face is Andy's, interested, pleased, not menacing at all. I am terrified, want to cry out, but his hand is over my mouth. It is Jaine's hand, Jaine's face in mine now. Then Kim. Then the little boy. They are all there. All pushing against me, fighting me, forcing me down. All of them except Nick. I am sorry I pushed him away, I want him back now. I can't see him, their faces are in the way. I know Nick is dead and I want him to come back. I didn't mean to send him away. I cry out for him but only the other names come from my mouth. They come running and I cannot explain that it is not them I want, it is Nick. Kim and Jaine and Andy and the little boy are all there but I want Nick. I want to find him, to explain that I didn't mean it, I want him back.

I am awake. It is freezing. I am huddled on the sofa bed with Jaine. I can see her in the half-light. She is staring at me. Like she knows something. Like I know something.

'I dreamt about Nick.'

'I know. I did too.'

We are both crying. I hold her, she cradles me. I kiss the tears on her face. Jaine kisses me, kisses my lips. It is not an offer, but a solace. We are both shivering, wrap goose-pimpled arms and legs around each other to try to keep out the cold. We can't. The chill is woven into the t-shirt I am wearing. Nick is dead and we want him back.

A long time later we both sleep.

This is what Jaine thinks:

Is she hurting like me?

I will not look through his things. I will just leave it all alone. I don't want to know. I don't want to be here. I don't want him to be there.

Does she hurt like me? I hope she does. I hope she hurts.

I'm scared. I want Nick.

37

I woke in Nick's t-shirt, feeling that he had to be close. He had to be close but he wasn't. He was still dead. Breath-stopping waking-up after the first day, coming to with a hint of maybe it was all a bad dream. Waking knowing you're kidding yourself. It was just after six in the morning. I'd been asleep for all of three hours at the most, a good half-hour of that taken up in cold-hell skating. Jaine lay beside me, eyes staring wide at the ceiling. We didn't speak. There was no point. Eventually a house-load of mourners dragged ourselves from restless beds, nodded smile-free hungover faces, making essential contact through swollen eyes, tender skin black-eyed with tear acid. The six of us drank weak tea and strong coffee in the silence of aftershock. We made a pointless communal breakfast of which only Jaine managed a few mouthfuls, careful of the baby, careful of her growing piece of Nick. I didn't get dressed for as long as possible, didn't want to surrender my protective Nick layer. Didn't want to return him to the real wife.

Andy had to go into work, so he could arrange to have the rest of the week off. The bureaucratic procedure of what would inevitably be permission for his absence meant he still had to put in an official motion to have his disappearance allowed. The form-filling that has become the lot of the modern British teacher does not buckle merely for the newly dead, not even for Ofsted's finest, like my husband. I, on the other hand, rang Mary and told her there wasn't a chance she'd see me for the next few days. Perks of having one's own business. One's own shared business. Despite the cool frost that had settled between us in the past few months, Mary was immediately all sympathy and understanding. Experienced enough to know how to deal with grief and used-to-be religious enough to know it was all shit anyway. I was permitted time off without even asking for it. I was given the permission because it was assumed that Jaine would need me totally, unimpeded by concerns of self-important business people. I was also given permission because if Mary had any suspicions about Kim and me, she also knew how many mobile phone calls I usually received from Nick, and while her stated concern had always been that I did not risk the business – other than that I could do what I wanted – her pursed lips had given away a more traditional displeasure at what she assumed were my other distracting possibilities. For a picture-perfect wife, she was clearly capable of imagining romantic hazards outside her rosy-glow suburban life. And for someone who had chosen to live within a tight bond of convention, she also knew how not to pry, to show sympathy and concern anyway. I blessed her for that.

By eight the phone had started to ring again. Jaine had showered and new-tear washed and was agitating to call the hospital for results and the hope of release for Nick's body. I was looking forward to running away and getting to my own house, where I could be alone and allowed a chance to cry like the grieving party I really was. I booked my return appearance for three in the afternoon when Jaine would need protecting from the smothering ministrations of her mum and dad. And when there would be guaranteed results from the hospital and my skills could be put to good use. All those years of office temping and car booking for demanding businessmen made me the perfect candidate for chief funeral arranger. I couldn't wait. Smiled sympathetically, took every task, agreed to anything that was asked of me, was perfect friend. Perfect broken heart well hidden inside the beaten breast of traitor bitch.

I handed over the t-shirt, returned the smell of husband to the grieving widow and left in yesterday's tired clothes. All comfort potential rinsed from them after an evening soaking up combined tears. Got back to our home and closed the door behind me. Quiet and cool, bliss reception for the overloaded mind. I turned on my mobile and checked my messages in case Andy or Jaine had called while I was driving home. I had switched it off before leaving because I was far too unsure of myself to trust that I could drive safely and deal with a phone in a moving vehicle. I dialled 901 and heard the nice lady tell me there were no new messages, then just as I was about to click her off I heard it. Nick. The last message I'd been left, two days old now, a message from him, knowing I was somewhere in the wilds of the north. Not knowing I was there with Kim.

'Hey, Lise, looking forward to seeing you tomorrow, even if it is in happy-couple land. Call me when the train gets near. I'll be waiting. I know you don't want to hear it but I'm saying it anyway. I love you. Bye.'

My knees buckled and I was on the floor. I listened to the message five more times, scanning each word for meaning, premonition maybe. The message of a man who would die within a day. Pointless. He knew as little as the rest of us, was probably still trying to work it out. I scrabbled to my feet and ran upstairs, grabbed the old cassette deck from under our bed and ripped a blank tape from the drawer. The three minutes it took me to unwrap the cassette from its thin plastic casing seemed to go on for ever, deliberately taunting me as I tried to capture Nick's voice before the message was lost to time. I actually had three days from the time of him leaving the message. I probably had at least another half a day in which to save it, but the urgency of pain was reaching far past any sanity I had left. I recorded Nick's message and then played it back another three times. I put the tape away at the back of my cupboard, a small piece of Nick hidden and held.

Then I ran myself a water womb and cried long and loud in the bath. Screamed into the cooling water, missed him, howled for the sort-of-us like I could never have imagined. All along I had hoped I was in charge. The relationship was my choice, I'd made it happen, I was in control. Bollocks. From the very beginning he had managed to eat into me, making me want more and more of him, needing him. Desire turned from cool lust into real love with no one to stop it burning me up. Whatever control I'd ever maintained had been wrenched from me the day before. Nick was in sole command and the bastard had chosen yesterday to prove it. Fucked off like some bored boy who gets fed up with the infatuated child-girlfriend, leaving her crying in time to Sinead O'Connor and Alanis Morissette, knowing it will never ever get better, no matter what her mother says. There was a moment of small relief in the cooling bath when I noted in my violent thrashing that I'd obviously moved on to the anger stage. Fast through disbelief into fury. No doubt there would be some charming guilt to look forward to next. I knew the death format, had gathered enough of the grief relay from watching Andy to know I'd just have to do it myself, all alone, no one to go through it with me. Same as anyone else's grief, intensely personal and incapable of totally honest expression in any form of conversation – because our words are not big enough and even practice never makes it any better. But this particular death-too-soon was still more. This one had the added arsenic aftertaste that there was nobody I could even tell half the truth to, no one I could confide in. My lover was dead and most of the world didn't know, was going happily about its business in that pop song kind of way, didn't know the sky had fallen in, the clocks had ceased to tick. My lover was dead and even the couple of hundred people who would have to be notified only granted him best-friend status in my life. Maybe they even thought they were his best friends too, many of them probably were. A group of mourners assuming we had a common level of pain. My mobile remained resolutely silent.

Somewhere through the grief and cold-bath scum I remembered Kim. Someone I could tell. Someone to care. I would be honest with her, tell her all about Nick. Even through the sodden-mask tears I remembered that just as there was a clear hierarchy of grief, there is also a pecking order for dealing with one's lovers. I needed to be careful with her. I would tell her gently. I would tell her so that she would understand and would be able to comfort me.

It's a pity I didn't also remember that no one ever really wants to be the other woman. Twice removed.

38

Sitting in Kim's lounge, looking out at the Thames, detailing all I thought and felt, pouring it out to Kim, who'd been surprised to see me at her door with no booking phone call beforehand, but who had offered me coffee anyway. A whole two hours before I was due at Jaine's to set in motion the unthinkable process of putting Nick in the ground. Kim was obviously not OK. And when I went to sit beside her on the clean linen couch, hoping to be held, comforted, hoping she might want to try to make better that which wouldn't be healed, I was met with stiff arms and a forced half-kiss on the shoulder.

'Ah, look, Lisa, I can't really deal with all this right now.'

'Oh. Right. I'm sorry. Are you supposed to be working? Am I interrupting?'

I hadn't given her much chance on arrival to say what she was doing. So scared to tell all and so determined to do so anyway, I'd just blurted it out the minute I got in, most of it in the hallway on my way through to the river-reflecting room. Told everything. Almost everything. Even I knew better than to let on the extent of the feelings I'd been denying to myself for the past few months.

Kim frowned at me like I was missing something, shook

her head. 'No. I was sorting through my notes from yesterday. I only got in at ten this morning.'

It was only yesterday. Time crawling on broken feet around the newly coffined.

'I wasn't . . . look, Lisa, I just don't really do the betrayed thing.'

I looked. It was a bloody big word but she wasn't laughing. Wasn't even smiling.

'No. Of course. But – betrayed?'

Seemed a bit much given my home circumstances.

'We've talked to each other for hours. You and me. Been places, laughed, had fun. Christ – we've had bloody fun! How could you not tell me about him?'

'You said you didn't want to know. We didn't talk about that sort of thing. You didn't want to talk about your family, your ex, you didn't want to know anything about Andy.'

'That's because I already knew he existed. I knew he was there. This is different.'

Too dim to know when to shut up. 'How is it different?'

'Well, it feels a bit fucking stupid now, but I suppose I felt special to be your only other one.'

Ah. Claims of special. A girl guilt twist I should have known was coming. Grief does terrible things to the female intuition.

'You are special, Kim.'

'I'm also one of your two other lovers. Seems a bit bloody greedy to me.'

I was too tired, my voice small. 'Yeah, I expect it does. It probably is. Don't think I haven't thought that myself.'

Thought it and ignored it. I'd asked for change and new and excitement. And also thought myself blessed to get it.

'So why keep him a secret? Did he know about me?'

'No.'

I didn't want to think about what he didn't know, what

he'd never know now. Couldn't bear how much he would never know.

'Then what the fuck have you been playing at?'

Impossibility of explaining. The museum-piece nature of half-words spilling out, trying to make sense and meaning nothing. I could barely have explained what I'd been doing just a day before, the day when it all seemed to work and I was happy, let alone in the state I was in now. I hadn't understood myself, hadn't wanted to start to analyse in case it all fell apart. I had only experienced and enjoyed.

I stuttered on in half-formed sentences, birth-strangling any meaning with my grief head. 'Not playing. Real. Wanting you. Really. Just wanting him too.'

'Them too.'

'Yeah.'

'Not good enough, Lisa. I would have preferred the truth. From the beginning.'

Fair enough. So would I if given the chance to ask for it. I tried to explain about the boredom, the desperate desires, the never felt before needing to have the different, the bliss of fresh skin. But even in explaining myself, I knew my words were inadequate and still, she wasn't really listening. My excuses as to why I had wanted her in addition to Nick clattered to the ground past deaf ears. She simply wasn't interested. I had crossed a boundary and it didn't look like I was going to get back in without a whole lot of questioning from the guilt police. Slowly, through the minutes of tired anger conversation it dawned on me that she wasn't merely pissed off that she hadn't known about Nick. It was also that I was asking too much from her.

'I can't handle all this shit, Lisa. I really don't want to have to deal with any of it, but I am certainly not prepared to take on this bloke's death as well.'

'Nick.'

'Nick's death, then.'

'Take on his death? What?'

'Your grieving. Even if I was in a more privileged position than it turns out I am—'

'You are.'

'I don't think so. But even if you had confided in me all along, I don't think I'd have been prepared to take on the responsibility of your grief. I don't do it myself and I don't really get it when other people do.'

Don't do it. There was an alternative to being in this pain?

'You've tried?'

'First lover died in an accident when I was nineteen. We were both babies. My mother died four months later. I was still a child. One of my oldest friends died last year. Slow cancer. Gave me a lot of practice in cutting off, getting ready. I am an adult now. I've worked out how to do grief. I don't do it at all.'

'Fuck. I . . . I had no idea. Why didn't you tell me?'

'It had nothing to do with you.'

Kim meant it. Her past, her feelings about the past – it all had nothing to do with me. She explained that not only did she not do grieving herself, she also didn't want me doing it. Not in her flat, not around her, not tainting her things with my tears. She was already pissed off with me for bringing my unhappiness to her house, my betrayal into her home.

Closed face blank like the grey Thames outside. 'I don't want to have to deal with your grief, Lisa, or your lies. It's not my job. I'm not your partner.'

'You're my lover!'

'Sadly not the only one. But yes, you're right, I am your lover. And it suits both of us, doesn't it?'

'Suits us? What?'

Too tired and sad to get the sharpness of her tone, I was still caught up in poor-me. Very dim.

'It's perfectly clear. I get a part-time lover who's also a friend, someone to play with, someone to enjoy warm lunch-times in gorgeous countryside, go to the movies, all of that stuff. Someone who doesn't get in the way of my work or my child. Someone who has a life of her own.'

'But Kim, you're also my friend.'

'One doesn't tend to fuck around on one's friends.'

'You're more than my other friends.'

'So tell them. Tell your other friends that your lover has died. Tell Andy. Tell Mary. If it's only my friendship you need you could probably tell anyone. Tell Jaine.'

'Of course I can't fucking well tell them.'

I started to cry yet again. Kim poured me another whisky, I slopped it into my rebellious mouth, lips dying to sob, tired of having to swallow instead.

'No, Lisa, you can't tell them. But you can't tell me either. I don't want to know. We have good times, you and me. And that's all I want. I wanted this affair. Jumped at the chance. Couldn't think of anything I'd like better. I like you, I fancy you and you came with no strings attached. I loved that.'

'I loved him.'

Refilling my glass.

'But you didn't love me.'

'I do. Did. I loved being with you.'

'No. You wanted to love me. It's not the same thing. Not even the same as wanting me.'

I didn't know if she was right, but I didn't have the heart to argue either.

'I was another challenge to you, another string to the bow that proved you could do it, get away with it. I'm not complaining, don't get me wrong. I quite admire what you've managed to achieve.'

'But?'

'But you can't start off with me only as an adjunct to

your two main courses and then decide I'm what you want to base your diet on. Whatever. Crap metaphor, but you know what I mean.'

Not really. I was getting to the stage where I didn't know what anything meant any more. She could tell.

'Lisa, listen. I was happy to be your occasional fuck. I never wanted any more than that. Well . . .' Laughing now, laughing at herself as well as me. 'I wouldn't have minded a more complete truth, as it turns out, but that was the extent of it. We weren't ever going to go any further than this. Good enough friends who have better than good enough sex. You're straight, I'm gay. You're white, I'm black.'

'And you think that's why we can't be together?'

'We don't want to be together.'

'But if we did, the black and white thing would make it impossible?'

'No, darling, the gay and straight thing would make it impossible. The black and white thing only makes it bloody unlikely. But it's not just that. You have no kids, I'm responsible for a child. You have a husband, I actively choose to be single. I told you I didn't want you to love me and I meant it. I didn't want you to ask for anything other than a good time from me. A spare-time relationship on both our terms.'

I could hear where this was headed, wanted to get up and walk out, but my legs weren't responding to any grief-filtered commands. My body had given in, surrendered me to the beating. My flesh is more Catholic than I am. She went on, pouring herself a still-bigger whisky, talking as much to the grey-spiked London silhouette outside as she was to me. 'I was just playing. And so were you. Which was perfect. That's all I wanted. Playing. But this . . .'

'Yes?'

'Well, it's like we started playing, only you had a bunch

of other lies you were hiding from me, and now you want me to understand. To make you feel better. You want my sympathy, having just told me you've been cheating on me. It's a bit fucking much, don't you think?'

No. I hadn't thought. Obviously hadn't thought. She was right, really – truly, incredibly right. Mouth finally took over where recalcitrant legs couldn't cope.

'I'll go. I'm sorry. I'll call you. I am sorry. I'll go.'

'OK.'

No argument from her. Relief flooding her body. Picking up my bag and putting on shoes with shaking hands. Her face was different, it wasn't the face I was expecting to see in this house. She was right. I was only used to seeing Kim smiling, happy to see me. I didn't know what she looked like angry. I didn't like what she looked like angry. I'd never wanted to see that look before, didn't want to see it now. Kim was so bloody right, but that didn't stop me feeling I was standing on the edge of a massive bridge and weaving uncertainly through the inevitable moment of should I jump or will you please, please push me?

Goodbye at the door. Kim cool, beautiful. Gentle. Me small and exhausted.

'I'm sorry I can't give you what you want Lisa. But it wouldn't be honest. I do feel sorry for you, but I feel a whole lot more angry than anything else.'

There are no farewells that don't sound like pop-song clichés. We didn't kiss and we didn't wave goodbye and I left her building, half an hour eternity to pull my messy self together before arrival at the death house. Chastened, confused, bloody sad and still with a small residue of confusion that didn't really understand what I'd done that was so bad, how it could have all gone so wrong. And beneath that, a small piece of child Lisa who still wanted things her own way, crying that it wasn't fair. I slapped her face and told her to shut the fuck up or I'd really give her something to cry for.

Walking to the Tube across pavement shards of shattered crockery.

39

Andy and I whisky-fumbled our way through the next three days in the welcome fog of being the designated copers, having to get things done. Nick was gone and vacant possession had been taken of the emptiness created by his going. What had been his space was now invaded by an army of grieving relatives and friends, each one arriving at the door bent down with a freshly cut travelling Dunsinane of weeping lilies. My stalwart husband and I were the first line of attack for getting it all done in time. That and the providers of tea and bite-size pieces of food of which Jaine was usually able to eat almost a third. Following her first day of admirable calm and strange dispassion, Jaine got down to the business of mourning in full – that is, at least half the time she was perfectly functional and sane, aware of the baby, aware of the pressing need to take care of herself and the daily growing foetus and even occasionally aware that there were people around who might need something from her. The rest of the time she was mad-bitch Medusa, grief-head and hands ripping through empty air, striking in words at her hideous misfortune and out at anyone who attempted to tell her what to do. I, on the other hand, was wonder griever – took to my tasks like the best of wet ducks. I was the chief bridesmaid, passing around dead cake to all and sundry. It was easy to ignore the best man – he wasn't there. Consummately efficient and pleasantly helpful and running myself into the ground for Jaine's every beck and call – perfect friend, wonderful mourner, pre-eminent helper, and not a single daylit second left over to think about how my stomach wouldn't stop churning, how I walked past his clothes and his things and couldn't bear that I wasn't allowed to cry into them at every opportunity and carried my mobile in my hugely efficient pockets just in case. Just in case it rang. Just in case Nick called. He wasn't going to call and of course I didn't have any hope that he would. But I wanted to pretend to myself it was still possible. Tiny pieces of 'there, there' to get through the disgusting truth of not here.

Andy took Jaine to do the business. Father-of-the-bride work. He went with her to get all the last gory details from the hospital, to register the death, pick up information packs from the funeral place we'd decided on – no good reason, they all cost too much, they all treated us like clients or customers rather than people, but at least one of them had a good phone manner. We went with the only interners who didn't offer a cheery 'good morning' when we called. We figured anyone who knew enough to answer their phone just with the name and line of business was likely to be a teeny bit more sensitive than those treating the subject in hand like another cheery day in Pollyanna's life. Death. No room for prisms at the window with so many white roses needing to be vased. Andy led Jaine out of the front door for the first time since she'd got back from the hospital, strong man strong shoulder to lean on, and I huddled to the mainline phone and began the information round. Bitch job of bearing bad tidings. Telling everyone that could be phoned, saying those words five or six times an hour and never getting used to having the feel of 'Nick is dead' in my mouth, no practice teaching me how to fill the following silence. It made me retch the ninth time as much as the first, questioning the impossibility of the phrase every time I said it. Went all through Jaine's address book and then turned my unwilling hands to Nick's. Andy and I were in there under L for Lisa. But we didn't need to be told. Then there was my mobile number too. Silly bastard had even added a pencilled exclamation mark after my name. I don't suppose he expected to die any time soon. I took the book and an eraser to the loo, smoothed away Nick's pencil. Hid in the toilet from the relatives who had moved into the flat to stake their grief claim, even though half of them hadn't seen Nick for years. Felt like a traitor to wipe him out so soon. Knew complicity with him for a second and briefly smiled at our little secret. Remembered it was not our little secret. All mine now. Fourth cry of the morning.

Once Jaine and Andy were back from agreeing with the Establishment that Nick had actually departed this earth and gone, quite possibly, to heaven, there were the death notices to be composed and agreed on. But first Jaine was to be laid out for her afternoon rest. Still the sofa bed. Still no desire to get into a bed that didn't hold her loved one. I knew how she felt. I remembered how he felt. Jaine wasn't anywhere near capable of sleeping for more than twenty minutes at a time, scared of dreaming, equally scared of waking up and remembering, but her doctor had suggested lying down regularly anyway. There was a slightly better chance that she might fade into sleep with her head on a pillow than if she was sitting up poring over the slow trickle of sorry cards the postman was forced to carry up four flights of steps twice a day. A trickle he no doubt looked forward to becoming a flood. Idle passing thought about whether or not postmen expected death-duty tips as they do for the extra load of the Christmas card rush. The lift in their building was only occasionally reliable at the best of times – one of the remaining parts of the block still to surrender itself to millennium cool – but it had very cleverly chosen the occasion of Nick's death to give up its own ghost too. We expected friends to break down at regular intervals, crying couples and threes huddled into corners where they hoped their sobs wouldn't disturb Jaine. Sympathetically pained machinery was a little more surprising. Everyone trod eggshells around Jaine's feet for a long afternoon while she worked out precisely how she wanted to tell the world that Nick was no longer in it. After four hours the terse dead-end was completed and, with Nick's parents' approval, the last page finally faxed through to newspapers. With Andy's credit card details. We were doing big spending that week. I would have done so anyway, guilt-edged gold card work has always been a favourite of mine, but in this case we were especially useful. The bank had thoughtfully frozen their joint accounts while they worked out if the woman who had lived with Nick for nine years and who was pregnant with his child was really his next of kin, since Nick and Jaine hadn't chosen to allow society to sanction their togetherness with a frothy white meringue and a morning suit. Mourning suit. They had assumed that making another human being between the two of them might be joining enough. I said all this without pause, without thought. It was what I believed. It was true. As it was also true that the creation of the baby had not stopped Nick wanting me, had not stopped me wanting Nick any more than a wedding ring on his finger would have done. That it was my job to persuade the officious bitch from friendly telephone banking of the validity of Jaine's position was a particularly delicious piece of hell irony. More karmic revenge. No one else understood my self-chastizing smirk, though. Probably thought I was controlling my features in an effort not to break into snotty tears yet again. Not far wrong there either. There have been times in my life when I positively got off on feeling like the bad girl, knowing sorry was just around the corner. This was not one of them.

By the next morning, the third after the big day of dying and Nick still hadn't rolled back the rocks and started chatting to the ladies in the garden, the various hospital doctors and analysts of the dead finally agreed that not only was he not the second coming but he had also died accidentally. We could have told them that straight away. At least none of us had come across any suicide notes in the sob corners of the flat. I didn't think the card I was carrying in my Filofax with the last line 'I'd die for your face, your fuck' quite counted. Not enough to bring it up in mixed company anyway. They said it was a congenital brain thing – no way of knowing it was going to happen, no way Nick could have prevented it. And we believed them. They were the ladies and gentlemen of the white coats and the long antiseptic corridors. We were grieving. They spoke in short sentences and soft voices especially designed for the newly hard of comprehension. And of course, they knew much more than we did. They'd made holes in his brain. We only loved him. Though it did occur to me that he might have been a little more circumspect with his use of Class A drugs if he'd known there was a particularly thin artery in his head just waiting to blow up at any moment. Or not. Nick had been known to drive with well over an acceptable alcohol limit in his bloodstream too. It was one of Jaine's reasons for preferring to use public transport as often as possible whenever the two of them went out together. As it turned out she could have saved a fortune on taxis and just let nature take its course instead. But then I wouldn't have had the pleasure of being part-time chauffeur to the Prince of Needing a Lift. Joy is a thin hologram glimmer in the early dead days.

There was, of course, the usual jockeying for position around the corpse, people arranging themselves in a top-heavy mourners' pyramid. Jaine the apex and Nick's mum and dad beside her and everyone else grabbing as large a chunk of the grief for themselves as possible. Endless repeat loops of 'I've known him since . . .' and 'He was my best friend/cousin/workmate . . .', phrases attempting to assert some control over the death chaos. No one doing it out of nastiness, just the usual desire to dance as close to the top table as possible. I settled for being Jaine's best friend. Anything else would have taken far too much truth to explain. There were also the useless, endless lists of what ifs. None of which made logical sense, none of which would have made a blind bit of difference, and every one there simply to torture our non-sleeping selves in the middle of the night when either Andy or I finally went home. We went home alone, alternating staying with Jaine, not sleeping on the sofa bed, no one sleeping in their empty couple-bed. Not sleeping in our bed either. Or maybe Andy was – I certainly couldn't manage it. In the five or six hours I was given to be by myself, I took the chance to muffle my screams into the welcoming pillow, to listen again to the leftover message, to beat myself up through the balled-fist duvet, to rock the agony out of my stomach and to feel on my skin how badly I missed Nick. Or perhaps it was even too soon to miss. I didn't yet miss him. That came later. In those first days all I did was want him. Like we'd first started fucking. Like we'd never started fucking. As if all the potential was waiting and pumping though me and there was never going to be a way to turn it off, to put him away. Wanting him in that way you can only want when there is absolutely no possibility of receiving. Wanting so it rips serrated-knife jagged from breast to cunt. A few hours of quiet in the middle of the night when I could begin to look at how badly this was all going. My very own grieving process. And still no way of being honest about just how crap it truly was that my friend's boyfriend was dead. No calls from Kim, no calls from Nick, just me and Andy being the perfect couple of chosen handmaids for our grieving buddy.

The secret love really is bliss, the glorious intensity of closeted passion, whipping around your blood and leaving a wordless kiss in the mouth. Secret grief, however, is exactly the same as any other grief, except you aren't allowed to do any of the things that might make the death pain something that can be borne for the maybe three hopeful minutes in each hour. The bottom line was that I wasn't allowed to talk about it. And, despite my lack of hands-on death experience until now, I knew enough Kubler-Ross to know that lunacy skipped down the silent road very quickly indeed. I thought of finding a therapist, but there were still cards to open and flowers to trim and Jaine to hold, and there certainly wasn't an hour to spare for talking to a stranger about what shit I was in. Nor did I want to detail the joys of my illicit liaison with Nick just so I could get around to explaining how I couldn't bear to have lost him. I thought about finding an open church too, but I knew that confession wouldn't do it either. There is no penance for the inconsolable tear queen, dancing alone in limbo.

And then it got worse. Bad things always do. Jaine wanted to see Nick.

40

The visit to the dead one had been discouraged from the start. When the wearers of the white coats gave their long-rehearsed and yet still poorly performed 'I'm sorry' speech at the hospital, they'd told Jaine she should hold him then if she wanted to. Told her it wouldn't be very nice later. It wasn't what people normally did. Not now. She'd be glad in the long run. In fact they used all the appropriate platitudes, thereby ensuring that a good five per cent of what they said actually went in. So Andy and I told them what Jaine wanted. They told us this wasn't a great idea. We told them she understood their reservations, but she wanted to see him anyway. They explained they'd needed to make holes in Nick's head, cut up pieces of his brain. Just to be sure he was really dead I suppose. We persisted. They stalled. Andy insisted. I realized that if I had to speak about Nick in terms of dead and cut up and cold one more time I might need to make a hole in my own head, just to release the pressure of the unspoken. Trepanning for the adulterous griever. Very Neal's Yard. Jaine wasn't listening to anyone's no-saying. The doctors had told her it wasn't a good idea, the pleasant-phone-manner man from the funeral parlour told her it wasn't a good idea. Her own doctor thought it was a terrible idea – shock, trauma, bad for baby, bad for Jaine, bad all round. Jaine, though, wanted to see Nick.

Wanted to say goodbye to Nick. Felt nasty and mean not seeing Nick, leaving him all that time in the hospital and now at the funeral parlour by himself. And she wanted me there with her.

It wasn't that I didn't want to see Nick. I mean, I was as scared as Jaine was about what he might look like. Scared that they had messed up his beautiful face. Scared in general of what I'd do, what I'd give away. But like her I did need to see him. Wanted to hold him one more time. Hundreds more times. To feel his hands cold and waxy and know they weren't going to be touching me again. Check out the closed blue eyes, the dead-hard soft lips. Like Jaine, I needed to know how dead he was, make sure he was really gone. I didn't especially want to confirm that truth in her company, but there was no way around it. No way over or under. One of those bulldozer, push-through moments. So we went. I drove us there. Didn't want Andy. Didn't want him to see us, see what we would be like. Didn't know what we would be like. When we got to the funeral parlour the good-telephone-manner man welcomed us in. Gave Jaine bottled water and me nasty instant coffee. Taking care of baby. Introduced us to his daughter – family business apparently. Now there's a thing to leave to your kids. She was the embalmer. Said some sweet nothings, that she could see he was a great-looking man in life. She thought it was OK we'd come. Said if we felt that strongly about it then seeing him was the only thing that was going to make us feel any better. That actually he wasn't as bad as some – the hospital hadn't done too much damage and she'd made a pretty good job of him herself, didn't think we'd notice too much. She was quite proud of herself. As well she might be. Perfectly respectable profession. Especially if you like working alone.

Jaine and I must have stood outside the door for a good five minutes, me just behind her, wanting to rush in, to grab him, but taking all my cues from her, being the good friend. It was the least I could do, considering. Eventually she sighed one big rasping breath and pushed the door open. There were no Hammer Horror creakings and the MDF portal swung back easily on its B&Q hinges. We have many movie images for the death scene, few of them anything like the sadly banal reality. The coffin was placed in front of the far wall. The painted brick draped in dark blue velvet, coffin lid leaning against one of the curtains. We walked across the room, walls falling back around us, the distance increasing as we got closer, floor trembling underfoot. Then Jaine was standing beside the coffin, raised hand shaking, wanting to stroke his beautiful face, wanting to smack his beautiful face, whispering to him. I stood behind her, ready to catch her should she fall, if it was too much. As if any of it could be too little. I didn't look at Nick until I saw her shoulders relax, concentrated my mind on Jaine until I saw her hand go down to his face, knew she would be OK. Stupid phrase. Knew she would be able to do what she had chosen to do. What we were there for. I looked at Nick.

He didn't look too bad, the daughter was right. He didn't look a whole lot like Nick either, though. Too pale, too Madame Tussauds, too half his head cut open. Too fucking dead. Jaine was holding his hand, soft fingers cold and nearly pliable, stroking his hair, crying quietly.

'Jaine, do you want me to leave you?'

Asking the right question, not bearing to think she might tell me to go, wanting to be her, wanting permission to touch him, wanting to kiss him.

'No. It's OK. Stay. I want you here. With me. Us. Me.'

Jaine patting her stomach and correcting her personal pronouns as she travelled the long distance from one to three to just two.

'Do you want to touch him, Lise? You can.'

Wanted to touch him, to hold him, to wake him up, to

make him explain himself, to beat shit out of him, to kiss him, to hold him, to make this bloody well not be. Sleeping Beauty him back to me.

'Yeah. OK.'

Moved beside her. Stroked his soft hair. Warm hair still. Warm air in the cold room. Warm from our breath, both breathing shallow and fast, both breathing extra for Nick. The scars weren't that bad. What we could see. What wasn't covered by buttoned-up shirt and jacket. Bright orange Ted Baker shirt, fine brushed cotton. Darkest blue Paul Smith suit in fine wool. Good choice. The largest scar was at the back of his head anyway, then a finer one around the hairline. Cut with care, just in case. In case we cared.

'Lucky he had such a good head of hair. All this floppy fucking fringe almost hides the mess.'

'Yeah. It's good.'

Agreement. Few words. The fewer the better. Less chance of crying. Screaming. Exploding.

'I told him he should grow out of having a fringe.'

'You did?'

'Last week. Said men in their thirties shouldn't have dandy fringes. Told him dads didn't have fringes.'

'What did he say?'

'Told me to piss off. We weren't having the best of days.'

Last Tuesday, then, they'd been fighting all morning and he'd come to meet me after work. We'd had a brilliant time together. Silly. Laughing. I loved his fringe. Something to grab hold of.

Jaine kissed his hands and turned around. 'I'm going out now. You can stay if you want. I've seen enough. This isn't Nick.' She stroked his head again, messed the fringe, ran her finger along the hairline scar, then traced his lips with hers. 'This isn't my Nick.'

Mine, though. I waited until the door closed behind her. Couldn't help myself. Kissed his hands, his face. Kissed his cold lips and lank fringe and blind eyes and stupid nose and fine-shaved chin. Kissed his lips again and came back for breath and his face was wet and my face was wet and he wasn't going to kiss away my tears. Not that he would have ever made such a crassly sweet gesture before, but it certainly would never happen now. Kissed the dead man one more time and then shook the tremors from my heaving body, hugged myself tight to literally pull myself together and drove his girlfriend home. Both girlfriends sobbing in the front seat with Jaine-chosen Carpenters in our ears. Karen singing *'Goodbye To Love'* with perfectly arranged end-of-verse broken voice. Just in case the tears weren't coming fast enough by themselves.

This is what Jaine thinks:

I think I was right. And I want her to cry.

But it doesn't really matter anyway. He's all mine now.

41

We buried him the next morning, and the polite shuffle of the before and after grieving parties was like the day Andy and I got married, waiting around the corner in all our bridal silliness, waiting for the late service before us to finish so we could get on with ours, and then leaving the church and smiling at the nervous next-to-be bridie as I left, just-made wife. There are too many people in London and not enough time to marry and bury them all. Nick's service, though perfectly timed to the last carefully allotted minute, was sweet and funny and right and very modern-priest low C of E and easy even for the atheists. Best-chosen songs for maximum tears, a couple of readings by shaking-voiced cousins, and then a walk outside, Nick shouldered by mates from drama school. Man-boy friends best dressed and biggest crying. His coffin was lowered into a six-foot hole, two inches shorter than Nick and still too deep, levered to the earth in a spring fever of pissing-down rain and a howling northerly wind. We were drenched in our new black elegance, Jaine especially beautiful and extra fantastically dressed. Having insisted on all black and real mourning, she'd gone shopping after we'd viewed the body and ended up in designer jersey silk. It took her three hours to find the perfect dress and I'd paid far more than too much for it. M&S and Dorothy Perkins may well have dinky little smocks and easy dresses for the mother-to-be, but high-street shops tend not to stock a comprehensive line in maternity mourning wear. By the end of the service we were soaked and shivering and all pushing Jaine to get herself and the baby back inside in the warm. She wanted to stay by the grave and cry but Nick's mother took control, generational genes delivering authority where none of her friends could. Nick would have been so glad to be inside the box where his good clothes and great hair weren't getting messed up. Except Nick was in the box and so no one was left to be glad. I looked down at the pale wood coffin and couldn't believe how deep six foot was. I threw down a rose from our garden and didn't believe it was possible to leave him there without screaming out loud. Then I turned to care for the widow. I made it look right.

It rained all morning until about eleven thirty, when southern sunshine arrived and a rainbow spread north from Crystal Palace. I could see it from Nick and Jaine's windows. I chose to discount the possibility that it was a sign Nick's spirit had relocated to Croydon.

Then there was a collection of disjointed hours, timed by the minutes since Nick's death, and each one looking like festivity but sounding like hell. A silent film camera would have recorded people eating little and drinking copiously, arriving at the beautiful minimalist flat and leaving some time after in direct correlation with their approach to a party. But the close-ups would have looked different. And the soundtrack was far from fun, too quiet except for the sobs breaking out every now and then behind closed doors, in huddled corners, strangled sounds of affliction making it through grimaced teeth, past lips that had promised they wouldn't break down in front of Jaine. At least not until Jaine broke down in front of them, gave them permission. Slowly the people went home – kisses for Jaine, kisses for the parents, a receiving line creating crumpled formality from the chaos. Nick's mum and dad were the last to leave of those who had to drive far, suddenly an old couple bewildered that they were now being forced to live out an inversion of their planned fate, Nick's dad touching the walls of the flat as if he might find a piece of his son in the perfect plasterwork, his mum squeezing Jaine's hands so tight that their ringed fingers bruised each other. By eight that night the guests had gone and the party was over.

Jaine packed slowly and left a couple of hours later for her mother's home to spend a few weeks in the realm of the quiet matriarch, difficult to disobey, who would ensure that even if she couldn't ease her daughter's pain, she would at least insist that the daily growing baby was taken care of. Jaine had always protested that her mother was too big, too demanding, and we'd all been happy to join in her omnipresent-mother myth. That night, though, the five-foot legend came into her own and Jaine was happy to be back in the vast embrace of the tiny woman. Andy and I saw them to the car and then climbed the stairs again to clean up the flat. Her flat. We worked hard together and talked little and met in passing with dirty plates and glasses to hold and cry briefly before going on. We left at one in the morning when the mountain of dishes was done, glasses washed and polished, rooms tidied and the flowers watered once more, dying and dead before Jaine's return, but watered anyway. I told Andy I'd lock up and meet him down in the car.

I heard Andy close the door and went into their bedroom. Opened Nick's wardrobe, breathed him in, soaked up what I could, listening for the tone of him, the sound of his skin. Held the material against my face and tried to absorb him. But he was already retreating from the flat, already leaving his clothes. Their scent was cooler than usual, perfume fading. Nick was further away. I turned off the lights and waited in the dark of the cold flat, tried to sense him in the hallway, but there was nothing. I felt nothing and cursed Nick for failing to haunt me. Double-locked the door behind me and walked slowly down the stairs to our car.

I went home with Andy. I went home alone.

42

There is no way round this. I did not tell the truth. Did not reveal. Will not confess. Absorption rather than absolution.

Kim and I ceased to interact on anything other than a purely business level. Once I had asked her for more than just the easy offerings of either juicy flesh or girlie friendship she could give neither. My offer, her choice. It was me who changed the boundaries of limited expectations, not her. Kim wanted to laugh and to fuck. I find it hard to fuck when I'm sobbing, body racked into my pillow. Sounds like laughter, looks like sex, is neither. And of course I lied to her too. She was right to be angry with me, I had hurt her. There is that. There will always be that. So – no playtime, no lover, no acquaintance-turned-friend. I missed the good lunches, missed the playing, the potential. She has promised me friendship again, maybe even desire, once I get over the needing. I do not know when that will be. If that will be. Falling plate smashes to the floor, no one hears the clatter of breaking china. I run away on splintered feet.

I lay awake on a cold night, unexpected rain beating away the early summer. I lay awake and could not bear that Nick was in the ground and cold, that it was raining on him. I cried because he must be lonely. I didn't want him to be alone in the dark.

The baby grew and Jaine divided her attention between

grief and imminent birth. She had a few short months to adjust, and then almost two weeks more – first baby, eleven days overdue. She did not adjust, but she did cope. Wonderfully. Jaine collected all the awards for finest widow and single mother supreme. I was presented with several compliments of the best supporting actress variety. I was good friend and antenatal expert and completely there for her and still resolutely missing inside – didn't deserve the Oscar, didn't put it on the mantelpiece. I was present at the birth of Jaine's daughter. Timed contractions, counted breaths, held and lifted and walked and ran, would have boiled towels and provided hot water if it would have helped. It didn't. Nothing helped. I wasn't Nick. It took far longer for this little scrap of girl to be born than it took for her father to die. And much more blood. Jaine was ill for a long time after, finally giving in to the big grief she'd put on hold while growing the baby. I held the slippery little girl and looked for Nick. Held my aching friend and listened as she told me of her dreams for the child, for her daughter, their daughter. This child would have it all. Everything except a daddy.

Weeks later I held the baby as the funeral vicar spilt holy water on her forehead and welcomed her into God's community. I renounced Satan and all his works with the best of them, with the rest of them. None of us quite sure what we were agreeing to, but agreeing anyway. I wasn't sure if God could hear me over the wailing of the child when I whispered my vows of obedience to the laws of the man-made God. I don't know that He can be bothered to listen all that often. Another plate falls and shatters in the quiet church, stained-glass light catches on the white shards, a Gaudi mosaic of crockery and passing colour.

I dreamt Nick and Jaine came to dinner. Jaine knew about Nick and me. Andy did too. It was all fine and no one minded. We ate bowl after bowl of ice cream, cookies and cream with whole cookies inside. Andy and Jaine watched football while Nick held me and we laughed at the baby, growing beyond her mothercare. I woke up smiling and two minutes later remembered to cry.

Andy and I were good to each other. Careful, gentle, grateful not to be Jaine, guilty as we held each other in eventual sleep. Nick's death made us take stock, look closely at the couple that we are. Andy does not know the clarity of this situation, knows only that Nick's death made him reassess his own mortality. He assumed my process was the same, assumed that in my grief I too was analysing my life. He was right about the analysis, but not the reasons. I do not have Nick and I do not have Kim and I lost much of me in that transaction. I lost much of my husband in that transaction, but didn't learn that until long after, didn't look at what I'd done to him until long after the end of raw grief. Andy believes he loves me. Says he will love me always. Andy has become much more vocal in his declarations of love. I do not choose to put his protestations to the test. There is no point. We are talking about having a baby again. Maybe I can do it. Maybe it isn't that big a deal. Everyone else does it. Maybe we can be happy.

I dreamt I opened an old shoe box. Nick's ashes were in a small plastic bag, but real ashes, not people ashes. Rolled up in a plastic lunch bag like dope. Flaky soft ashes, grey. My passport was in there too. Old passport, old picture, old Lisa. There was a stone, a carnelian, mounted on a large gold base, like an oversized cuff-link. And a tiny jewellery box I had kept as a child. It was broken. I gave the stone to Jaine in my dream. The stone mattered to her for some reason. I did not know what the dream meant when I woke up. I don't know what it means now. I have never been happy with symbols. I am much more likely to understand flesh and words. And blood.

I cannot bear that Nick is dead and yet I have to. I do not

understand that my heart keeps beating while Nick's weak brain made his stop, don't know why this has happened to me, and yet all my childhood half-believed Catholicism and guilt would offer me many reasons. As would my adult awareness and the basic call never to betray one's girlfriend. Except there aren't good reasons. I did not make Nick die through my sinful actions, nor did he depart this earth because he was Jaine's boyfriend and we were having an affair. Nick's death was not karmic retribution for my transgression. Even I am not that powerful. He died because a thin vein carrying the blood in his brain stopped doing its job. It is that arbitrary, was that pathetic. One whole life finished from a tiny piece of non-cooperative flesh. He had not even been feeling poorly, a bit tired. It simply was a moment of occurrence and most of the world didn't blink at the notice in the newspaper. Nick is over and so is my playtime. I had my cake and ate all of it and in the glee and in the gluttony there was joy and pleasure greater than I could have dared to expect. But I do not yet know if the pain was worth it. There may have been some gains, it is too soon to say. Last plate falls. I do not feel it rip at me. The scars are now so much thick skin, the blood just another liquid.

I dreamt he had not died and our affair had gone on. More hotels, B&Bs, a little more lying, much more laughter. We did not continue for long. When his daughter was born Nick discovered family and responsibility and married the woman who was his real wife anyway. Kim found a proper lover, full-time lover, and we returned to just good friends. Years later we all had other affairs with other people and the passing of time made our months of semi-together so much less important. When I woke up I knew this would have been truth. Perhaps it was not a dream. A five-in-the-morning daydream. I knew then that I would have preferred to have simply stopped wanting Nick than to still love and mourn him.

I dreamt I had not bothered with either of the affairs. That I had not ever wanted more and I had stayed good wife and therefore did not have to deal with the grief. I had broken no boundaries, experienced no bliss. When I woke up I was disappointed until I realized the good-girl life had been the dream. Nick really was dead. And therefore the affair had been real. And that pleased me.

There is no solace for grief, and time does not heal. It puts a patina of age on the scars, simply makes the pain last longer. There is a day when you wake up and notice you're not crying. Time has not healed anything, it has just made you used to the pain.

I did it, though. Had the excitement, had the fun and the playing. Offered up the prayer, got my wish. I run in autumn evenings again. I hear Andy call for me to be careful as seven o'clock begins its descent into darkness, but these nights I stay well clear of other people's uncurtained windows. I cross busy roads to avoid the temptation of comparison. I have had another birthday and did not wait for revelations. The Jesus year is over and done with. I know he would have first revealed himself to the whore, and I waited in the garden far longer than the requisite three days. Nick didn't come back. I am happy enough with Andy.

And I will make happy enough suffice.

Until I can't.